# FAIRY GODMOTHERS, INC.

Also by Saranna DeWylde

*How to Lose a Demon in 10 Days*
*How to Marry an Angel in 10 Days*
*How to Seduce a Warlock in 10 Days*

# FAIRY GODMOTHERS, INC.

## Saranna DeWylde

ZEBRA BOOKS
Kensington Publishing Corp.
www.kensingtonbooks.com

ZEBRA BOOKS are published by

Kensington Publishing Corp.
119 West 40th Street
New York, NY 10018

All Kensington titles, imprints, and distributed lines are available at special quantity discounts for bulk purchases for sales promotion, premiums, fund-raising, educational, or institutional use.

Special book excerpts or customized printings can also be created to fit specific needs. For details, write or phone the office of the Kensington Sales Manager: Attn.: Sales Department. Kensington Publishing Corp., 119 West 40th Street, New York, NY 10018. Phone: 1-800-221-2647.

Zebra and the Z logo Reg. U.S. Pat. & TM Off.

First Zebra Trade Printing: January 2021

ISBN-13: 978-1-4201-5314-9
ISBN-10: 1-4201-5314-5

ISBN-13: 978-1-4201-5317-0 (ebook)
ISBN-10: 1-4201-5317-X (ebook)

10 9 8 7 6 5 4 3 2 1

Printed in the United States of America

For the bit of fairy godmother in each of us . . .

# Prologue

Petunia "Petty" Blossom happened to have an extra gleam in her twinkling eyes on that particular morning. Much to her sisters' chagrin.

First, spring had come to Ever After, Missouri (they only had winter in December), and the fairy godmother sisters had set about their duties bringing the town to lush and vibrant life. To any nonmagical person on the outside looking in, the sisters looked like a trio of kindly grandmother types who had run slightly wild in their youth, but who now baked cookies, enjoyed gardening, and collected cats.

The sun was high in the clear blue sky, and fat birds singing their songs of young love dotted their unfortunately naked cherry tree. Several squirrels waited patiently, clasping their tiny little paws together as they looked back and forth between the fairies and the tree. Petty hoped she wouldn't have to disappoint them.

"I don't know what you're smiling about, Pets. We're all going to hell in a rather thorny handbasket." Bluebonnet sighed and slapped her wand against her hand as she tried, and failed, for the fourth consecutive time to bring a bloom to the cherry tree that dominated the backyard of their gingerbread-style cottage.

"Decidedly cherry-free, I might add." Jonquil crossed her arms over her chest and scowled.

The scents of magic and their herb garden flooded her

awareness and she grounded herself in the moment. She allowed herself to feel the magic of the green grass and rich, loamy earth beneath their cedar deck, and she recalled childhood memories of her sisters.

When they first got their wings.

Their first wands.

Learning to be magical.

And she filled herself with all the love she could summon.

Love for her magic, for her darling charges, and, of course, for her sisters. Petty bumped her ample hip into Bluebonnet's and a zing of magic crackled from the wand and produced exactly one perfect bloom.

"How did you do that?" Bluebonnet frowned.

"Stop frowning, Bon-Bon. It'll give you wrinkles," Jonquil said.

"You've already got wrinkles." Bluebonnet stuck her tongue out at her sister, but then quickly checked her compact to see if she had, in fact, developed the ever-dreaded wrinkles.

"So what? I'm not afraid of my age. I just know how terrified *you* are." Jonquil returned the rude gesture.

"Sisters. You know, we could argue until kingdom come, which is going to be soon if we don't do something. Or, we could get to the talking about *how* I brought a bloom to our sad, little tree." Petty pushed her glasses up on the end of her nose. They were more a fashion statement than anything, but she liked the effect.

"Yes, fine. Let's get to that." Bon-Bon rattled her wand again and then looked around. "Oh dear, I hope the neighbors didn't see."

"Stop shaking the poor dear. You're going to give him motion sickness," Jonquil said.

"I am not."

"Yes, you are. If you'd just—" Jonquil reached for the wand. Bluebonnet was not about to have any of that nonsense.

She jerked the wand away, but it slipped out of her grasp and when it hit the cedar planks of their deck, it shattered into toothpicks.

"Look what you did!" Bluebonnet cried.

Petty could see that things were about to go decidedly south, and that wasn't something they had time for.

"Love!" Petty shrieked.

Both of her sisters turned to look at her.

"Excuse me, what?" Jonquil asked as she tucked her silver-white hair behind her ear.

"Yeah, what?" Bluebonnet added. "Love?"

Petty nodded. "Yes, exactly. That's our answer."

Jonquil sagged down into a deck chair, unmindful of the dirt now on her bright-yellow dress. "We can't even bring spring to Ever After. How is love our answer?"

"It's the problem *and* the solution," Petty continued. "The world is running out of love. That's why we're running out of magic."

"That sounds like hippie woo-woo to me." Bluebonnet wrinkled her nose and leaned against the cottage door.

"We're fairy godmothers, but the magic of love is hippie woo-woo? This is why we're going extinct. Honestly." Petty shook her head. "No, seriously. I'm telling you that's how I made your magic work. I thought about how much I love you."

"And you only got one bloom?" Jonquil cackled.

Petty narrowed her eyes. "It was the best I could do because we're all low. So much strife, hardship, and fear. Those things both drain love and make it stronger. For us, I fear it's drained our compassion, our empathy, and yes, our love."

"So what do we do?" Bluebonnet bent over to pick up the toothpicks and tried to reassemble them in a way that represented her poor little murdered wand.

"The answer has been right in front of our noses for the longest time. Look at where we live. It could be the premier wedding destination." Excitement lit Petty with an ethereal glow.

"I hate to break it to you, sister dear, but Nowhere, Missouri, is never going to be a premier wedding destination. Have you been smoking the wormwood?" Jonquil scrutinized her sister for any signs of being in a chemically altered state.

Petty huffed. "Nowhere is in Arizona. I got my picture by the sign. See?" She whipped out a picture of her standing by a sign in the middle of the desert and one run-down, vandalized building that might've, at one time, been a gas station. "We live in *Ever After.*"

The picture disappeared into the nothingness from whence Petty plucked it.

"Humans don't normally come to Ever After. There's a reason we're not on any maps," Bluebonnet said.

"Well, we're just going to have to change that, and I know just how to start," Petty began.

"We're all ears," Jonquil replied, and began working her bare fingers in the dirt of the flowerpots that sat waiting for her attention.

"With Lucky and Ransom," Petty said. "They both owe us favors."

Bluebonnet made a face. "Oh no. No. No. That's an awful idea. Don't you remember what happened the last time we meddled in their lives?"

"I know. Whatever. They're adults now. I'm sure they've forgotten . . ."

No. Everyone present knew there was no way *anyone* had forgotten.

Petty cleared her throat and continued. "This is also our chance to try to help Lucky with her *un*lucky. Regardless of what that could do for the town wells, and our magic, isn't that our job? We're their fairy godmothers. They've withstood the trials. They've battled through the long night. It's time they get their Happily Ever After. They've earned it."

Jonquil gave a heavy sigh. "Well, you know we can only meddle so much. They have to make the choices themselves. You can lead a prince to his princess, but you can't make them kiss."

"Oh yes, we can. That's what poppets are for. But that's neither here nor there." Petty straightened her apron. "Are you in?"

"If we can convince the town, it might be worth a shot." Bluebonnet looked out at the magical, lone bloom on their cherry tree.

"I just don't buy it." Jonquil shook her head.

"You know with fairy dust, you have to believe. That's the magic." Petty tapped her foot with obvious impatience.

"I thought it was love." Jonquil snorted.

Petty stopped mid–foot tap and her eyes narrowed. "Jonquil, so help me . . ."

"Fine. Fine. *Fine*. I believe." She coughed. "I guess. Whatever."

"Good. Sisters, get out your best meddling outfits. I'm going to call a meeting with the town council. We're about to put Ever After on the map!"

# Chapter 1

Lucky Fujiki had always hated her name.

Whenever she had too much time by herself, like now, waiting at the park for her partner-in-crime and ride-or-die bestie to drop her kids off at school, she thought about it.

Lucky tried to focus on the ducks flapping in the melting pond, the first blooms of spring on the trees, which were pushing forward much too early by the way, and the landscaped grounds.

Nope. No chance. Because if she stared at the ducks too long, they'd get agitated. Or the tree would get struck by lightning. Or the grounds . . . well . . . who knew, really?

She hated her name so much.

Not the Fujiki, she was more than good with that one.

*Lucky.* What the hell? That was just asking for trouble.

Why couldn't her mother have named her something traditional like Akira, or Keiko, or even Tatsuo? She had a friend named Keiko who was very successful.

The world didn't fall apart at the seams whenever Keiko walked by.

That was all Lucky wanted, to be able to move through the world without the fabric of the universe coming undone.

Of course, there was an ancient Japanese proverb that fit her situation nicely: "Shit in one hand and want in the other, and see which one fills up first."

No, on second thought, that wasn't Japanese. It was a universal truth. Really, she could want and wish as hard as she could and it wouldn't change her situation. Although, her mother would argue that point endlessly.

She hated her nickname, too. "Un-Lucky." Yay her.

Her mother, of course, had told her it would pass, but what did she know? *Her* name was Fortune, and she'd lived up to it with no problem at all.

*Lucky.* She spat on the ground.

"Whoa! Friendly fire!"

Lucky looked up to see her best friend, Gwen Borders, holding out a cup of coffee. From the looks of it, a mocha chip caramel latte, hopefully with a shot of blond espresso. And whipped cream with a hearty dusting of cinnamon.

She needed a lot of sugar and caffeine to maintain.

"Sorry, Gwen. Thanks for the fortification." She accepted the cup gratefully.

"Bemoaning your name again, huh?" Gwen sat down next to her on the park bench.

"Like I do every day."

Gwen took a drink of her coffee and sighed happily. "I talked to the woman who does my tarot cards about your problem. She said that you're out of alignment with the universe. So if you could just figure out what's causing the misalignment, you'll be good as gold."

Lucky wrinkled her nose. "What does that even mean?"

Gwen shrugged. "Hell if I know. I just give the woman money. Maybe you should go see her? I could book you some sessions. Then you can ask your questions."

"You've got kids who are going to need a college fund. You don't need to be spending your money on me and my problems. Especially not on some 'hippie woo-woo,' as my godmother likes to say."

Gwen grinned. "It is absolutely my pleasure to spend all of Jake's money on frivolous and stupid things. Plus, I get cash every time I pay with his card. It gives me an excuse to take out more money for my little nest egg."

Lucky scowled. "You know, if it wouldn't affect you and the monsters, I'd go give him a daily dose of bad luck." She turned to look at her friend. "I really don't know how you and the kids are immune to my bad vibes. I'm grateful, but I wish I knew how it worked."

"So you'd only inflict it on people who deserve it?"

"Yep." Lucky took another sip of her coffee and luxuriated in the sweet warmth on her tongue.

"Oh, don't look now, but there's PTA Nancy."

Lucky looked around the park and saw a woman go into Gaston's Tea Shop across the street.

PTA Nancy had been making Gwen's life miserable, and to be honest, poor Gwen already had enough misery on her plate.

"You know, I think I need to buy some tea for my god-mothers." Lucky stood.

Gwen flashed a half grin. "We shouldn't. I mean . . ."

"Oh, but we should. She's awful."

"Do you think this is considered using your powers for good?" Gwen asked.

"Probably not. *I* think it's a good cause, though." With that, Lucky marched with purpose toward the tea shop, and Gwen followed close behind.

"Really, I need to send them a little something. I got a care package last week of cookies. Petty's peanut butter chocolate chip, Jonquil's raspberry windmills, and Bluebonnet's pump-kin cranberry cookies." Lucky stopped to pull a small baggie out of her purse with two of each cookie inside and handed it to Gwen. "Almost forgot."

"Your godmothers are the best. They definitely deserve tea." Gwen nodded as she stuffed a cookie in her mouth.

They went inside Gaston's Tea Shop and immediately,

Lucky was drawn to a fat ladybug teapot. That was definitely going to Petty because she was round, happy, and mostly good luck, too.

"Ope!" Gwen cried, and grabbed her wrist as she reached for it.

When Lucky looked down, she saw that her sleeve had caught on the edge of the glass shelving. One more move and she'd have murdered the display. Gwen untangled her, and Lucky grabbed the teapot.

"Thanks," she murmured.

"*Lucky* I was here, huh?" Gwen grinned.

"You think you're funny." She hugged the teapot to her chest.

"I know I'm funny. I'm a freaking delight."

"Gwen Borders, is that you?"

Lucky knew without turning to look that the woman speaking was PTA Nancy.

Gwen's face contorted into a fake smile. "Nancy. Nice to see you."

"Is it, though? I had the feeling you'd been avoiding me after you saw me having dinner with Jake. . . ."

Lucky had to fight the urge not to swivel her head around on her shoulders like an owl.

"Since we haven't spoken since then."

Gwen waved her off. "You know how it goes. I've just been busy. I'm glad Jake wants to help with the Spring Sock Hop. The kids will be so happy he'll be able to chaperone. He never gets to attend these things. He's always so busy."

Gwen hadn't told Lucky about this.

And maybe Jake had just been discussing the dance, but Lucky had a sense for when people were lying, and that story reeked like hot garbage.

"Ah yes, well, he . . . uh . . ." Nancy coughed. "Volunteered you to bake all the snacks. We were hoping for allergy-free. Can you do vegan, gluten-free, nut-free chocolate chip cookies? That way everyone is covered? We'll need about three hundred." Nancy smiled.

"Of course. It's not a problem." Gwen's smile was real this time, and Lucky knew it was because she loved baking, and a challenge. Gwen had grown up in a place where they didn't have a PTA, didn't have Spring Sock Hops, and she definitely hadn't had a mother who baked cookies.

"Anything for our little darlings, right?" Nancy smiled back.

Lucky wanted to puke.

For a hot minute, she considered it. Everyone in town was used to her mishaps and if she happened to spew Technicolor glory all over PTA Nancy, no one would know it had been on purpose.

Of course, that would mean giving up the delicious coffee she just snarfed and Lucky was not about that life.

Instead, she shoved the ladybug teapot at Gwen and launched herself at Nancy.

Not to pummel her face like Lucky wanted to do, or even to ralph in her hair, but to give her a giant hug.

And rub her bad luck all over the woman.

"I'm so glad my niece and nephew have such great people to advocate for them. So. Glad." She tightened and released the hug with each sentence. Just to make sure the woman was good and covered with Lucky's definite *un*luck. Then she stepped back and beamed at her with a bright smile.

"I . . . thank you." Nancy coughed. "I didn't know Gwen thought so well of me."

Gwen got in on the action. "Oh, Nancy. I should do more to show it. You work so hard on all the events and running the PTA. I mean, even though you're not the president, you always take charge. You get things done."

Which was all code for the fact PTA Nancy, from the stories Lucky had heard, was a raging shitlord.

"I should really get going." Nancy shrugged uncomfortably.

A long silence reigned before Nancy coughed and headed to the register.

"That was pretty brilliant. I thought her eyes were going to pop out of her head like one of those pooping animal keychains. You know the ones? Where you squeeze them and their eyes bulge and so goop squishes out of their butts?"

Lucky laughed. "That's amazing. It's too bad you didn't get a video."

"I've got it on replay in my head right now. Where it's going to stay forever and ever."

"You didn't tell me Jake went out to dinner with her," Lucky said.

Gwen shrugged. "It is what it is. I don't care if he's cheating on me. I just care that it's with her. And they both think I'm stupid."

"Any chance you think they were actually working on the sock hop?"

Gwen snorted. "About as likely as winning the lottery."

"I'm sorry." Lucky reached for Gwen's hand and squeezed. "I've got a shovel and a tarp if you need me. . . ."

Laughing, Gwen pulled her in for a hug. "Thank you. You always know how to make me laugh."

Lucky hugged her back, once again grateful that she was immune to whatever black cloud hung over Lucky's life.

Unless this thing with Jake was somehow her fault. . . .

"No, stop it," Gwen said.

"What?"

"I know what you're doing. Jake made his own choices. I made my own choices. Neither of them has anything to do with you."

Lucky gave her a half smile. "It would kill me if my . . ." Lucky struggled to find the right word. "My curse, for lack of a better word, harmed you and the monsters in any way."

"Lucky, I don't know what I'd do without you. You're my best friend. I'll take having you cursed over not having you at all." Gwen perked. "Hey, maybe that's your problem. Maybe you are *cursed*. You've got three godmothers. Maybe they're *fairy* godmothers and your mother forgot to invite one of the fairies to your christening and she was pissed and cursed you or something."

Lucky snorted. "Dude. This isn't Sleeping Beauty. I'm not *that* fair of face. I mean, pretty fair, but not fairy-tale princess fair. Or really fair of disposition either, now that I think about it. Weren't those the fairy gifts? Plus, I was fine until *him*."

"Maybe his . . . um . . . moment where he was out of alignment knocked *you* out of alignment. Maybe if you saw him again?"

"That's the meanest thing you've ever said to me. I don't wish bad things on him, but *oh my God*, how do you expect me to look him in the face after that debacle?"

"He was the one who drove his little car into the wrong garage. What do you have to be embarrassed about?"

Lucky looked up at the ceiling. Her face on fire as she still burned with embarrassment from that ill-fated night so many years ago.

"Look, things happen during sex. One time, Jake was—"

"If we could not talk about this anymore, that would be great. I don't want to imagine Jake having sex."

"Okay. Fine. Me either, honestly. But . . . maybe you should talk about it. It doesn't have to be with me, but I'm sure he's forgotten about it, too."

"Unlikely."

"Oh, hey . . . look. Nancy is still trying to check out."

Lucky watched as Nancy pulled card after card out of her wallet and none of them worked.

They crept forward silently for a closer look.

"Everything okay, Nancy?" Gwen asked.

"There's been some kind of mistake," Nancy said. "All of my cards have been declined."

"Here. Let me help you." Gwen pulled out one of her credit cards.

"Oh no. I couldn't ask you to."

"You're not asking. I insist. How embarrassing. I'm sure you'd come to my rescue if the situation was reversed. Right?" Gwen said, and handed her card over to the clerk.

Nancy looked down at her phone. "Oh my God. All of my cards are maxed out. There are charges in Hawaii. California. Florida."

"That sucks," Lucky said, helpfully.

Nancy grabbed her tea and darted out of the store.

"That sure worked fast. It's rare that you get to observe karma in action. Usually, it doesn't hit until long after you don't care anything about watching it slap the person in the face."

Lucky shrugged. "Happy to be of service." Then she looked at the teapot in Gwen's hands. "Oh, I need this wrapped and shipped," she said to the clerk.

"Oh, right. You need to get them some tea to go in it, too," Gwen reminded her.

"The Russian Caravan, I think. Petty likes strong flavors. Maybe some blueberry rose as well."

"All good choices," the clerk said, and added them to her order.

Just then, Lucky's phone rang. She pulled it out of her bag, but the screen was cracked and she couldn't tell who was calling. Which drove her nuts. She didn't answer the phone for just anyone. People who called without texting first were savages.

Of course, it was most likely one of her godmothers. She took a wild guess.

"Hello, Petty."

"My sweet little good-luck charm. What are you doing? Are you busy?"

Lucky tried not to snort. Petty behaved as if Lucky didn't

break things everywhere she went. It was rather endearing, honestly, because it seemed like she didn't actually notice.

To Gwen, she said, "I'm going to take this outside. Can you . . ." She nodded to the teapot.

"Sure."

Lucky handed her a credit card and stepped outside the shop, barely missing a shitting pigeon flying overhead. That *was* actually very lucky. Maybe things were about to change.

"I need a favor, darling."

Lucky wasn't sure what she could do for Petty, but most likely she was down for whatever shenanigans the old dear had cooked up. "Sure. Anything."

"Be careful what you agree to, sweet pea."

How bad could it be?

Of course, this was a question that she'd learned not to ask. Or at least, she'd thought she'd learned that lesson.

"I need you to get married. Well, fake married. On Valentine's Day."

"What's that?" Lucky wasn't sure she'd heard her correctly.

"You should get your ears cleaned. Maybe you have impacted wax? I'm sure I spoke quite clearly. I need you to get fake married. All of us do. Fairy Godmothers, Inc. is in the pooper. So is Ever After. We need to draw in more tourists. More business. A high-profile wedding will put us on the map."

Lucky coughed. "Petty."

"Yes, dear?"

"Are you stoned?"

"Why does everyone keep asking me that? No, and even if I was, it's a good idea."

"I . . . no. I mean, me? High-profile? You know how I break things."

"Yes, but now you're going to fix it. Trust me. This is exactly what everyone involved needs."

Lucky consoled herself that even if she agreed, there was

no way in hell they were going to find a groom who would fake marry the Master of Disaster.

"Who is the groom?" She laughed when she said it, but a sudden feeling like a wrecking ball smashed into her gut.

She knew before Petty spoke.

But no, it couldn't be.

They wouldn't.

*He* wouldn't.

"Now, don't hang up on me."

Lucky did just that. She hung up on her godmother.

Of course, Petty called right back. Lucky considered not answering, but she knew better.

"No."

"Darling, yes. And it's time for the two of you to clear the air. Plus, he's our best bet. Heart's Desire Chocolate is the biggest chocolate maker in the world. He uses fair-trade, organic cacao and uses best practices to ensure there's no slave labor, protects the rain forest, and he's America's Sweetheart. The press loves him. It'll be a fairy-tale romance the public can get behind. And getting married in Ever After is just too perfect."

*Get behind.*

Lucky rolled her eyes. Her godmother was either oblivious or being a raging smart-ass. Lucky wasn't usually sure which, and that was definitely one of Petty's superpowers.

"I think you've forgotten we're *his* godmothers, too."

"Well, that's just incestuous."

"Pish posh. How soon can you get here? And you should bring Gwen and the monsters. They'd get a real kick out of Ever After."

"I'm not doing it, Petunia." She'd used her full name. Petty had to take her seriously.

"We can do this the hard way or the easy way." Petty's tone was sweet, but there was steel under that syrup.

"It's like you forgot who I am. I have to do everything the hard way."

"What if I told you this could fix your little problem?"

"I'd say you're a shrewd tactician."

"I am. But I also think it's the key."

Petty was usually right about most everything, but Lucky didn't think she could face him. It had been too long and . . .

"Please, Lucky. Jonquil and Bluebonnet and I just don't know what else to do. We need you both."

It was the please that got her. Right in the guts.

"Okay, fine."

"You won't regret it."

"I'm already regretting it."

"See you soon, lovie."

As soon as she hung up the phone, another pigeon passed overhead.

And this time, he didn't miss.

# Chapter 2

Ransom Payne couldn't have been more pleased with this quarter's sales predictions.

They were through the roof.

But he knew they would be.

That was the benefit of having not only fairy godmothers, but a tiny sprinkle of fairy dust in the soil of his cacao farms. It gave his chocolate that little something extra. All he'd had to do was promise the godmothers he'd ethically source his materials and take care of the environment. All of those things were important to him, so it wasn't any kind of sacrifice. This was the kind of business he'd wanted to run.

The kind of man he wanted to be.

The fact that it made him richer than Midas didn't hurt, either.

He leaned back in his chair and surveyed his kingdom. Err . . . his office. This wasn't somewhere he'd ever expected to be. Not when he'd first started. Not until he found out his godmothers were actually *fairy* godmothers. The real deal.

He'd started in a garage with some grow lights. Now, he had a penthouse office, more money than he could spend in one lifetime, even with all of his charitable contributions, and he'd crossed almost every item off of his bucket list.

Except a family.

Sure, his best friend worked as his assistant, he had the godmothers. They were his family, but he wanted a wife—a partner. He wanted children.

Roderick, his best friend, stepped inside the double doors. "A Miss Jonquil is here to see you."

"Did she bring cookies?"

Jonquil toddled in behind Roderick. "Of course, I did, darling. Of course."

"You're supposed to wait until I tell you that you can go in," Roderick said, but his tone was patient and kind.

"Do I ever?"

"No, Miss Jonquil."

"But I do bring you cookies." She handed an overstuffed basket to Roderick. "There you go, dear. Now, off with you. I have some important business to discuss with my godson."

"Important business." Roderick nodded, but accepted the basket with a grin. "I can be bribed."

"Cookies are my superpower," Jonquil said, and handed the other basket to Ransom.

Ransom didn't even try to pretend he wasn't drooling for his godmother's cookies. This batch was the best he'd ever tasted, so he was sure she was going to ask him for a favor.

The godmothers usually traveled as a trio, unless they had a mission. Jonquil and her cookies were the big guns when it came to Ransom. Although, if they ever needed anything, Ransom was more than happy to help them. They were family. He loved them dearly.

Also, *cookies*.

"While I enjoy bribes, you know that you don't have to bribe me," he said around a mouthful of cookie.

"You might need it for this favor."

He stopped midbite and eyed her. Her "grandmother glow," as he liked to call it, was extra glowy today. Her round cheeks were pink, and her white hair was pulled back into a bun with a crown of yellow flowers. And her dress was especially starched, swishing when she walked. Yes, she'd gone the extra mile today.

"What is it?"

"So Ever After is in trouble." She took a bite of her own cookie, seemed to think about it before stuffing the rest of it in her mouth. "Not my best work. But I was stressed. Sorry, dearie."

"Tastes fine to me."

"Savage," she said with no real rancor. She handed him another cookie.

"So what is it? How can I help?"

"The town is losing all of its magic. Why, when Bluebonnet tried to bring the cherry tree to bloom, we got nothing."

"What does that mean?"

"It means we need a way to refill it and fast, or Ever After is going to fade away, as will what's left of the magic in the world."

"Do you need money?" He had that in abundance, but he didn't know what else he had to offer them that could help.

"We need something money can't buy. We need love. So we need you to get married."

He proceeded chewing calmly and swallowed before he spoke. "Well, that's all fine and good. I can get married, but I need to do this little thing called falling in love first. Don't think I haven't tried. I've been on some of these dating apps; I even let Roderick set me up, which was horrible."

"You haven't let *us* fix you up."

He cocked his head to the side. "Why do I suddenly feel like this conversation is going to take a turn I don't like?"

Jonquil smiled at him. "Don't you trust us?"

"I know you."

"Of course, you do, dear. Of course." Jonquil smiled a rather large smile. "But you don't have to get real married. Fake married is fine."

Yes, this conversation was definitely taking a turn down an ugly road. He pinched the bridge of his nose.

"Please explain to me, Godmother, how getting fake married will help restore the love in Ever After?"

"I thought you'd never ask." Jonquil perked. "See, it's a publicity stunt. That's what you call it, right? All the press with billionaire chocolate magnate getting married in Ever After, Missouri, quintessential small-town USA. If you do it, others will do it, too. We have a whole plan. Turn the castle into a B and B, hire a team of wedding planners, magical caterers . . . it will be the best thing ever. People will flock to get married in a fairy-tale town. Especially after seeing yours done right on Valentine's Day. It doesn't get any more romantic than that."

"Don't you run the risk of exposure?"

"That's the genius part. Everyone will just think it's part of the kitsch. People will get the real fairy-tale weddings to celebrate their love, and we'll get to thrive again."

"If I agree to this, I assume you already have a bride picked out?"

"Oh yes. She's beautiful, and it's a perfect second-chance romance."

"*Second chance?*" His eyes narrowed.

"The papers are going to love it."

"Oh no."

"Oh *yes*."

"No."

"You don't even know who I'm talking about." Jonquil rolled her eyes.

"Yes, I do. *Lucky.*" He said her name like a curse.

Jonquil gave a delicate cough. "Maybe you do. But listen. It's time for both of you to forgive each other."

Was it possible she hadn't forgiven him after all of this time? He'd forgiven her for telling everyone about it. Although, he supposed . . .

"I have forgiven her."

"Have you? Then why haven't you spoken to her?"

"To be fair, she hasn't spoken to me, either."

"The last time you spoke, what did you say to her?" Jonquil gave him a stern look with a raised brow.

He'd swear that woman could stare down the worst criminal and make him confess with only that look.

"We tried to let you two work this out on your own. We can't help too much. Especially since we're low on magic, but by the gods, you two are the single most stubborn creatures on earth. I could push a recalcitrant donkey up Everest before I could get either of you to do what I want."

"Maybe what you want isn't what we want."

Jonquil snorted. "Of course, it is. You just have to realize it. I'm the fairy godmother, remember? I know things."

"Well, she said some mean things to me, too."

"She did." Jonquil nodded. "But is that how we deal with being called out on our behavior? Hmmm?"

Ransom sighed. He hated being treated like a kid, but she was right. "You're right. No, what I did was wrong, regardless of what she did. Her actions are a separate topic, and we can address them after I make amends for what I did," he recited.

"Some lessons do stick."

"I just don't think this is a good idea. Why can't Roderick get fake married to Lucky?"

"I heard that," Roderick called back into the office. "Not a chance. You'd murder me in my sleep."

"There is that," Jonquil said.

They were right. Despite everything, he did still have feelings for Lucky. How ridiculous was that after all of this time? After everything that happened, that should've been closure enough.

But the idea of seeing her again . . . of being in the limelight, someone would dig up that story and it would explode from the gossip rags like an awful comet.

"You're not that boy anymore, Ransom." Jonquil touched his hand. "You're a grown man with a successful empire. And we need you."

It was the "we need you" that got him.

Ransom made a secret promise to himself when he discovered magic and his godmothers had helped him start his business and make it what it is today. He swore if there was ever any way he could help them, he'd do it without question.

He hadn't expected it would come at such a personal cost. He hadn't imagined any future where what they'd need from him would rip his heart out and tear down the idea of himself it had taken him so very long to construct.

Of course, if one silly mishap from the past could tear it all down, maybe he needed to start over anyway.

"Ransom, one more thing."

He looked up into Jonquil's wide, and kindly, blue eyes. "What?"

"She already said yes."

He coughed. "I didn't say no. I . . ." Saying yes would make it real. Of course he was going to say yes, but Ransom was having trouble getting the words out of his mouth. Making the commitment outside of his own head.

"I know this is scary, but we believe in you."

Yes, the godmothers had always believed in him. Although, he'd always had the fairy dust as a backup. He couldn't fail with fairy dust, right? Maybe they could just dust him for this?

No, he knew there was no magic like that of the human heart. They couldn't make you brave, or change who you were deep inside.

This would be all him.

Roderick had come back inside. "Since I was eavesdropping, I figured I might as well come in and offer my two cents."

"Yeah, thanks for that. Privacy, man."

Roderick shrugged. "Whatever. You were going to give me the play-by-play anyway. Is this the woman from college?"

"You just eat your cookies and mind your business," Jonquil advised.

"Everything Ransom does is my business. I'm his assistant and his best friend." But he didn't hesitate to eat another cookie.

Jonquil made a face, but relented. "Yes, it's that woman." Then her eyes narrowed. "I suppose if Ransom is getting married, then you should be in attendance. You'll need to be the best man."

"Yep."

"Lucky's best friend is about to be single." Jonquil eyed him pointedly.

"No thank you."

"You haven't even met the woman."

"I don't have to meet her to know I don't want any part of her." He leaned against the desk. "I'm sure she's lovely, but I am not interested in a relationship right now."

"Doesn't matter, if the relationship is interested in you."

"That's true," Ransom agreed. "Sometimes, it just happens."

"No, relationships don't just . . . happen." He wiggled his fingers to accentuate his point. "They take planning. Work. Effort."

Jonquil nodded. "They do at that, but you find yourself doing those things for the right person. You want to do them."

"Nope, and you can keep your fairy dust or whatever to yourself, ma'am."

She laughed. "No fairy dust needed."

"I'm all for fake best man duty. You know I'm always up for an adventure. But the rest of it? No thanks."

"We shall see." Jonquil grinned. "So you'll do it?"

"Yes, I'll do it. I'll fake marry Lucky Fujiki."

"Good. I'll see you in Ever After, then? We'll have our publicity people get started."

Dread sank like a rock in the bottom of his gut, but he nodded.

Jonquil stood up on her tiptoes to hug him and kissed his cheek. "You're the best godson we could ask for. All will be well. Eventually. You'll see."

"It's the eventually I'm worried about."

Jonquil headed toward the door, but stopped in front of Roderick. Instead of kissing his cheek, she gave it a solid pinch. "Sweet boy, we'll get you right as rain soon enough."

"No more meddling. You're not my godmother."

"I think yours had an accident on her broom on the way to Bora Bora."

"That would explain it." Roderick nodded in all seriousness.

Jonquil waved her goodbyes and after she was gone, Roderick turned to Ransom.

"Does she really believe she's a fairy godmother?"

Ransom studied him for a long moment and considered his next words carefully. "Do you doubt her?"

"I know they gave you the seed money for Heart's Desire, but . . ."

Ransom eyed him.

"But . . ."

He continued to eye his friend.

"You're fucking with me. You don't believe all that nonsense. This fake-marriage thing is just an excuse to get you in a room with Lucky."

"Maybe it is, maybe it isn't. But you can't deny that the chocolate is good."

"Because you worked on it. You put all of your blood, sweat, tears, and heart into a product."

"I did. But Jonquil, Petunia, and Bluebonnet really are fairy godmothers."

"I'm on some kind of prank show, right? If I say I believe you, a crew is going to come out of their hiding places and—"

Ransom shook his head. "Nope, they're the real deal."

"Where the hell is my fairy godmother, then?"

"Jonquil just told you she's still recovering from an accident on her broom." Ransom laughed. "That's probably why she brings you cookies, too. They're really wonderful ladies. I'm so relieved to finally be able to tell you the truth. I hated keeping that from you."

"Say I believe this. What else are you keeping from me? Are you really a dragon who hoards chocolate?"

"Maybeeeee." Ransom grinned and ate another cookie.

"So Ever After. It's actually magical?"

"Yep."

"Huh."

"You're taking this much better than I thought you would, honestly."

"Yeah, I'm still hung up on Jonquil's prediction for me with Lucky's friend. I don't like it."

"You've never met the woman."

"She's still married."

"But she won't always be. The godmothers know these things. Their specialty is love."

"Don't want it."

Ransom shrugged. "You can't fight fate."

"I don't believe in that crap. You know that."

"So you can accept there are fairy godmothers with real magic, but you don't believe in fate?"

"Considering I met one and, really, it explains so much. The easiest answer is usually the correct one, so I'm just going to roll with it. I figure if you get one over on me, that's fine. You know what you've got coming." Roderick grinned. "By the way, this fake-wedding thing? Consider me still on the clock."

Ransom rolled his eyes. "As if I don't actually pay you a robber's fortune anyway."

"You couldn't live without me."

"You're right." Ransom grinned back. "So, uh, I guess we should get ready to go to my doom."

"It's not going to be that bad. No one is going to call you The Boy Who Missed. They stopped doing that when you made your first million."

"Let's hope you're right about this, too."

Roderick stood. "I'm always right. Obviously. But would it matter if I wasn't? The godmothers need you."

"Right again." Ransom sighed.

Even though trepidation coiled tightly around him, something warm sparked in his chest and Ransom wondered if the flame between them would still burn as hot after all of these years.

And if it could burn through the shame of the Incident.

# Chapter 3

As a child, Lucky had spent a few summers in Ever After with her godmothers, and she was thrilled to be able to share some of that magic with Gwen's kids now. Even though it was the end of January, it was a perfect day in Ever After. Unseasonably warm, but beautiful.

The sun shone overhead, the trees were thick and lush . . . come to think of it, the only time she'd ever seen snow in Ever After had been the one Christmas she'd come to visit. Snow on Christmas Eve and Christmas Day.

She supposed a town named Ever After had to be a little different from the rest of the world. Or at least, that's what her inner child hoped.

And speaking of children, the three-hour car ride hadn't been too awful, and Brittany and Steven were entranced by the little fairy-tale-style cottages, the town square, and the abundance of wildlife that allowed the children to get ridiculously close as Lucky took them on a walking tour of the town.

If Lucky didn't know better, she'd swear all the animals had some kind of silent agreement with the children that they could get close as long as they didn't touch.

Brittany and Steven laughed and squealed when one gray squirrel with a giant, puffy tale threw an acorn at another squirrel when he seemed to take one from the first squirrel's pile. They made sounds at each other that sounded like a laser gun. *Pew. Pew. Pew.*

The children couldn't stop giggling.

"I can't believe we've never come here with you before," Gwen said.

"I totally should've brought you to visit sooner. I'm glad you're here now, though. The kids seem to be having a great time."

"Who wouldn't? This place is so cool. You're so lucky that you got to spend time here as a kid."

Normally, she would've cringed at the use of the word, but Gwen was right. "Yeah, I am."

"I can't believe the godmothers rented a cottage for the kids and me." Gwen shook her head. "I also can't believe that more people don't know about this place."

"They will after the fake wedding."

"When does he get in?" Gwen didn't have to specify which he she meant. They both knew.

"I don't know. I don't want to think about it." She pointed to the edge of town at the castle that looked like it had been plucked directly from the Brothers Grimm. "Look at the castle."

Gwen looked up at the spires rising out of the forest, and a path into the woods seemed to become more visible.

"We're actually in a fairy tale. I don't want to go back."

"Not even for your stuff?" Lucky teased.

Gwen bit her lip. "You know what? Not even for my stuff."

"I'm sure the godmothers could help you out with that, if you're serious."

"Really? You think? I don't know what I'd do here. How I'd pay my bills."

"Specialty baking. You were going to bake three hundred allergy-friendly cookies like it was nothing. I'm sure with a booming wedding industry here, they'll need something like that."

"Yeah, maybe." Gwen was quiet and thoughtful as they wandered down the quaint path.

"Oh, hey. We should take the kids to the fountain. It's on the way to the castle. Come on." Lucky led them through the forest.

The trees arched like a cathedral overhead, and the path seemed to open up for them, almost as if the forest itself invited them to explore her leafy depths.

The sounds of the gurgling water led them onward, and warmth swelled inside her chest. She hadn't been to the fountain since she was little. It was her safe place. Where she went to think, to plot, to be with her thoughts when she thought that the whole world was coming down around her ears.

It was especially amazing during summer evenings when the fireflies danced and flickered long into the warm night.

Except when they emerged into the carefully manicured little park, they were not alone.

Lucky knew before the figure standing by the mermaid fountain turned around that it was *him*. She hadn't seen Ransom in years, but she'd recognize his broad shoulders anywhere, and the way his dark hair curled just under his ear.

"I'm gonna puke," she murmured.

"Aunty Lucky's gonna yark," Steven echoed.

"Shh," Gwen said. "She's fine." But she stopped short and held the children's hands. To Lucky, she said, "You're fine. You're not gonna puke."

"Yes, yes, I am."

"You should listen to a person when they say they're going to be sick," a deep voice said from the other side of the fountain.

"I think I know my friend, thanks." Gwen scowled at the man who emerged.

He looked familiar. Lucky thought she might have seen him somewhere before. He was obviously one of Ransom's friends.

"Do you know her better than she knows herself?" The man arched a dark brow.

Lucky noticed that he was handsome. Not as handsome as Ransom, of course, but there were few creatures on heaven or earth that were.

"I do. Not that it's any of your business," Gwen growled.

Her best friend bristled next to her, and for a brief moment, she was terrified that Gwen's immunity to Lucky's bad luck was going to run out. Lucky was definitely going to be sick. Why was her stomach like this around him? He hadn't even turned around to face her yet.

She considered running back down the path the way she'd come, but Lucky had known this moment was coming since she'd agreed to this charade.

Ransom had agreed to it as well, she reminded herself.

"Of course it's my business. I'm Roderick, the best friend, the best man, and the personal assistant. We can't have little Lucky here puking all over the groom, can we?"

At that moment, Lucky knew that he knew. About the Incident.

That shouldn't have surprised her. Everyone knew. Of course he did. She'd become an urban legend, a cautionary tale they told coeds about the dangers of all the sins to be found on campus. From eating the cafeteria sushi, which she didn't, to drinking, which she didn't, and to having sex. Which she almost gave up on after the Incident.

"Really? You're an asshole." Gwen rolled her eyes at him.

"Asshole," Brittany repeated in her little voice.

Gwen didn't correct her, and she began to sing a song made entirely of "asshole." She skipped around, singing and doing a little dance, stopping every so often to point at Roderick.

"You're not going to correct her?" Roderick drawled, with doubt scrawled across his features.

Ransom still hadn't turned around. Lucky wondered if he was still as embarrassed as she was. That gave her a small measure of comfort.

"I teach her not to lie." Gwen smiled.

"I can't believe Jonquil wanted to set us up. That's the worst idea in the history of bad ideas." Roderick snorted.

Gwen bark-snort-coughed. "That has to be a lie. Jonquil loves me. She'd never saddle me with you. Plus, I'm married."

"Not for long, it seems."

"Thank God for that." Then, a stricken expression crossed her face and she looked at the kids.

Steven hadn't noticed anything, but Brittany stopped and wandered back over to her mother.

"It's okay, Mama. We'll live in Ever After and you can marry someone else. But not *him*." She stuck her tongue out at Roderick.

Lucky slid a glance to Ransom to see that he'd finally turned around.

The years had been overly kind. Not that she expected he'd look like a mole person or anything, but where there had been the first awkward bloom of male youth, there was a man. His jaw had been a sharp angle, but now it was a bladed edge. His shoulders had once hinted at the way he'd fill a space, an outline of the width and breadth of the muscle to come. He moved with the confidence and grace of a man used to power. The only thing that hadn't changed was the depth in his eyes. The warmth and kindness there that made her fall in love with him so many years ago.

Roderick and Gwen, the kids, everything faded away at that moment. It was as if the two of them had been caught in a bubble outside of time and space. The sound of her heartbeat in her ears was like listening to the ocean in a shell.

Lucky didn't want any of the old feelings that surged in her chest. She didn't want to remember how much she loved the way he smelled. How natural it felt to move closer to him, because that had ended so well the last time.

Why did he have to smell so good?

The bastard actually smelled like chocolate.

What an asshole to come to this meeting smelling like her favorite thing in the world.

Worse? He looked down at his feet just for a second before raising his ridiculously blue eyes to meet hers once again. It was endearing. It was devastating.

Then he gave her that half smile that had always given her a case of what Lucky liked to call "Turtle Syndrome." It made her want to throw herself on her back, and stay there, much like a turtle that couldn't seem to right itself.

He was the first to speak. "It's good to see you."

"I didn't expect to see you," she blurted.

"At all?" He gave her a full grin. "Since we're getting married, I'd say you have to look at me at least once."

She pursed her lips. "You know what I mean."

They stared at each other again for a long moment. His eyes moved over her, and his perusal made her squirm. Ransom wasn't gross about it, he wasn't objectifying her or treating her like a fuck doll, but the butterflies in her stomach had started cannibalizing each other. It was getting ugly in there.

Lucky wrapped her arms around her stomach.

"Are you okay?"

"Why, you scared?" She mentally slapped herself. Why was she such a dick? He'd been nothing but gracious and she was acting like a spoiled brat.

Except, he didn't seem to take offense. He actually laughed. "Nah, I've dealt with worse."

Then he winked.

He. Fucking. Winked.

It brought back all the shame and horror from that night, that final night, when everything had shattered around them.

If he hadn't winked, it would've been fine. She didn't know why the wink enraged her so much, but it did. Lucky would've called herself out on her own bullshit and she could have settled in for a nice pretend wedding.

But instead, he'd winked, and her carefully constructed wall that was supposed to keep her safe shattered into a million, tiny, stupid pieces.

"Nope, I'm out." She turned to walk away.

"Oh, hey. Come on. It's either laugh or cry. Everyone else has already laughed. Why can't we?"

She spun on him. "We're supposed to pretend like it didn't happen, Ransom."

"But it did. Have you forgotten it? I sure haven't."

Heat rushed her entire body.

"I . . . When I applied for my first loan to start the business, I heard them talking about me before I went into the loan interview. The Boy Who Missed. If I couldn't figure out how to fuck, I'd never be able to navigate my own business. I didn't get the loan."

"You went in anyway?" Lucky studied him, something like admiration blooming in her chest. Not that it was a surprise he'd go in anyway. That was the kind of guy Ransom Payne was.

But Lucky, she didn't know if she'd have had the fortitude.

"Of course, I did. Screw them." He smiled at her. "And I don't bank there. I advise everyone I know not to. I pulled out of a deal with a distributor because they still bank there."

"Petunia is definitely your godmother."

"Her nickname is Petty for a reason."

She couldn't deny that being here in this same space with him fed something inside of her that she hadn't known was hungry.

He exhaled heavily. "It *is* good to see you, Lucky."

"Yeah, it's good to see you, too."

"See, this won't be so bad."

Of course, that was the wrong thing to say. Those words were to the universe like a red flag to an angry bull. Or so Lucky was sure.

"Don't jinx us." Lucky looked around, trying to spot the

form their destructor would take. No birds overhead to shit on her. At least there was that.

"I don't believe in that."

"Well, you sure did when you said I was a curse."

"We both said a lot of things. It was a high-stress situation. I think we can forgive each other." He took her hands in his. "Can't we? Even if it's just for the godmothers?"

He was right. Plus, it was for the godmothers. That's what mattered.

"Of course. It was a long time ago. I was always more embarrassed than anything."

"Me too," he admitted.

Her mouth was moving before she had a chance to censor herself. "I guess we should spend some time together before all of this goes public. Get to know each other again."

"Are you staying at the godmothers' or the castle?"

"The godmothers'. I guess we'll have to move to the castle when it's time for the show."

He nodded. "I'm at the godmothers', too. Looks like we'll be sharing the attic suite."

"Okay, that's a lot more togetherness than I'd planned on." She bit her lip. "It's so weird. Why didn't I ever see you here when we were kids? How did I not know they were your godmothers, too? Not until . . . well . . . after that time I don't want to talk about."

"I don't know. It's weird, though. Right?"

She nodded. "So weird."

Suddenly, she was aware of the world again. Their little bubble had been popped by little fingers. Brittany and Steven were pulling her away from him, begging to go to their cottage.

"I think I have to go."

He smiled. "Dinner, then? Bluebonnet is roasting a chicken."

"Dinner," she repeated, numbly. "Dinner."

Lucky allowed the children to lead her to Gwen and they

walked back down the path toward the town proper, where guest cottages sat fat and happy, with rounded roofs shaped like red-spotted mushroom caps from a fairy tale.

"That's the guy? Oh my God. His friend is a first-class asshole, but he's . . . Girl. *Girl*."

"Yeah," Lucky mumbled.

"Hey. Guess what?" she said as they continued walking toward the cottage Lucky had indicated was theirs.

"Huh?"

"Nothing bad happened. There were so many opportunities. You had an upset stomach, the woodland animals, the birds . . . so many crows. I thought for sure you were going to get shit on. Again. The fountain could've malfunctioned. It was all fine."

"I didn't see the crows!" She looked up to the sky to make sure she wasn't in any immediate danger before she continued. "No, it was not all fine. He still makes me stupid."

"Why is that bad?"

"It just is." Lucky huffed and stuffed her hands into her pockets.

"I thought we were going to the castle?" Brittany asked.

"We'll go later. We're going to be spending a lot of time at the castle, right, Lucky?"

"Yeah, sure." She was still in a daze.

"Will the buttface be there?" Brittany asked.

"That's not nice. He was an asshole, but we don't insult people with how they look."

"Why not?"

"People can control being jerks. They can't control how their DNA combined to make their face."

Brittany was thoughtful for a moment. "Okay. I suppose."

"It's this one," Lucky said, and came to a stop in front of the largest mushroom structure.

It had a solid wooden door, with a giant brass key on a

long chain sticking out of the lock. Yellow and purple flower buds huddled tightly in their bed, waiting to unfurl.

Brittany stuck her nose on one and sniffed so hard, it almost went up her nostril.

"I hope they bloom while we're here!" Brittany sniffed again.

"Maybe they will," Lucky said.

"I have a sneaking suspicion who we're going to be neighbors with." Gwen nodded at the cottage next to them. It also had a key in the lock. The rest of the cottages were sans keys.

"Yeah, me too. Sorry about that. The least the godmothers could do was wait until you're divorced."

Her godmothers were amazing, but they're meddling was legendary. It all came from a place of love, of course. But it was exhausting trying to constantly thwart their matchmaking efforts.

She really hoped their business would take off. Not just to take care of them and help the town, but to keep them occupied with their version of fairy godmothering and matchmaking other people instead of herself.

"I should tell you something." Gwen leaned on the door for a moment before opening it and ushering in the kids. "Guys, go pick out your beds while I finish up with Aunt Lucky."

Lucky shook off her fugue and kissed the kids' foreheads before they went inside. Then she gave Gwen her full attention. "What happened?"

"I told Jake we weren't coming back."

"You what?" Lucky was shocked, but that quickly melted into happiness. Jake and Gwen were miserable together, and she wanted nothing more than to see her friend happy and fulfilled.

"Yeah, I . . . after what happened in the tea shop, it was satisfying to see PTA Nancy get what she deserved, but why put myself through that? I don't want to be bitter and hateful. So . . . I took the leap. I don't know where we're going to land, but I just had to."

Lucky hugged her friend tight. "It's going to be okay. You're going to get through this, and you know the godmothers will help you. Me too. Anything I can do. You're going to be so much happier. You'll be free."

"Same to you, toots."

Lucky narrowed her eyes. "I hate it when you quote my good advice back to me."

"I know." Gwen laughed. "So what are you going to do about it? I think you should sleep with him. That's when things started going horribly wrong instead of just a little wrong, right? And it doesn't look like it would be a chore, if you know what I mean."

After seeing Ransom again, she wasn't so sure she would ever be free. She couldn't stop thinking about his smile, the way he smelled, his hands . . . oh, his hands.

She'd be lying if she said she didn't want to feel his hands on her body again.

While remembering what had happened the last time was an anti-aphrodisiac, she reassured herself he had to have made progress since then.

Gwen's idea was unwelcome.

Unwanted.

Most likely the stupidest thing she'd ever considered.

But her whole life had gone even more wrong that night when . . . Lucky took a deep breath and realized she had to face it. She had to let the memory bloom fat and ugly in her mind. She couldn't look away. Not anymore.

Ransom had pressed forward eagerly, fumbling in the dark, and had made entry into the exit-only portion of the ride. It had been just the tip, because when she shrieked, he immediately withdrew.

She'd started that awful nickname by screaming he was a loser Harry Potter who didn't know what to do with his wand. He was The Boy Who Missed. For better or worse, it had stuck.

"Maybe you're right. Maybe I do need to go to bed with Ransom."

"That's the spirit!"

He was willing to marry her. So it shouldn't be too hard to get him into bed, right?

Lucky had a sneaking suspicion that things were going to get a lot worse before they got better.

Especially since she just realized she hadn't called her mother to inform her of her upcoming fake nuptials.

# Chapter 4

The scent of Bluebonnet's rosemary roasted chicken did strange things to Ransom Payne.

It stirred all of his appetites.

Every. Single. One.

He understood why the scent of the chicken made him think of home. It was his favorite dish, and it stirred happy childhood memories. Ransom wanted to swim in them, experience that joy and warmth for as long as he could. A simpler time when all he had to worry about was tracking mud from the creek on the godmothers' freshly waxed floor. It reminded him of summers that seemed to last forever, bedtime stories, and midnight ice cream sodas.

Except now, these memories stirred other longings. He wanted his own children to run and play in the creek, to spend long summers chasing each other and climbing trees. He wanted to help teach them about growing things in the godmothers' garden. He wanted to have to buy the godmothers a bigger table so their giant family could eat meals like this together.

After one bite of the chicken, and seeing Lucky across the table from him as she laughed at something Jonquil said, her dark eyes sparkling with mischief, he wanted those summers, those memories, and those children with *her*.

God, but she was the most beautiful creature he'd ever seen.

He was struck by her beauty with the same force as the first time he'd seen her walking across the quad.

Even when she'd tripped over a gopher hole.

He remembered their first kiss. The moonlight had shimmered on her smooth skin, and her lip gloss had smelled like strawberries. Tasted like them, too.

They'd been in the middle of the lake, and he'd planned a candlelit picnic on the rowboat. Drawn together, she'd pinched out the candles almost effortlessly as she leaned in to meet him.

That kiss had been like hitting him with a bat.

Or maybe it was just because their boat had capsized, dumping them into the cool water.

But the heat between them hadn't abated, they'd laughed and swam to shore and made out there, with the fireflies dancing around them until dawn.

Ransom reminded himself that this wasn't what he was here for, and no matter how much the idea appealed, the two of them were not meant to join in that way.

They couldn't be.

They'd tried to complete the deed several times, and each time had been a bigger disaster than the last.

Skinny-dipping in that same lake had resulted in leeches that got much too close to delicate goods.

A tornado had hit the cheap motel they'd tried off I-70 and had ripped the roof off of only one room. (Thankfully, no one was actually hurt.)

When the equestrian team had gone on its fall break, they'd been making out in the barn and as soon as Lucky had asked him if he wanted to have sex, they were charged by feral pigs. Ransom, being determined, had decided they should climb up to the loft, but a mutant wasp colony had taken up residence.

God, they should've stopped after that. But did they? No. They were in love.

They'd gotten close in the back of his car, but then the engine caught fire.

Lucky looked up at him then and offered a soft smile.

That softness on her beautiful face, the way she looked at him, it was all worth it.

For a moment, even as aroused as he was, he wondered if they could have a life together without sex. It wasn't the most important part of being with someone.

He'd fucking miss it, that was no lie.

But he still loved her, still wanted her as a person as much as he had all those years ago.

They could adopt children.

Because sex was always when things had gone bad.

Then he realized that his train of thought was on crazy tracks. They didn't know each other anymore. They weren't the same kids they were in college. Just because she was stunningly beautiful didn't mean he should be building fairy-tale castles in the—

*Fairy tale. Castles.*

Ransom didn't like the connection that just sparked in his brain. He looked down at the bite of chicken on his fork and raised an eyebrow at Bluebonnet.

"Something wrong with your chicken, dear?" Bluebonnet asked.

"I don't know. *Is there?*" Had the meddling old dears put some kind of love potion in his food? That was the only thing that made sense. He knew they weren't above that kind of thing.

"Whatever do you mean?" Petty asked.

"You know damn well what I mean," Ransom said.

"The chicken tastes delightful, as always, Bon-Bon." Lucky took a drink of her cherry blossom tea.

"Lucky likes it," Bluebonnet said in defense.

"I didn't say I didn't like it. We're already here to help you. Don't meddle," Ransom warned.

"I hope you don't mind that you're sharing the attic suite," Jonquil said, as if there wasn't already a discussion going on. "We thought you two should spend some time together before the press descends on our little town."

"Or before we can escape each other at the castle?" Lucky asked.

"Precisely," Jonquil agreed easily.

Ransom put down his fork and glared at each of his godmothers in turn.

"Ready for dessert?" Bluebonnet asked, blinking her eyes with faux innocence.

He narrowed his eyes, but then picked up his fork again. If she'd done something to the delicious chicken, he was already under its influence. No reason to go to bed hungry.

"Not quite."

Lucky took seconds.

Then thirds.

He wondered if she knew the truth about the godmothers. She didn't question that there always seemed to be more chicken. Even though no actual, living chicken had eight breasts.

"Godmothers," Lucky began after chewing a bite. "Would you mind if Gwen and the kids joined us for dinner from now on? She's left Jake and I'm . . . we're her only other family."

Petty gasped. "This is fantastic news."

"Like you didn't know," Ransom said with a snort.

"Well, I mean, I knew it was coming. I just didn't know when." Petty puffed with pride.

"I had another idea," Lucky continued. "I know there's already a bakery in town, but if you want to be a wedding town, you're going to need more than one. Gwen didn't bat an eye when the school asked her to bake three hundred allergy-friendly cookies for the bake sale."

Jonquil trilled. "I see exactly where you're going with this and it's marvelous. She and the kids can continue to stay in the cottage until the business is up and running. The town could all chip in to get her started. She could take over for Red and Grammy. They're looking to move farther out into the country and start a ranch. They've wanted to for ages."

"I can't wait to tell her!"

"Does she need help collecting her things from the soon-to-be ex? I could send Roderick," Ransom offered.

Bluebonnet smiled and for a moment, she looked almost vulpine. "Oh, that would be just perfect, don't you think, Lucky?"

Lucky laughed. "I don't know if I'd say it was perfect. They didn't exactly hit it off."

Ransom snorted. "Actually, Brittany called him an asshole."

"Did she?" Petty arched a brow. "Well, children are the tellers of universal truths."

"They'll figure it out. But it can't hurt to help it along. That would be lovely if you could send him a textural," Bluebonnet replied.

"A text, Bon-Bon," Lucky corrected.

"Whatever." Bluebonnet waved the words away with her left hand while she stuffed a golden, buttered roll in her mouth with the other.

Lucky met his gaze across the table and for a moment, the rest of the world fell away. It was only the two of them.

And Bluebonnet's damned chicken.

"Lucky, why don't you tell Ransom about that new piece you're working on?" Petty prompted.

"We're adults. We can figure out how to talk to each other," Lucky said.

"Well, then do it. I'm watching new witch hairs grow on Jonquil's chin waiting for you two to have a conversation."

Jonquil gasped. "You are not." She rubbed her thumb over her chin.

"No, Petunia has confused herself again." Bluebonnet narrowed her eyes. "She caught her own reflection on our grandmamma's silver.

"Bluebonnet, so help me—" Petty began.

"Lucky, would you like to walk in the backyard before dessert?" Ransom blurted.

"I would." She pushed her chair back and headed out the back door.

"What is your problem? How are we supposed to pull off a wedding in two weeks when you three can't stop bickering?" Ransom demanded.

Petty sniffed. "Oh, go for your walk. You handle your end. We'll handle ours. We've been doing this a lot longer than you."

"Maybe start getting it right, then."

Jonquil made a sound that was not unlike that of a startled bird. "Insolent boy. We should zap your bottom."

"Or turn you into a toad for a week," Bluebonnet threatened.

"I can't woo the girl if I'm a frog, now can I?" Ransom grinned, sure of himself.

"It can be done," Petty said with a surety that made Ransom cringe. "But our Ransom has never been a frog. We save that for special cases. Everyone is on edge. We really need this to work."

"I know, Godmother. But give us a little space, okay?"

"We've given you several years of space. Really, it's above and beyond, I think," Jonquil informed him.

"Yes, Godmothers. But you do remember this marriage is fake?"

The three old dears flashed him their best smiles and nodded.

Ransom arched a brow. "Uh-huh. Well, you know to be legal, we have to sign a marriage license. Which we're not doing."

"We said we understand, darling. Do run along. She's waiting under the cherry tree." Jonquil came over behind him and nudged him toward the door.

He allowed them to usher him outside and they closed the door behind him, leaving him mostly alone with Lucky.

"I can see their sweet little faces in the window watching us," Lucky said. "They look like little kids in line for an ice cream truck."

"I know. They want so desperately for this to be real."

Lucky pressed her lips together and looked down at her feet for a moment. It seemed as if she had something to say, but ultimately decided not to share whatever it was.

"Do you think the town really needs help? They seem like they're doing okay."

"I think it's a front. They don't usually bicker like that. A little back and forth, for sure. But there's an edge to them. I think they've been struggling."

"Question, and feel free not to answer if you don't want to." Ransom cleared his throat. "Well, let me have it."

"If the town is struggling so hard, if our godmothers are struggling so hard, why don't you just give them the money? They gave you the seed money for Heart's Desire, after all."

"That's a fair question." But he didn't know how to answer it. It was obvious now that Lucky didn't know about the fairy part of their godmothers. That they didn't need money. They needed love to fill up their magical wells. "You know I would, if they'd take it."

Lucky looked around his shoulder back to the window. She made a motion with her hand, waving them away. "For the love of . . . everything. How are we supposed to talk with them perched over us like pigeons on a bag of bread?" She shook her head. "I know they love us, but . . ."

"Yeah, it feels a bit like being in a fishbowl. Much like how we're going to feel when the press gets here."

"That terrifies me."

"Me too."

She snorted. "Thanks."

"No, I didn't mean . . . Me. Not because of you."

Lucky bit her lip. "Honestly, if it was because of me, I wouldn't blame you."

He remembered her reaction to seeing him by the fountain and he understood it. "None of that is your fault. You don't have any control over it."

"I have control over what I do. Who I spend my time with." She looked up at him. "Who I touch."

The way that she looked at him now, like she was thinking about touching him. That couldn't possibly be what she was thinking.

Could it?

No, no. Even if it was, he wasn't going there. It could only end badly for both of them.

"We should probably get our stories straight. I was thinking it would be easier to lie if we came up with them together."

A lie. Right. That's all this was.

"Good idea." He stuffed his hands in his pockets to keep from reaching for her. "It's not all a lie, though."

"No," she agreed softly. "Can I ask you something else?"

"You just did?"

"I mean . . . something real."

"Of course."

"My friend Gwen thinks that we should sleep together. I kind of do, too."

He coughed and took a moment to breathe before replying. "Is that the question?"

"Maybe."

"Lucky . . ."

"It's okay if you don't want to. I wouldn't either, if I were you. I mean, a tornado, feral pigs, wasps, leeches, fire . . . Actually, I'd probably run screaming."

Ransom tried not to think about how he was being offered something he still desperately wanted. "Why does she think that?"

"I've always been unlucky, but things didn't start to go horribly wrong for me until our near misses. She thinks if we followed through, that would bring my old not-great luck back. Which is better than my *un*luck."

"So it's not because you're still attracted to me?"

"Oh for . . . Have you seen yourself? Of course, I'm still attracted to you. A board would be attracted to you."

He felt his lips curl into a self-assured half grin. "Oh yeah. Tell me about it."

"Not a chance. I'm definitely not feeding your beast."

"That's not what you said five minutes ago."

She gasped. "I don't know what I was thinking. You're awful." The smile on her face said she didn't believe any such thing.

Stuffing his hands in his pockets worked for only so long. She was so close, and she smelled so good, and she offered everything. He reached up to touch her cheek, sliding his thumb over the elegant arch.

"Maybe we should get our stories straight first."

Her skin was so soft, and he remembered what it was like to touch almost every part of her body.

"Our stories." She nodded and turned her face into his palm.

"I suppose it would go much like it is now. We ran into each other after these long years apart, and nothing had changed. We both knew we wanted forever. So we decided to tie the knot in the quaint little town where our godmothers live. We decided we get the fairy tale."

If only that were true.

What would he give to make it true?

"Wouldn't that be nice?" she murmured, her lips brushing against his skin.

He knew he shouldn't kiss her.

But when she turned her face up to his, the polarity between them was undeniable.

She rose up on her tiptoes, and he bent down to meet her.

Their lips collided and for a solid minute, he was in heaven. Lucky felt so good in his arms, and everything was right with the world.

Lucky melted into him, her arms around him and her body pressed so tightly against him. She tasted like the cherry tea she'd been drinking and sunshine. He couldn't get enough. She seemed as hungry for him as he was for her, which pushed his need even higher. He wanted to taste her every desire, push her higher than she'd ever been, and stay that way with her until the stars burned out.

Until the scent of cherry blossoms exploded around them. Which in and of itself was rather lovely, but the tree began to creak and groan, and even though Ransom was sure he was in mortal peril, he couldn't bring himself to stop.

Not until Lucky broke away and looked up at the branches of the tree above them.

*Holy God*, she mouthed.

Ransom looked up just in time to see a cherry the size of a grapefruit drop like an anvil. He pushed Lucky out of the way and barely dodged the missile himself.

Only the tree shifted and groaned, heavy with the ridiculously large fruit, and more of the cherry brethren followed to cannonball to the ground below.

Lucky and Ransom made a mad dash for the back porch as the rain of monster cherries continued.

He turned around to take stock of the devastation and that's when he saw it.

A dark-red softball-size cherry comet headed right for his face. Ransom's brain screamed at him to duck, to move, to do anything but stand there and wait for it to hit him in the face.

Unfortunately, his body didn't obey his mind and the missile made contact with his face.

Damn, but that thing had weight. Even though it split apart on contact, some of the flesh of the cherry found its way up his nose and it packed a devil of a punch.

So much so that to Ransom's utter humiliation, the cherry, as they say, knocked him the fuck out.

# Chapter 5

Lucky was horrified.

As she looked down at him, prone on the couch, where she and the godmothers had managed to drag him, the little voice in her head got stuck on a loop. And that loop was that this was all her fault.

She knew the risks when she'd tried to entice him, but Lord, that man could still kiss. Lucky missed kissing him. Missed feeling his arms around her.

She missed *him*.

But all of those mishaps—correction, flukes or coincidences—were because of Lucky and her *un*luck.

Everything had been mostly fine until she kissed him. So basically, she just had to keep her paws to herself.

Or her lips.

She looked down at where he lay on the overstuffed old couch, his face stained with red smears from the cherry attack.

"This is awful," she whispered.

Ransom's eyes fluttered.

"See, he's fine. I told you he'd be just fine," Jonquil reassured her.

"I feel like I was run over by a truck," Ransom groaned, and then sneezed into a kerchief, blowing errant cherry bits out of his nose.

"A cherry truck dear, yes," Petty agreed.

"Where did they all come from? I don't understand. There was only one bloom when we went outside. It's like my very existence conjures bad luck."

"Don't be so dramatic," Bluebonnet replied. "Of course, it doesn't. Why don't you help us get Ransom upstairs?"

"I can get myself upstairs," he grumbled while he struggled to sit up.

Lucky helped him up, but then stepped back. "I'm so sorry."

"It's not your fault," he said.

"But wasn't it?"

"Did you direct the tree to make grapefruit-size cherries and fling them at me?" Ransom asked her.

"Of course not."

"Then it's not your fault."

"Definitely not your fault," the godmothers said in unison.

"You know what I mean."

"Just help me upstairs, please?" he asked her.

"Are you sure you want me to?"

"Go on, dear. Go on. We'll bring dessert up to you later," Jonquil said.

"Don't use the white washcloth for that cherry juice. There are red ones in the drawer and some homemade scrub in the rose petal jar that will take it right off," Petty called up after them.

After they shuffled up the stairs and into the attic suite, Ransom sank down on the twin bed that was the closest to the door.

Lucky had always slept on the one closest to the wall.

Nothing about the upstairs rooms had changed.

It still smelled of vanilla and cinnamon, and the scent washed over her, enveloping her in familiar safety.

Being a cottage attic, the room had a lot of odd angles and shapes. The two twin beds were positioned by the coolest window to ever exist. With a couple of pulleys and levers, it folded

out into a balcony and overlooked the backyard and the possessed cherry tree. As a child, Lucky used to pretend that she
was Rapunzel and trapped in an enchanted forest. Well, sometimes she was Rapunzel, but other times she was the witch.

Most of the time she was the witch, if she was honest with
herself.

Farther into the room was a living room space, with a TV
that got only three channels and still had the old VCR and
VHS tapes on the shelf underneath it. And against the far
wall was a mini kitchen.

Those visits in her childhood made her feel so grown up
to have her own sink, fridge, and microwave. The fridge was
always stocked with cherry cola and chicken fingers, even
though she would tiptoe downstairs for midnight ice cream
sodas. So much of what Lucky would call the magic of childhood she'd experienced here with the godmothers.

However, the crowning glory of the attic suite was the
bathroom. It took up as much room as the bedroom portion
and had a giant Roman bath, where Lucky used to spend
hours pretending she was a mermaid.

"This place was a castle for a kid," Ransom said. "So many
nooks and crannies to explore. So many worlds to build and
experience. This place brings back so many memories."

"I still think it's so strange I never saw you here." Lucky
had often wondered at the connections between Ransom and
the godmothers, but they'd never spoken of it.

"Nothing really surprises me with the godmothers anymore." He pulled himself up off the bed and wandered into
the bathroom.

"You seem to be feeling better." Relief flooded her.

"I think I was more surprised than anything else and I got
cherry juice in my eye."

They both knew he'd actually lost consciousness for a moment, but she was content to let him believe he was simply
surprised.

"Here, let me help." Lucky pulled out the washcloth and the rose soap Petty had suggested. "Sit down."

Ransom sat on the edge of the Roman bath and Lucky set about scrubbing the proof of their almost indiscretion from his face.

"That was insane. I wouldn't believe it if I hadn't seen it for myself."

His fingers closed around her wrist, sending electric jolts through her whole body, and their eyes met.

It was almost as if the cherry tree incident hadn't happened, even though the proof was right there on his face.

Lucky wanted nothing more than to lean down and kiss him, but she looked away and tugged softly at her arm.

He released her and she continued her work. Before long his face was as clean as if it had never happened.

"There. All better."

"Do you still think that we should try to finish what we started?" he asked.

He obviously wasn't going to let this go. The man didn't have the survival sense the Lord gave a flea.

And neither did she, honestly.

She still wanted to do exactly that—finish what they'd started all those years ago. Only she didn't get to make decisions based solely on what she wanted.

"How can you even ask that after what happened?" Her eyes widened, but then she wilted and sank down next to him. "How are we going to get through our fake wedding? All we did was kiss, which is what we have to do when we get married, and a cherry tree went all exorcist. What's going to happen to our guests?"

"I'm sure the godmothers have it in hand."

"I'm not."

A trio of cackles danced up through the windows from the outside, and Lucky ran over to look and saw her godmothers running around the yard, their ankles red with the cherries they'd stepped on and baskets and baskets full of the monster fruit.

"Well, the godmothers are thrilled with all those cherries."

Ransom came up behind her. "You know we'll be eating cherry cakes, pies, jams, and jellies until we die, right?"

"Dried cherries. Candied cherries. Chocolate-covered cherries. Cherry tea."

"This might send them right over the edge into cherry coffee."

Lucky considered. "That doesn't sound too terribly awful. But a little bit awful." She was thoughtful for a long moment. "I'm sorry, Ransom."

"Stop, it's not your fault. I wanted to kiss you as much as you wanted to kiss me."

"But we can't."

"We could try again. Right now," he offered.

"And risk the whole cottage falling down around our ears?" She sat down on her own bed and leaned with her head in the bowl of her hand.

Ransom eased down on his bed. "It would teach the godmothers not to meddle, wouldn't it?"

They looked at each other and then said in unison, "No."

They laughed, and it was the deep kind of belly laugh Lucky hadn't felt all the way to her bones in a very long time.

"Don't forget to 'textural' Roderick."

"Oh yeah. You know, maybe the godmothers are wrong on that. Roderick and Gwen, I mean."

"You think? They're not usually wrong about much."

"They're wrong about us. You think they could be wrong about two couples in the same week? Is it possible?" Ransom gave her a gentle smile.

That smile melted her heart into goo.

And other parts of her.

Why did it have to be the one guy she couldn't have?

Lucky needed some air, some distance. She shouldn't

be crying over spilt milk, but that's exactly what her heart wanted to do.

"I need to go call my mother. I'm gonna take a walk."

"I'll catch up with Roderick and maybe text me Gwen's number so I can coordinate?"

Lucky pulled out her phone. "I have a hard time texting."

"How did you do that?" He motioned to the cracked screen.

"Oh, you know. The usual. I sat on it."

She wrote down Gwen's number for him and headed downstairs and out the front door. Lucky didn't want to make this call, but she knew she had to do it before the godmothers did. Her mother would be so hurt if someone else told her.

Plus, she didn't trust the godmothers to tell her that this was, in fact, a *fake* wedding.

She walked down the winding path to the creek and checked to make sure she still had a signal. Lucky took a deep breath and exhaled.

She realized Gwen's plan had appealed to her because she wasn't over Ransom Payne. She wanted to be mad at him, blame him for everything. It was easier than blaming some stupid thing she couldn't control.

Lucky had to push that thought out of her head, too, because she thought of the one person who could have controlled it. The one person who had given her her name.

But it wasn't actually her mother's fault, either.

It had been a long tradition for the women on her mother's side of the family to name them after things you wanted for your child. Beauty, Peace, Fortune, and . . . Lucky.

Using voice recognition, she said, "Call Mom."

"Darling! I hope you're calling to tell me when you're coming to visit?"

"No, Ma. I'm at the godmothers' house."

"I should be offended you go to visit them more than you do me."

"You're always traveling. Just when I find out you're in Paris, you're off to Sofia."

"That's what trains and planes are for."

She wasn't quite sure how to broach the subject, but she might as well just get it over with. "I'm getting fake married on Valentine's Day, and it would be nice if you could come."

"Congratulations! This is wonderful news. Who's the groom?"

"You did hear the part where it was fake, right, Mom?"

"Fake, shmake. Tell me." Lucky could hear her mother's dainty shrug in the tone of her voice.

"Ransom. The guy from college."

"I'll book my flight now."

"Don't you have questions?"

"Like what?" Fortune asked.

"Like *why* we're getting fake married? Why it's on Valentine's Day? I don't know. Stuff?"

"I figure you'll tell me everything I need to know when I get there. I have some things to tell you as well."

"If it's about your wedding to my dad, I don't want it."

"Of course not. He's old news. Wait, unless . . . should I find him?"

"I wouldn't invite him to my real wedding, so you don't need to go to any trouble for the fake one."

"If you're sure. . . ."

"I'm very sure."

"There's something in your voice. What's wrong? Tell me."

Her mother always knew. It was kind of silly that Lucky was trying to keep it from her. "We'll talk about it when you get here, okay?"

"Can you find me a cute place to stay? I'm sure with the wedding coming up so soon all of the cottages are rented."

"They're turning the castle into a B and B, so I can probably get you a room there."

"That's a fantastic idea. I don't know why they didn't do

that sooner. The beautiful old thing was just rotting up on that hill. Have you heard the story about the owner? The kids used to say he was a cursed prince."

"Oh, please. That's taking the Ever After shtick a fairy tale too far."

"Is it? I suppose we'll see about that."

"You know what I'd rather know about? I want to see where you grew up. I don't know why it's such a big secret. It's not like Ever After has a wrong side of the tracks."

"Oh, it does. But that's not where I grew up. I suppose it's time to show you everything."

"And maybe there will be a clue how to break this curse."

"Perhaps. If only you'd stop thinking of it as a curse. It's not."

"You're not the one who has to live with it."

"No, I'm just the one who has to watch the being I love more than my own breath live with it."

Lucky sighed. "I'll see you when you get in. Love you, Ma."

"Love you, too, Lucky Charm."

The call ended.

Lucky Charm. Her mother refused to get it through her head that she was not, nor would she ever be, a lucky charm. The things her mother chose to accept and incorporate into her thinking were always a surprise.

She hadn't blinked an eyelash at this fake marriage announcement, or at whom she'd be marrying.

Although, what had Lucky expected? Her mother knew her well enough to know that when she decided to do something, no matter how foolhardy, well, that was just the way things were going to be and nothing was going to stop her.

Lucky sat down on the bank of the creek and took her shoes off to dip her piggies in the cool, clear water of the creek.

It had seemed so much bigger when she was a kid. A lot of things had.

She didn't know how she was supposed to go back to that room and sleep, with Ransom in the next bed over, and pretend like nothing was wrong.

Although, maybe she just had to convince herself that was the case. Nothing was wrong. Everything was fine. Everything was as it should be.

She hadn't thought about Ransom Payne in—oh, but that was a lie. She couldn't lie to herself. That wouldn't do anyone any good.

She still felt all the old feelings.

And some new ones she hadn't expected.

Everything came surging back. Like a fever.

That's what these feelings were, an infection. She needed a cure and she definitely wasn't going to find that sleeping in the same room with Ransom.

Something else was afoot, though. Lucky just didn't know what.

Her mother was acting weird.

A naked cherry tree had bloomed to full, and one might even say demonic, life.

Ransom thought that Bluebonnet had added something unthinkable to the chicken. . . .

What exactly could that have been?

Well, she told herself, being unthinkable meant she shouldn't be able to think of it, didn't it? Lucky shook her head, trying to rattle those idiotic thoughts out of her brain.

She didn't know how she was going to get through these next two weeks.

Lucky loved and appreciated her mother, and she was grateful she was coming, but she didn't know what she'd do without Gwen and the monsters.

She'd left many a care beside this creek, but she didn't think childhood magic was going to work this time.

Lucky stuffed her shoes back on and trudged back toward the cottage while evening fell soft and quiet.

When she got back to the house, all of the commotion had died down and the godmothers were in the great room with a small fire going.

Petty was pitting and slicing giant cherries, Bluebonnet was carding yarn, and Jonquil was knitting. It made a peaceful and homey picture.

"Did you call your mother, child?" Petty asked.

She nodded and waited for the godmothers to ask about what else had happened with Ransom, but they didn't.

Instead, Petty said, "There's some blueberry tart if you'd like to take some up to bed with you."

"It's pretty early for bed, don't you think? I'm grown." Lucky grinned.

Jonquil giggled. "You do what you like, dear. But we're going into the office bright and early tomorrow. We need to meet with the publicity people and get this thing on the road. You and Ransom will have meetings with the caterer, dressmaker, you'll need to pick colors . . ."

"We're fine with whatever you want," Lucky said as she snatched up several of the blueberry tarts.

"Oh no. You have to choose. It'll be good practice for the vendors," Bluebonnet corrected.

"When are we moving to the castle?" She stuffed an entire tart in her mouth.

The flaky crust melted on her tongue, and the rich blueberry filling was a treat she needed to taste again.

"Already ready to be rid of us?" Petty teased. "They'll have your rooms ready soon."

"Hopefully in time for Ma. Otherwise, I don't know where we'll put her."

"Sure, he'll have room for her. But you two are getting one of the new honeymoon suites. Phillip is doing a whole wedding wing in the castle. There are multiple ballrooms, a giant kitchen, oh, so many amenities. You should go take a bath. You'll be right as rain," Jonquil interjected. "Go on, then."

"And just maybe, you'll get an ice cream soda when you get up," Petty added.

Lucky slid into a chair at the table. "I need one now."

Petty put the cherries down, Bluebonnet her yarn, and Jonquil her knitting. They drifted toward her, almost like they had wings, and they enfolded her in a gentle, yet still-fierce hug, and then they set about making her an old-fashioned ice cream soda.

Petty got the ice cream.

Jonquil got the chocolate syrup.

Bluebonnet got the soda water.

As she sat at the table, she had the urge to swing her feet as she had when she was a child. Her godmothers doted on her and when they finally sent her up to bed, she was reminded of why she'd do anything for those dears.

Even face the prospect of breaking her heart all over again.

# Chapter 6

"Our poor little lovie." Petunia sighed after Lucky went up to the attic.

"Poor darling," Jonquil agreed.

"Except, the cherries, sisters. The *cherries*." Bluebonnet's eyes were wide as saucers. "And look at my wand!" She pulled it out of her apron pocket and waved it around like a sparkler, showing off its tiny blue comet trail.

Jonquil pulled her wand out. "Oh look, mine too!"

"That's because the kids love us," Petunia said, but then grinned as wide as her face would let her. "But the cherries, that's because they love each other! I knew we were on target with those two."

"Then we really need to do something about Lucky's lack of luck," Jonquil said. "If Ransom was almost murdered by a mutant cherry . . . I just don't think we can take any chances."

"You know we're immune to her . . . ." Bluebonnet seemed to struggle for the right word. "Gifts. So they should be okay as long as they're under our roof."

"They can't stay under our roof, though, can they?" Petunia sighed.

"I don't see why not. If that's the only way to give them Happily Ever After, they can stay upstairs forever." Jonquil trailed a picture with her wand in the air, watching her yellow comet trail dance.

"I'm just glad Fortune is on her way. It's time for her to tell Lucky the truth. About herself, and about us," Petunia said. "I feel like we're lying to her."

"That's because we are, but it's what Fortune wanted. She thought it best." Bluebonnet looked up the stairs. "Remember when she was little? Her little pigtails bouncing around as she bopped through the house singing?"

Petty began working on the cherries again. "I do. She was the sweetest little thing. I love it when we actually get to know our charges and can be directly involved in their lives. It makes their Happily Ever Afters so much better." She ate a bite of cherry. "All Happily Ever Afters are satisfying, but these are the ones that really fill my heart."

Jonquil tapped at her temple with her wand. "Think, think, think."

Bluebonnet nodded. "I should find my thinking cap. I made one in 1697, but I haven't been able to find it since 1880." She turned her head sharply to Petunia. "And not one word out of you about that."

"Me? I wasn't going to say anything." But Petunia smiled.

"I've got it!" Jonquil squealed. "Fortune thinks she used up Lucky's good luck during her delivery."

Her sisters nodded.

"It was a tough delivery. Without us, they both might have died." Bluebonnet's bright-blue eyes welled with tears.

"Never mind that, now. She's okay. They both are." Petunia patted her sister's shoulder.

"Back to the topic at hand," Jonquil demanded in an uncharacteristic tone that sounded much more like Petunia. "We all seemed to have forgotten that Lucky was born here."

"We didn't forget. I just said—" Bluebonnet began.

"She's been living out of alignment! We don't stay long in the outer world because of the same things. Our magic gets wonky. So her luck is wonky!" Petunia said.

"But wait, though. If it's just an alignment thing, why is she still having trouble with Ransom?" Bluebonnet asked.

"That's what I'm trying to figure out," Jonquil replied.

"What if . . . what if all of this with Ransom isn't *un*luck at all? I can't believe we didn't think of this sooner." Petunia's eyes were alight with mischief.

"That look in your eyes, Pets. What are you thinking?" Jonquil prompted.

"It's a gauntlet. We're fairy-tale creatures. Ransom has to prove himself. It's a different manifestation of True Love's Kiss. He just has to love her, despite the world falling down around them," Petunia said.

"Oh, that's it." Jonquil waved her hand. "Should be fine. I mean, tornados are fine, right?"

Petunia sighed. "No, listen. It's all going to be fine. I know it is. We just have to keep pushing them together."

"Gently, and from far away?" Bluebonnet asked.

"Exactly. I mean, just look at how they powered up our wands. That's the power of love," Petunia said.

"I think you're forgetting that the kids love us, too. It could easily be their love for us that powered up our wands," Jonquil interjected.

"That's true, but it wasn't their love for us that made our cherry tree explode. Oh no, that was all the fire that burns between them," Petunia said. "By the way, do you have the publicity people on this wedding yet? There are arrangements to be made."

"I'm getting there. I've been trying to handle coordinating with Phillip at the castle, but you know that's kind of hard since he spends his days in the mermaid fountain. Green." Jonquil arched a judgmental brow.

"I'm not going to apologize for that. He was being an ass. Maybe I should've turned him into a donkey, so then the outside could match his insides. Besides, it's not my fault he hasn't found anyone who wants to kiss him." Petunia crossed her arms over her chest.

"Well, he wasn't going to help until you agreed to remove the spell," Jonquil tossed back.

"I've long forgiven him, honestly. If there was a way to undo the spell, I would've done it already," Petty confessed.

"That's what I told him. And also, that every woman in Ever After has already smooched his dumb green cheek and if he wants new prospects, modifying the castle into a B and B is the only way to get there."

"Jonquil, you're brilliant," Bluebonnet said.

"Thank you." Jonquil grinned.

"Yes, quite." Petty nodded. "Okay, so plan of attack. Announce to the news outlets that the Chocolate Baron himself—"

"Isn't he a prince? A chocolate prince?" Jonquil interrupted.

"Oh no, a king. Definitely the King of Cacao," Bluebonnet said.

"Eh . . . maybe we'll just go with successful entrepreneur?" Petty decided. "We should get with them about a guest list. And colors. Let's help them pick colors."

"No, listen. I have a better idea. Why not a Cinderella wedding? We're fairy godmothers. Ransom will look so handsome in a Prince Charming getup and Lucky . . . oh Lucky. She'll look beautiful in pink," Jonquil said.

"They have to choose it. We have to make them take ownership of this thing. The more real it feels, the better it will be for everyone," Petunia said.

"That's a little mercenary, don't you think?" Jonquil asked. "I don't like using the kids."

"We're not using them," Bluebonnet spoke out. "We're killing two birds. Three, actually. We get them to fall in love. Or admit it. Whichever. Their love is the final goal of this whole charade. The fact that it will bring our town back to life is a bonus. And our wands, a gift. We told the kids why we wanted them here." Bluebonnet pressed her lips together. "Well, mostly. We told them we needed them. They are giving this to us of their own free, and mostly informed, will."

"Feels kind of sketchy to me." Jonquil made a moue with her lips.

"Well, what would you do?" Petunia asked.

"Mind my business," Jonquil answered.

"We are minding our business. Our charges are our business," Bluebonnet said.

"Okay, but when is it a fairy ring too far? We're supposed to give them the tools to help themselves, not outright meddle. This feels like meddling. I don't like it."

"So noted," Petunia said.

"But we're not going to slow down?" Jonquil asked.

"No, we can't. We've got two weeks to pull this wedding off and to bring life back to Ever After."

"Have you considered that maybe our time has passed? Maybe the world doesn't need us anymore?" Jonquil questioned.

"Honey, I think your blood sugar is low. Let me get you an ice cream soda," Bluebonnet said, and grabbed a giant cherry. "Yes, cherry chocolate, I think."

"Oh, me too," Petunia said.

Jonquil rolled her eyes but didn't refuse the treat when her sister handed it to her. After taking a sip, she said, "I just want to make sure we're doing this for the right reasons."

"There's no arguing that we will reap rewards from this, but so will everyone in Ever After. I don't think that's selfish. Is it?" Petunia asked.

"I don't think so. No." Bluebonnet shook her head.

"What if Ransom and Lucky decide they don't want to do it? Then what?" Jonquil asked, drinking down the last bits of the cherry chocolate goodness. Then she dropped the cup and pressed the heel of her hand to her forehead. "Curse it, brain freeze."

"Put your tongue on the roof of your mouth. It helps," Petty promised.

"I guess I did need the sugar," Jonquil said.

"See?" Bluebonnet said in a motherly tone.

"Still need an answer to that question."

"We're not going to *make* them do anything," Petty said, obviously offended at the suggestion.

"What about the chicken? Did you do something to it, Bon-Bon?"

"Well, I might've added some extra seasoning," she confessed.

"What kind?" Petty demanded.

"Oh, the kind that makes you feel your feelings. It was just a little boost." Bluebonnet blushed.

"Bon-Bon!" Jonquil chastised.

"It was just a little nudge. It didn't make anyone feel anything that wasn't there. You know we can't manufacture what's not there."

"I wonder if your nudge had anything to do with the cherries?" Petty's brow wrinkled with concern.

"Oh no! Do you think it could have?"

"If the spice was to amplify feelings—"

"No, no! It doesn't amplify anything. It doesn't make those feelings any stronger, it just makes them present. For instance, if you'd locked away an emotion, it's a key for the lock. That's all," Bluebonnet swore.

"Maybe let us in on it next time? I invited Roderick, Gwen, and the kids to dinner tonight and that might've been a disaster if they'd come," Jonquil said.

"It would've been interesting, that's for sure," Petty replied. "Is Roderick's FG really on the injured list?"

"Yes, and really, with everyone's powers low, she's having a hard time recovering." Bluebonnet took a delicate sip of her soda.

"Gwen doesn't have one, but I think she needs our help

anyway. No, she *deserves* our help. Her love for Lucky is true and steadfast. We should all be so . . . well, I was going to say lucky, but you know what I mean." Petunia grinned.

"Fine," Jonquil agreed. "You're right. Gwen is amazing. I saw in my crystal ball that Jeff, no . . . Jack . . . What's his name?"

"Jackass?" Bluebonnet supplied helpfully.

"Yes, that one," Petty nodded.

"Oh! Jake. Yes, he's awful. Gwen deserves better. But I think we should leave them alone. Jake is going to serve her with divorce papers. And before you ask me anything else, no, I don't know any other details. The ball is foggy."

"Foggy balls!" Bluebonnet chortled.

Petunia giggled.

Jonquil wrinkled her nose. "You two are awful." But she giggled. "Anyway, let's do like we said and help Gwen get established here. She needs to find who she wants to be before we go mashing her up with Roderick."

"I'll give you that one," Petty said.

"Oh, will you?' Jonquil snorted. "I'm only right."

"Yes, yes, you're right," Bluebonnet agreed. "We need to have a chat with Gwen about baking the wedding cake, and Red and Grammy. Let's go round them up!"

"Nope, can't. It's a full moon, dear. Grammy is *busy*, as you well know," Petty said.

"Darn."

"And it's late. Have you looked at the time?" Jonquil yawned.

"It's not even midnight." But Petunia yawned. "I have to get these cherries prepped if we hope to use them. It would be a shame for them to go to waste."

"No, instead they're going to go to waist." Bluebonnet pointed at her midsection.

"I have always held that if my wings can still carry me, I'm fine." Jonquil fluttered up a few feet off the floor and then landed gracefully. "Still good. Bring on the cherry pastries!"

"Speaking of our charges, has anyone heard from Juniper? How is her next book coming? Do we need to send the muses?" Petunia asked.

"You just can't stop meddling, can you?" Jonquil laughed as she said this, no real bite behind the words.

Petty looked as if she were about to argue, but then laughed, too. "Nope, it's just how I'm wired."

"She's doing great," Bluebonnet said. "Finishing up her next novel on a writing retreat with her friends in Ireland."

"How did I not know about Ireland?" Petty asked.

Bluebonnet shrugged. "You know how absentminded she is, always living in other worlds. She usually tells one of us. That's what matters."

"Too right." Petty nodded.

A sudden thump echoed from the upstairs and everyone's eyes widened. They looked at each other in silence, each of them fighting hard not to laugh.

Jonquil was the first to speak. "Stop it, the lot of you. Nothing untoward is going on up there. After the cherry tree, it wouldn't."

"Explain the thump, then?" Petty demanded.

"Shh!" Bluebonnet demanded.

They were answered with another thump, then another.

Bluebonnet and Petty giggled, but Petty was the first to compose herself.

"I have cherries to see to."

Bluebonnet burst out with a full-bodied cackle. "I guess you do."

"Oh, stop." Petty couldn't contain another giggle. "This is serious work."

"You guys are actually the worst," Jonquil said with a roll of her eyes.

"Literally, even, as the kids say." Bluebonnet cackled again.

"Keep flapping that cake trap, Jonquil, and don't just see if I decide to turn my powers on you," Petty threatened.

"Don't you dare! I'm quite happy where I am."

"Obviously not." Bluebonnet nodded slowly. "I think I agree, Pets. I think Jonquil should be our next project. Who were you thinking of?"

"I don't know yet." Petty tapped her chin and three very long hairs uncurled and wrapped around her fingers. She gasped and zapped them with her wand. "Oh, now we're playing dirty."

"You'll get more of the same, Pets, if you try to use your fairy magic on me," Jonquil growled.

"You'd never know it, would you?"

"I . . ." she began.

"Sisters!" Bluebonnet hissed. "We should go to the shop. We do have work to do. After all, if things go like we've planned, Fairy Godmothers, Inc. is going to be busy as a fat bee." She sniffed. "And let's give the kids some privacy."

"You're right, Bon-Bon. Just let me get my shawl."

"There's a reason magic spells end at midnight. We're old. We should be in bed. I'm missing my *Midsomer Murders*," Jonquil grumped.

"Pish. You're not missing anything, you old bag. We've got a DVR." Bluebonnet rolled her eyes. "But you stay here if you like and we'll just plot without you."

Petty wrapped her shawl around her shoulders. "And you can't complain when things aren't being done as you'd like them."

"Fine, I'll go. But I think I need another chocolate cherry ice cream soda."

"That's the spirit!" Bluebonnet set about making another, but when another crash from upstairs echoed down to them, she used her magic to finish. "We should be off!"

Lucky's voice echoed down to them. "Don't worry, God-mothers. We were just moving the furniture around."

"Hehehe. We weren't worried," Petty muttered.

"That's fine, dears. Do what you like. We're running to the shop for some late-night strategy. See you in the morning!" Jonquil called out.

"That's the spirit, Jonquil!" Petty said approvingly.

"Well, I do want them to be happy." Jonquil tightened her own shawl.

"Shall I walk you?" Ransom was on the stairs, and they could see he was wearing a T-shirt and pajama bottoms.

"No, don't trouble yourself, we're fine. Ever After is virtually crime-free. We're safe enough. Off to bed with you," Petty said. Then she turned to her sisters. "Crank the heat high enough to roast a partridge."

Bluebonnet adjusted the modern thermostat *and* zapped a fire in the hearth that would heat the whole house.

"Consider partridges roasted." Bluebonnet grinned. "I'm so glad Petunia isn't plotting my matchmaking."

"Who says I'm not?" Petunia grinned back.

"If you're plotting mine, I'll give you more than just chin hairs. I'll give you warts, too," Jonquil promised.

"Love is for everyone," Petunia reiterated. "Even the three of us. Warts and all."

"We'll just see about that." Jonquil spun around and headed out into the night, with her sisters following hot on her heels.

# Chapter 7

The attic room that was usually very comfortable had suddenly become an oven.

Sweat slicked down her back and she desperately wanted another shower, but she was enjoying this time just talking with Ransom like they used to. Before everything went to crap.

"Sounds like the godmothers have gone out for the night," Ransom said from his bed.

"That's a terrifying thought. I can't even imagine what kind of trouble they could get into at midnight in Ever After."

"I know, right?"

"Maybe when we moved the couch around they had . . . ideas? I think they're trying to give us some privacy." Her face flushed from more than just the heat.

"It feels like they cranked up the heat, too. Are you hot?"

"I'm dying. Can you open a window?"

Ransom got up and not only opened the window, but used all the cranks and pulleys that converted the window into a small balcony.

"That's fantastic." Lucky rolled onto her back as the cool night air rushed inside the sweltering room. "I don't know how you're not dying."

"I'm used to the heat. Cacao doesn't grow in cool places, you know?"

"I assume you're very hands-on." She immediately thought

about exactly where she wanted his hands on her body. Why had she done that to herself?

"Yeah, I like to stay very involved from planting to harvesting. I'm responsible for my business, not just in what I produce, but how I produce it."

"What's your favorite chocolate?" Lucky asked, trying to distract herself.

"I've been experimenting with ruby chocolate. It's this beautiful blush color and the taste is unlike anything else." He went to his bag. "I actually brought you some, but it's probably melted."

"Ransom, you know me. If it's chocolate, I'll lick it off the wrapper. I don't care."

He laughed. "Yeah, I know you. I actually thought of you when I decided to add ruby chocolate to Heart's Desire's offerings."

"You did?"

"It was unique. Like you."

She snorted like a pig. "Nuh-uh."

No way had he been thinking about her. At least, not in any good way. How could he after everything that had happened? She was definitely sure he hadn't made a business decision based on something that reminded him of her.

"No, really."

He continued to rummage in the bag and pulled out a foil-wrapped shape that had once been a bar. As he held it up, it bowed to her, slumping over in his grasp.

Ransom muttered an oath.

"I don't care. I'll eat it anyway."

In that moment, she wanted it more than she'd ever wanted any other chocolate in her life. He'd thought of her. He'd brought it to her. That chocolate, that particular bar, it was going in her face one way or another.

"It won't be the same." He held up his hand. "Look, it's gross."

"Don't care. I want it."

"You won't get the right notes. It'll be even worse if I put it in the refrigerator." He held it up by the edge of the wrapper and chocolate oozed out over his fingers. Then he put it in his other hand and wrinkled his nose as he so obviously realized both hands were covered in ruby chocolate.

Lucky got up on her knees and reached out for the chocolate. "You brought it all this way. Just give it to me."

"No."

She narrowed her eyes. "If you'll recall, telling me no has never turned out well for you."

"Just this one time, trust me." He put the chocolate back in his other hand and looked around the room, seemingly searching for a solution to the chocolate mess that wasn't Lucky.

"I do trust you, but not when it comes to chocolate."

He laughed. "Lucky. I'm considered an expert when it comes to chocolate."

"Not if you're trying to keep it from me, you're not. Maybe you are an expert in chocolate, but you're lacking a certain set of survival instincts."

He laughed again. Lucky loved the sound of it. Deep and rich, just like his espresso dark chocolate tasted.

Not that she'd been buying Heart's Desire Chocolate since it hit the market. Not that at all. She loved the espresso dark chocolate, the bacon milk chocolate, and she had a peculiar love for the lemon ginger dark bars.

"No, no. Seriously. Just wait. I'll have some flown in."

Lucky wasn't impressed. She didn't want any flown in. She didn't want a different bar. She wanted that one, that one that had currently smeared half of itself all over his fingers. "*You* just wait. You brought that one for me and I want that one."

"Well, you're not getting it." His tone of voice seemed to indicate that this was his final word on the matter.

It wasn't Lucky's.

She wasn't sure if it was the cocky grin, or the confidence in his stance, or if it was simply that he told her no.

But she wasn't going to stand for it.

Err . . . sit for it.

No, instead she launched herself at him like a chocolate-seeking missile. She plowed into him, and he stumbled backward, falling onto the bed with her right on top of him. Lucky didn't stop to think about their precarious position.

Nope, she didn't stop to consider she'd straddled him like a pony at Churchill Downs.

Or that there was no chocolate left in the wrapper and everything worth tasting was all over his hands.

Or that given her precarious position, she definitely shouldn't have licked the blossom-pink chocolate from his fingers.

Not in the least.

Not until his finger was in her mouth, the chocolate was on her tongue, and she heard a faint moaning sound that had to be coming from her.

The ruby chocolate was the best thing she'd ever tasted. It was like sour berries dusted with sugar with a chaser of white chocolate. The whole flavor palette was a journey in itself.

"Luck-eee," Ransom growled.

Or maybe it was a groan, she wasn't sure. She wanted to hear it again. So Lucky surrendered to the mad desire pounding in her head, her heart, and between her thighs and took a long, languorous lick of the chocolate, then sucked his finger inside of her mouth.

It wasn't about the chocolate anymore.

Which was really saying something considering Lucky's great and terrible love of all things cacao.

His lounge pants did nothing to hide his reaction, and her own sleep shorts were useless as a barrier between them.

He was hot and hard, and his body wanted her.

Despite everything that had happened between them from the distant past to only a few moments ago, he still wanted her.

The man was a glutton for punishment.

Her lips fell apart, but he didn't reclaim his finger.

Instead, he just looked up at her, all intensity and heat.

She imagined they looked pretty stupid, but even that thought didn't break the spell that had woven itself around them.

Lucky reached out a tentative hand to cup his cheek, but with the other pulled his hand away. "We absolutely can't."

Even though she absolutely, desperately wanted to. She already wanted to taste more of that chocolate, more of the salt on his skin, and more of all things Ransom.

Ransom nodded. "Absolutely, positively not."

Only his hands went to her hips and his fingertips burned into her skin, seared her to the bone. He brought her forward to center her even more intimately against him.

She braced her hands on his shoulders and leaned her forehead down to touch his.

"The chocolate was good. Thank you."

"It'll be even better when you experience it as it's meant to be experienced," he whispered.

Lucky's breath caught in her throat and she tried to school her breathing, her thundering stampede of a heartbeat and her shaking hands. She exhaled with a delicate shudder.

"Oh, I think this is the best way to experience chocolate. Don't you?"

He smelled so good, and the warmth of his skin under his T-shirt scalded her palms, grounded her in the reality of him.

She wanted to rub her cheek against his, to feel the rough stubble of the day's growth of beard, to mark him as her own. Lucky tried to push that thought out of her mind. He wasn't hers and he couldn't be, even though the here and now felt so good.

Ransom tilted his chin up so the carved marble of his lips was only a breath away from her mouth.

She couldn't think.

She couldn't breathe.

All she could do was feel.

Even though a voice in the back of her head screamed for her to stop. Begged her not to test the fates like they had underneath the mutant cherry tree.

Oh, would he taste like cherries?

Or chocolate?

Her lip quivered and she was lost. Lucky would've surrendered to what was between them if Ransom hadn't whispered against her lips.

"Kissing is out. Penetration is out. But there are more ways to bring this thing to fulfillment between us."

His hands slid down from her hips to cup her bottom and he thrust his own hips up to meet her.

Desire was a supernova that incinerated her from the inside out.

"Don't you think we're tempting fate," she managed, breathless and wanting.

"I don't believe in fate. I believe in here. I believe in now. I believe in us." He pulled her forward again. "I believe in this."

Lucky wanted this more than anything. The feel of him against her, the way his breath caught, too, when she shifted her hips, and most of all how he accepted that there were some things that they couldn't do.

He didn't care.

He wanted what they could have together.

That was an aphrodisiac in itself.

Except, she realized that maybe she was the one who couldn't accept there were things they couldn't do. This felt good, more than good, it was . . . but what it wasn't was enough. Lucky wanted everything.

His hands smeared the chocolate up under her shirt, and his hands cupped her breasts, his thumbs teasing her nipples. Each brush of his fingertips sent another jolt of need through her and she rolled her hips in time with his ministrations.

"Maybe I can't kiss your mouth, but maybe I can kiss other places."

She helped him peel her shirt off and gasped when he took her nipple in his mouth.

Lucky decided this was the only other sanctioned and approved use for chocolate. Ransom Payne could lick it from wherever he liked.

Although, probably her luck she'd end up with a monster yeast beast and—

"Lucky?" His voice pulled her out of herself.

She looked down and met his eyes.

"There you are, baby. Stay with me. Don't think about all the what-ifs. Just be here." He searched her face. "Unless you don't want to be. We don't have to do this."

"I want to."

"Show me."

Lucky ground her hips against him, the friction between them sending her need soaring. She moaned.

"Take us there."

She moved again, tentatively, and his body movements mirrored hers, taking them both deeper into a dark sea where nothing but sensation and touch mattered. Every touch, every shift, every new friction pushed her beyond bliss, and she rocked into the ecstasy.

"I dreamed of this for so long," he confessed.

Their actions grew more passionate, more furious as they reached together for that impossible high, that beautiful place that hung among the dreams and stars.

When they reached their pinnacle together, Lucky thought for a moment that she was actually dying.

She couldn't breathe and as the bliss exploded out from

her core in concentric circles, she swore the middle of her forehead went numb and for a single moment, she actually saw stars.

They sank down on the bed, wrapped together, but instead of enjoying the moment, the release, she waited.

Lucky waited for the price of their pleasure.

She waited for something awful to happen.

The longer it took to manifest, the more fear welled up inside of her.

"It's all fine, Lucky. Nothing bad happened. We're here. We're together. And it was so damn good."

Lucky let him tuck her against his strong, hard chest. "Was it enough?"

"It was for me."

Lucky decided that she must be a total and utter asshole because while it was good, it wasn't enough. She wanted more of everything. More intimacy. More skin. More touching.

More of everything.

Maybe that was her problem. Maybe she'd always wanted more than what she could have.

"But," he prompted.

"But nothing."

"There's more. I can feel the words waiting to be said."

"It wasn't enough for me," she confessed.

"Don't tell me you didn't get yours, because I've got a wet—"

She slapped his arm gently midsentence. "I didn't say I didn't get mine. I just want everything. All of it. This isn't fair. Neither one of us deserves this."

"I'd say we both got a good start on what we deserve."

Lucky huffed. "I can see we're not going to get anywhere with this conversation in our current state."

He pressed his lips to the top of her head. "Don't ever think I don't want more from you. I want everything, too. But we can't have it. This is what we can have. All I'm saying is I'll take this over nothing."

"But for how long, Ransom? How long until it's not enough? How long until you realize you did yourself dirty by settling for half a relationship."

"There's more to a relationship than sex. So much more. In fact, we'd spend more of our lives out of bed than in it. So we can't have what people think of as a traditional relationship. Who the fuck cares? It's not about them. It's about us. It's about what we want our lives to look like."

"And this . . . this is what you want your life to look like?" A small, delicate seed of hope planted itself deep inside of her and took precarious root.

"If that's what we can have, then yes."

She closed her eyes and breathed deeply, letting his words wash over her like the balm she didn't know she needed.

Or wanted.

Whenever she imagined a life with someone, it was never like this. Her curse was always broken. She'd never thought about a commitment to someone with . . . this thing hanging over them.

She'd been able to have sex with other men. What a cruel twist of the knife that it was the one she truly loved whom she couldn't be with.

He pulled her tighter. "We'll figure it out."

"Yeah? Well, maybe I'll take you on a date after our wedding," she teased.

"See? This is perfect. We'll have our first date after our wedding."

She snorted. "In case you've forgotten, we already had a first date."

"Anything with leeches doesn't count." He shuddered.

"Fair."

She couldn't help the sense of dread that settled on her shoulders like an icy embrace. Suddenly, she had to get away from him. Lucky was covered in chocolate and stinging waves of something she couldn't name. Something that left a taste in her mouth that wasn't unlike sour regret at what could have been.

Lucky realized she didn't actually believe that this could ever work. Except in that secret place where that tiny seed had buried itself and demanded to be heard with a roar of a lion.

Stupid thing.

She had to get away from him.

From this. From these feelings that she wasn't ready to feel.

Lucky shifted, and the bed made a sound like a dying bear.

They froze and looked at each other, waiting for what would come next.

Seconds ticked by, and when nothing happened, Lucky launched herself from the bed in almost the same manner she'd launched herself onto Ransom earlier in the evening.

"Shower!" she called out as she fled to the giant bathroom.

Ransom laughed. "You're not getting away from me that easily. A baseball team could shower in there."

He followed her into the shower.

Dear Lord, he was naked. Well, of course he was naked. He was getting into the shower. One couldn't clean themselves properly if they were fully clothed.

She couldn't take it.

But she wanted to. Oh, did she ever want to take it.

She rolled her eyes at her own thoughts.

Lucky was determined to ignore the hot, naked man in the shower with her. When he squeezed out some of the godmothers' homemade apple shampoo and lathered it into her hair, it didn't weaken her resolve.

Not. In. The. Slightest.

Worst lie she'd ever told.

She relaxed back against him as he worked his fingers through her hair.

"See, I told you there was more to this relationship stuff."

"I don't want to talk about it, Ransom. At least, not until after the wedding. We need this to go smoothly."

"All right. Let's rinse." He nudged her back under the hot spray and worked the lather from her hair.

Lucky missed being touched. She missed casual intimacy.

She missed human connection. She'd been so afraid her bad luck would rub off on the people she loved that she was an island.

She was getting exactly what she wanted, but it had been denied to her for so long, it was almost too much. Lucky was afraid to like it. Afraid to surrender to it.

As soon as her hair was rinsed and her body was chocolate-free, she dashed from the shower and wrapped herself in a towel. Only when Ransom exited the shower behind her, he looked like a dream come to life.

And like a dumbass, she found herself sitting on his bed instead of hers.

He grinned and with a laugh, pounced on her.

Which was totally and completely the wrong move.

The bed screamed, or maybe it was the floor. A sharp sound like a crack of thunder rent the air, but it wasn't thunder.

It was splintering wood.

The floor dropped out beneath the bed and they both screamed as the bed dropped like a stone in the ocean to crash into the living room below.

Lucky, realizing neither of them was actually hurt, looked up into the gaping hole above and saw what seemed to be a family of mice looking down at them and wringing their little paws with what could've been construed on a human as worry.

She blinked, and they were gone.

Along with her sanity, she was sure.

"Guess that other shoe dropped," she mumbled.

"Right through the floor," he agreed, obviously dazed.

She wrapped the blanket around herself and trudged back up the stairs. "Guess I'll see you tomorrow at the dressmaker's."

"Lucky," he began.

"There's a hole in the damn floor, Ransom. It's a miracle it wasn't worse."

As if in answer, the bed that had previously been in one piece cracked in half, off-loading Ransom to the floor.

He looked up at her. "I'm going to figure this out, Lucky. I swear to you."

"Don't make promises you can't keep. It'll just be harder in the end."

"I can see you don't believe me. After what happened between us, you don't have any reason to. We left each other when we needed each other most, but we were still young. I'm a man now and I'm not going anywhere. I swear."

# Chapter 8

Petunia's screech of surprise stabbed straight through to Ransom's spine and jarred him from a dead sleep.

He jerked up off the couch and tumbled, once again, to the hard floor. Ransom decided he was definitely too old for this. He fought to a sitting position and leaned his back against the couch.

"Petty. Can you not?" He rubbed his temples in misery.

Ransom had a crick in his neck from the too-small couch, a headache that raged like a thousand sugared-up toddlers banging on metal pots with serving spoons, and his eyes had been cemented shut with glue and sand.

"Can I not? Boy, what have you done to our house?"

Jonquil, instead of being upset, just giggled. "Petunia, it looks as if you got exactly what you wanted, judging by the hole in the floor and the broken bed."

Bluebonnet tittered. "Oh dear. Jonquil is right."

"I didn't mean for them to . . ." Petty waved her hands at the mess in front of them.

"Magic has unintended consequences, our grandmamma always said." Jonquil nodded knowingly.

Petty sighed and looked upward at the hole in the ceiling. "Where's Lucky?"

"Upstairs. Sleeping. Like I would still like to be," he grumbled. "We're both okay, in case you were wondering."

"Pish. If you'd been hurt, I'd have known it." Petty pulled

out her now-crackling wand, but Bluebonnet grabbed her hand.

"Nuh-uh. Not yet. Not until Fortune gets here," Bluebonnet said.

"Oh, fine. It looks like you two will be moving to the castle sooner than we anticipated," Petty replied. "Well, how did this happen?"

Ransom fixed her with a hard stare. "Exactly how you think it happened."

"Oh. Oh my stars." Petty blushed. "Well, I guess we don't have to worry about that part of the relationship."

"Can we not talk about that right now?" Ransom considered punching himself in the face just so this could be over.

"When are we going to talk about it? You've only got two weeks," Bluebonnet said. "Speaking of which, we need to get some breakfast and get moving. We told you it would be an early morning."

Jonquil just shook her head and waved her wand and yellow sparkles of magic filled the air. An iridescent bubble formed around them and Jonquil tapped it with the wand. It wiggled and jiggled.

"There. Solid. She won't be able to hear anything we're saying. Bubble of silence. Now, do go on," Jonquil said.

"Thank you, sister. As I was saying—" Bluebonnet began.

"No, no more of this." He shook his head but was immediately sorry. Ransom put a hand to the back of his neck and squeezed for a long moment. "Lucky has been through enough. Every time you guys try to throw us together and something bad happens, she's traumatized."

"What about you? Are you traumatized?" Bluebonnet asked gently.

"Well, no. But you have to admit, I got bashed in the face with a satanic cherry and my bed fell through the floor. My batting average is not what you would call good."

"Tsk. Tsk. We don't like the S-word in this house," Jonquil reminded him.

"Sorry, Godmother." Ransom knew they'd been called all manner of nasty things whenever the wrong humans had discovered their existence. "But come on."

"Yes, I understand." Jonquil nodded. "But we think we know why this is happening."

Ransom perked. "By all means."

"We have two working theories. Lucky was born here. Her mother was lost and alone when she came to us, and we're wondering if because she was born here, that she must abide by fairy-tale law. She might be living out of alignment," Bluebonnet said.

Ransom nodded. "Okay, that's logical. Except for the part where she's back in Ever After, so she should at least be creeping toward some semblance of alignment."

"Maybe," Petty said, sitting down on the floor next to him and taking his hand in hers.

Ransom looked into her sparkling blue eyes and he found a sense of peace wash over him. He was filled with a sense of love, safety, and pride. Like he could do anything.

"What are you doing, Petty?" he asked her.

"Nothing, sweet boy. Just letting you know how much we all love you. How much we believe in you."

"Oh no," he said, but he squeezed her hand back. "I remember when I was a kid and I thought I couldn't do something, one of you would hold my hand like this and give me an extreme case of good self-esteem. What are you going to ask me to do?"

"The other working theory is"—Bluebonnet sat on the other side of him—"Lucky is a fairy-tale creature. What prince wins his princess without a quest or some kind of gauntlet? Maybe Lucky's *un*luck is the part of the story where you have to stay true to who you are, what you know to be right. Then you get your Happily Ever After."

"Bon-Bon, what if we just don't get that?" Ransom asked. It *was* possible that he and Lucky just weren't meant to be.

Instead of being offended like Ransom thought they'd be, the three of them clucked their tongues.

"Ah, youth." Petty shook her head.

"To be so naïve again," Jonquil said.

"If you have a fairy godmother, you *obviously* get a Happily Ever After. This is just that part of the fairy tale, kiddo." Bluebonnet patted his hand.

"So what am I supposed to do?"

Petty grinned. "We're glad you asked. Your quest is simply this: love her. As she is. Can you do that?"

He nodded.

"With no hope of curing her ill luck?" Jonquil added.

A brick crashed in his stomach. No, he didn't know if he could do that. Actually, no. He was certain he couldn't do that. "You don't understand."

Petty snorted. "Of course, we do. You don't want her to suffer. So obviously, you want to save her."

"Yes, dear. You'd be quite the jackass if you didn't," Bluebonnet said helpfully.

"You've been using that word a lot, Bon. I think we may need to wash your mouth out with Mama's lavender soap. You're not setting a good example," Jonquil teased.

"But wait. So I'm supposed to love her, but not want to save her?" Ransom wondered if his dear old godmothers had taken bumps to the head. "That makes no sense."

"It will. Listen, you two need to get ready. Our appointment for Cinderella and Fella is in approximately thirty minutes. Get ready!" Petty popped the magic bubble and shooed him toward the stairs like an errant child.

"I'm starving and Lucky will be, too." Ransom paused on his way up the stairs. "You know we'll both be awful if we don't get some food."

Lucky's face appeared in the hole in the ceiling. "Food?"

"You'll just have to save up your hearty appetite to try the wedding cake samples," Bluebonnet said.

"Oh, there's cake? I can wait for cake." Lucky's face disappeared.

At the sound of her voice, Ransom was reminded of the previous night. Of his hands on her pert breasts, the expression on her face as she surrendered to him, to pleasure.

The idea that he wouldn't get to experience her like that again was a punch to the solar plexus. He had to put it out of his mind, though. She said she didn't want to talk about it until after the wedding, so he'd do his best to respect her wishes.

He knocked on the door. "Can I come in?"

She opened it, dressed in jeans and a thin green T-shirt. "You look like crap," she blurted.

"Sleeping on a couch built for fairies will do that to you."

She snorted. "Just because it's not Ransom-sized doesn't mean it was built for fairies."

Actually, it *had* been built for fairies. Fairy godmothers.

He wanted to tell her so badly. Anything else felt like lying.

He registered a flutter of movement out of the corner of his eye, but when he looked, there was nothing there. Still, Ransom could've sworn he saw a mouse tail.

If he caught the damn things sewing his tux for this sham wedding he was going to . . .

Well, he was going to what? Nothing, that's what. He was going to smile and say thank you and give them some cheese or apples. He knew how the story went. The godmothers were more than capable of blasting mice out of their cottage, so if they were here, they were here because the old dears wanted them.

"Did you see it, too?" Lucky grabbed his arm.

"I thought I saw a mouse, but it was just a shadow."

"I thought I saw them last night after we fell through the floor."

"Maybe. I mean, it's an old house. And you know how Jonquil feeds any animal that makes its way into the yard."

Lucky pursed her lips. "They seem like they're smarter than your average mouse, don't you think? I mean, have you ever noticed how tame all the 'wild' animals are in Ever After?"

"The people here live in harmony with nature. There's no industry, really. It makes sense." He shrugged, even though every word out of his mouth stuck on his tongue like stale peanut butter.

"Uh-huh. Is there something you're not telling me?" She eyed him.

"What—" No, he wasn't going to ask her what she thought he wasn't telling her. That was deceitful, and he couldn't lie to her. "Wait until your mom gets here. Then we'll all talk."

Lucky crossed her arms over her chest. "Now, I really don't like this. So whatever this secret is, everyone knows but me? Thanks a lot."

"At least I'm not lying."

"I guess there is that." She rolled her eyes.

Ransom didn't say anything else, but instead grabbed a pair of jeans and a blue polo shirt from his closet and started to dress.

"Are we there yet, darlings? Move it, move it, move it!" Petty ordered from belowstairs.

"Hold your dumplings, Petty! We're coming. Jeez," Lucky grumbled.

"That's fine, dears. Take as long as you like," Bluebonnet called sweetly. "It's just we won't be able to walk and we'll have to let Pets drive The Beast."

The Beast was a cherry-red, 1955 Chevrolet Bel Air convertible and while it was a beautiful, pristine piece of machinery, Petty was actually the worst driver to ever sit behind a steering wheel.

Ransom was sure the town had some kind of warning system when Petty slipped the key into the ignition. Townspeople locked up pets, children, and even themselves when Petty Blossom got behind the wheel.

They double-timed it down the stairs.

"Are you sure you don't want me to drive," Petty asked with a big grin.

"No!" All of them said in unison.

"Just asking." She adjusted her spectacles on the end of her pert, little nose and wrapped a pink lace shawl around her shoulders before heading out the door.

The walk to Cinderella and Fella was a short one and took them along a manicured path that was made of hand-cut pink stone and ended in a carefully planned town square that Ransom was sure was going to be like catnip for the tourists they were hoping to draw here.

Each building was shaped like the business it housed. Cinderella and Fella was an A-line building painted to look like a ball gown. Grammy's Goodies looked like a fat, old-fashioned, wood-burning cookstove, and to be honest, Ransom didn't know if that was a good choice in a town that was made of fairy tales. What with witches, candy houses, ovens, and such.

Bernadette's Beans, the coffee shop, looked like a French press, and Snow's Market was shaped like a giant apple. The whole thing was just too much.

Honestly, he loved it.

Ransom watched delight wash over Lucky's face as she took in the little town. He noticed she breathed a heavy sigh, as if she'd just put down a heavy burden. He could tell Ever After was a balm to her.

Maybe this was where she belonged, like the godmothers had said?

The godmothers hurried them along into Cinderella and Fella and when the door opened, glass bells tinkled lightly to announce their presence.

"Rosebud? It's the godmothers! We're here with the happy couple!" Bluebonnet called out.

The place smelled of roses, too. Not a heavy, cloying fragrance like old perfume, but the lightest touch of a blooming rose lingered in the air.

Suddenly, Lucky gasped and she grabbed his hand and jerked him over to a far corner. She didn't stop to look at anything but the silk creation that stood almost like it waited for her. It was impossibly iridescent, almost as if the colors shifted between green and purple. For all he knew, maybe it did.

Gwen was suddenly beside them and they were oohing and aahing together, but Ransom didn't notice much of anyone besides Lucky.

She reached out a tentative hand to touch the dress, but he watched as she stopped herself and an expression of longing fell like a shadow across her face.

"Go ahead," a new voice called out. "Touch it. It's yours, if you want it."

A young woman came over to the group. She was a pretty little mess. Her blond hair was tucked up into a bun and held there with all manner of pins, fabric scissors, and some other bits and bobs he couldn't name. She wore a pink sweater set and white slacks, with a pink rose pinned to her lapel. Her pockets were stuffed full, and she had a measuring tape wrapped around her wrist.

Lucky looked back and forth between the woman and the dress.

"Go on," Petty urged. "It won't bite."

"I promise," the new woman said. "By the way, I'm Rosebud Briar. I'll be your dressmaker."

"Nice dress for a fake wedding," Roderick said as he came up to stand beside him.

"It's a nice dress for any wedding." Rosebud narrowed her eyes at him.

"Hi, I'm the maid of honor. I'm Gwen. That's—"

"Asshole," Brittany interrupted her mother.

"I see," Rosebud said, fixing Roderick with a hard glare. Then she turned her attention back to Lucky. "After speaking to your godmothers, I thought this material would suit you best, but this is about you and Ransom. If you don't like it, we can do something else."

"How could anyone not like it?" Her hand still hovered over the fabric. "I don't want to hurt it."

"My darling, you can't hurt it. Stainproof." Rosebud smiled, then looked from side to side, as if she pondered something very important. "Yes, yes, I believe it's flame-retardant as well."

"I definitely need that." Lucky nodded and looked back at him.

For a moment, Ransom forgot that this wasn't real. He was looking at his bride and she'd found The Dress. The One. She was asking him what he thought and for a moment, his only thoughts were what she'd look like coming down the aisle to him and their future.

He remembered what the godmothers had said. He had to love her unselfishly. His thoughts at the moment were all about himself.

"It's beautiful, Lucky. You should try it on," he said.

"Should I? I mean . . . it doesn't matter, right?" Lucky replied.

"Of course it matters!" Gwen interjected before anyone else could say anything. "You are going to be on national television. You want to look your best. Oh, you're going to need something new for the press junket, too."

Rosebud grinned. "I think I have just the thing for that, too. I've put together a small selection."

"If I go with this dress, what colors will we go with for Gwen and Roderick?" Lucky asked.

"I was thinking that we dress everyone else in white and

let the bride and groom wear the colors. This is what I was thinking for the groom." She pulled out an iPad and showed it to Lucky and Ransom. "While you're looking at that, can I get anyone anything? Water? Tea? Wine?"

"Bourbon?" Roderick asked.

Ransom didn't need to see Gwen to know that her eyes rolled so hard she was lucky to have kept them in her head.

He turned his attention back to the iPad and saw what Rosebud had planned for him. He'd expected it to be a traditional tux, but this was different.

The military-style tux jacket was double-breasted and cut from the same material as the dress with sharp, precise lines that would mold well to his body, and she'd planned for him to wear dove-gray breeches and shiny black Hessian boots. He'd look just like a fairy-tale prince.

Lucky looked up at him. "You'd wear this?"

"Why wouldn't I? It'll make my shoulders and my ass look amazing." He winked at her.

She snorted. "No trolling for dates at our wedding."

The godmothers peered around them to look at the iPad and they made the appropriate noises of pleasure and praise.

"My, my. Rosebud has outdone herself," Jonquil said.

"Lucky still needs to try on the dress!" Rosebud said when she returned with a tumbler of bourbon for Roderick.

"I get a dress, too, Mama?" Brittany asked.

"Yes, but let's have Aunt Lucky try her dress on first."

"Oh yes!" Brittany said.

"Aunt Lucky's gonna be so pretty!" Steven added.

"You're the sweetest little monsters ever," Lucky told them.

"Don't forget," Bluebonnet began. "We're waiting to hear back from the organizer on the junket. Do you need a new suit for that, Ransom?"

"Whatever you think," he answered.

"This is your event, too. What do you think?" Rosebud asked.

He knew what they were doing. The godmothers wanted them to engage in the process. So they'd feel ownership. So they'd forget it wasn't real.

"Who am I to say no to a new suit?"

"Fantastic! Let me get Lucky set up in the dressing room and I can show you my ideas." Rosebud grabbed the dress and led Lucky away.

She turned around to give him one last look over her shoulder and she smiled.

He smiled back, but Bluebonnet's words echoed in his ears like gunshots.

The press junket.

Where people would forget he was a billionaire philanthropist, and all of his hard work would be erased by four words.

The Boy Who Missed.

That wasn't who he was anymore. That wasn't who he'd ever been. He was more than four words. He was more than a single moment.

Ransom knew he shouldn't even worry about it. If they brought it up, it didn't matter. He couldn't spend his life hiding from a stupid moment in his past.

That logic didn't stop the dread that curled like a serpent at the base of his spine.

# Chapter 9

Lucky was the first to admit she was afraid of the dress.
It was too pretty.

Too fragile.

Too pristine.

Things that fell into any of those three categories were not things that Lucky was to be trusted with.

As she was shuffled into a spacious dressing room, she had the urge to warn the pretty Rosebud about what could happen.

"I know you said this was stain-proof and flame-retardant, but I sort of have a thing."

"Oh, your godmothers told me all about you. I'm prepared," Rosebud assured her. "You'll see."

Eh, Lucky thought it was more likely that Rosebud would be the one to see. Not that she wanted it that way. She hoped against hope that the sweet Rosebud Briar was prepared for Lucky.

Or un-Lucky, as the case happened to be.

She changed out of her clothes and wriggled into the dress.

Then something amazing happened.

Something that convinced Lucky the dress was magic.

Looking at herself in the mirror, she didn't see un-Lucky Fujiki. She saw herself. She was elegant. She was beautiful.

From the delicate swan arch of her neck to the inherent grace in her movements.

She'd never seen herself that way. She'd never felt graceful or elegant. Not ever.

Lucky decided she was never taking the dress off. It was going to have to rot off of her body. She didn't want this feeling to end. She couldn't go back to being un-Lucky.

When she emerged from the dressing room, Rosebud gasped. "You look beautiful."

"I feel beautiful," she said. "How did you do this?"

"Magic, of course." Rosebud grinned. "Let's show everyone, shall we?"

Lucky followed her back to the main area, where most of her nearest and dearest waited.

Gwen was the first to speak. "I need to take a picture for your mother!" She whipped out her cell phone and snapped a few shots.

Lucky smiled and the monsters ran up to her, both wanting to be picked up. She didn't hesitate and hauled one up in each arm.

"You guys are getting too big for that," Gwen admonished.

"They'll never be too big," Lucky corrected.

"Even when I have my big teeth and a white dress?" Brittany asked.

"Well, kiddo. You're going to get a white dress for the wedding and you've got some of your big teeth. Are you too big?"

"No," she said with a grin.

"When I'm too big, I'll pick *you* up, Aunt Lucky," Steven informed her.

She put the kids down when she felt Ransom's eyes rake over her. Lucky managed another smile.

"Well, what do you think?"

"He's speechless," Roderick answered for him.

Ransom just nodded in agreement.

"It's absolutely perfect," Petty reassured her.

Then her stomach growled long and loud.

Rosebud laughed. "Oh dear! I bet you were saving your appetite for the cake tasting. Well, let me just get some measurements from all of you and we'll get you on your way. If you could all please walk single file through that trellis by the dressing room, it'll get your biometrics."

Lucky found it strange that no one questioned that the ivy-covered trellis was going to take their measurements. Everyone lined up single file and they walked through the trellis. It made a strange sound as it finished each one of them.

"I want to go again," Steven said after his turn.

"And you may, but not until after everyone else has gone. Little boys grow very fast, so we might need another reading," Rosebud replied.

What they were doing with tech these days was incredible.

"Lucky, you can change now, if you'd like," Rosebud said.

"No, I don't like. I want to wear it forever."

Rosebud's laugh was like the glass bells over the door. A light, magical sound. "That's the best compliment you could give me. Thank you."

It wasn't a compliment. Lucky never wanted to wear anything else. She wondered if all the clothes from Cinderella and Fella would feel like this dress. She didn't think it was possible because nothing could be like this dress.

But she trotted back to the dressing room and peeled the dress from her body with reluctant hands.

She sat with it in the room for a long moment, just allowing her fingers to glide over the material, to watch the shimmer of color as she did.

Her stomach again reminded her that while the dress was nice and all, it was time to eat and if she didn't, there would be actual hell to pay. The first burning sting of hunger erupted in her stomach, and she knew she'd better move her backside if she wanted to enjoy the cake.

When she emerged, she didn't see Rosebud anywhere and

she didn't know what to do with her perfect, beautiful, holy grail of a dress. She took several tentative steps and heard what sounded like Rosebud singing.

Lucky followed the sound, but she didn't find Rosebud.

She found a dress form with a lovely pink satin and tulle dress in progress, but that wasn't what made her stop short.

It was the mice holding bobbins of thread. A doe with her head in the window watching, a rabbit perched on the window sill next to the doe.

And the fattest cardinal she'd ever seen in her life with a needle in his mouth.

She froze.

They froze.

All except for the bunny. The bunny's nose continued to twitch, and it was as if that kept him free of whatever spell trapped the rest of them.

He looked back and forth between the group of sewing animals and Lucky like he was watching a tennis match, only no one else moved.

Finally, the cardinal dropped the needle.

"Caw?"

Lucky narrowed her eyes. That bird sounded like a human making fun of a bird. This had to be some kind of practical joke.

"Shit, that's not it." He puffed up all of his feathers.

Lucky opened her mouth to scream. To her, it seemed as if her mouth had been open for centuries before any sound erupted, but when it did, it sounded like the scream of someone dying.

The deer jerked back and bounced her head on the window sill, the rabbit screamed back at her, the mice scurried away, and the cardinal, bless his heart, tried again.

"Chirp chirp?"

Lucky couldn't move; her legs were rooted to the spot. She

tried to run, but her whole body stiffened and she fell over like a fainting goat.

The cardinal landed on her forehead and he put his beak down to her nose. "Got a cracker?"

Suddenly, she was aware she was surrounded by people. The godmothers, Rosebud, Gwen, Roderick, even the kids, but it was Ransom she looked for. Ransom she wanted to see so that she knew she was safe.

He was on his knees next to her in an instant.

"Are you okay?"

The question stopped her cold. Was she okay? No, definitely not. She had to be hallucinating. There was no way she'd just seen an obese cardinal sewing a wedding dress. No way in hell.

It had to be a hunger-induced hallucination.

"I think so," she mumbled.

Rosebud looked sheepish. "I'm sorry if my dear little Bronx startled you. He has quite the vocabulary, don't you?"

The bird landed on her shoulder and rubbed his face on her cheek. He really was very cute.

"I could've sworn . . ." she started.

"What did you see?" Ransom asked.

Looking around at all the concerned faces, she couldn't bring herself to utter the words. "Nothing. I think I'm just hungry."

Ransom helped her to her feet, his hands warm and steady. Just the contact with him calmed her and made her feel safe.

"Good thing I'm done with you for the day and you can get on to the delicious cake tasting! Grammy is an amazing baker. You'll love everything," Rosebud assured them.

"When will everything be ready?" Jonquil asked.

"In a day or two. Shall I have it sent up to the castle or to your house?"

"The castle," Lucky answered.

"Oh, I've just remembered one more thing. If the gentlemen will wait outside?" Rosebud asked.

Steven waited with Brittany, but Rosebud shooed him out as well. "No, no. You too, young man."

"Is it secret girl talk?" Steven asked, but didn't wait for the answer. "I bet it is. That's okay. We'll talk about secret boy stuff."

When he was gone, Rosebud was instantly on point. "So, I know this wedding is mostly a publicity stunt, but your package includes honeymoon lingerie. I usually match it to the dress, but I thought I'd give you a choice. Green, purple, or do you want it to match the dress?"

"If it matches the dress, will it be made from the same material?"

Rosebud smiled knowingly. "You like that fabric, do you? It's good stuff. I can do that, but there's an extra cost involved."

"Oh. How much?" Lucky deflated.

"A favor."

"What kind of favor?"

"Well, I won't know until I need it, will I?" Rosebud teased.

After seeing a sewing bird, she wasn't sure she could trust the dressmaker, but when she looked up at her godmothers and saw the warmth on all of their faces, she remembered she could trust them. They wouldn't have brought her to a place that could hurt her.

Even if the damn cardinals helped make the dresses.

"I can promise it won't be anything that goes against your moral fiber," Rosebud said.

"Don't do it," Gwen hissed in her ear. "Something's off."

Normally, Gwen's advice was gold, but she wanted more things made out of that material. She couldn't imagine what it would feel like to have lingerie that made her feel that powerful, graceful, and beautiful.

She'd wear it all the time.

"Yes," she agreed.

"Good. I'll get started on it right away." She looked at the godmothers. "Yes, dears. I think this is going to be good for everyone."

"I told you so," Petty said.

"You did. When is your shop going to be open?" Rosebud asked. "I need a fairy godmother."

"We can talk after the wedding, unless it's an emergency," Petty said, and the godmothers circled Rosebud. "Is it an emergency?"

"No, no. I'm fine. We'll talk then." Rosebud then turned to Lucky. "Thank you for trusting me with your dress for your magical day."

"I . . . thanks for doing it?"

When her stomach growled again, Gwen linked her arm with Lucky's.

"I think we need to eat something," Gwen said. "I could eat a horse."

"I could eat a dragon," Brittany said helpfully.

"I bet Grammy has some dragon cookies, if we hurry," Jonquil said, and held out her hand for Brittany.

Brittany took her hand. "I want a fairy godmother. Can you be my fairy godmother?"

Jonquil beamed. "Of course, I can."

The two skipped ahead, with Petty and Bluebonnet right behind them. Gwen and Lucky lagging behind.

The bakery wasn't far, just a few shops over, but Gwen obviously had something on her mind.

"What's up?"

"This place, Lucky. I don't know."

"I know what you mean. I thought for sure I saw a bird sewing a wedding dress. There must be something in the water."

"I can't believe you agreed to owe that woman a favor. You don't know her."

"No, I don't. But really, what's she going to ask me to do? Knock off the head of a rival crime family? I doubt it."

"I don't know. I'd watch that show." Gwen giggled.

"I would, too."

"So what was so special? It's a beautiful material, don't get me wrong, but when you were talking about the lingerie, I knew you'd do anything to get it. That's not like you."

"I can't explain it. It made me feel . . . beautiful. It made me feel graceful. If I could have everything I wear every day for the rest of my life make me feel that way, I'd pay anything for it."

"Lucky, you *are* beautiful."

"I notice you didn't say graceful."

"Well, who is? Even the most accomplished ballerina falls on her ass now and then."

"There's a life motto for you. I should have it printed up like those 'Live, Laugh, Pray' signs and change my name to Karen."

Gwen cackled.

"I need to make a confession."

"What did you do? What happened? Did you sleep with Ransom?"

"I . . . we'll get to that."

Gwen squealed like a happy pig.

"No, no. Wait. The godmothers and I have been scheming upon your behalf."

"Oh, not Roderick, please say you didn't . . ."

"As if. No, that will work itself out in its own time, or it won't. But I didn't want to drop this on you blind. After the wedding, we were thinking instead of trying to get you established on your own, you could take over for Grammy and Red. If everything works out."

"I haven't thought that far ahead. I don't know if I want to bake."

"You could figure that out, too."

"I did have some ideas for your wedding cake."

"Oh, and no pressure. That's why I wanted to tell you."

"I'm lucky to have you and the godmothers looking out for me." Gwen put an arm around her.

"You know I hate that word."

"What? I am lucky."

Gwen laid a big smack of a kiss on Lucky's cheek and for a moment, Lucky didn't feel *un*lucky at all.

# Chapter 10

The inside of Grammy's Goodies smelled like graham crackers and frosting.

Lucky wanted to dip her face in a trough of whatever it was and never come back out. She also noticed a ridiculously large pizza on one of the family-size customer tables.

It was heart shaped.

The godmothers took the kids over to a table and sat down. Brittany was attached to Jonquil, having decided that Jonquil was now her fairy godmother, and Steven sat between Petty and Bluebonnet.

Crayons and coloring books were found, and the group seemed quite happy to carry on as they were without a thought for the pizza.

"Now that's what I'm talking about! That is for us, right?" Ransom headed straight for the pizza.

"Yes, it's for you." A redheaded woman came out from around the counter. Her skin was pale as milk and she was ample hipped, just like a purveyor of sweets should be. She had a warm smile, and her hands were covered in flour. She wiped them on her apron before reaching out to shake Lucky's hand.

"I'm Red. Grammy will be here in just a minute. She had a late night last night."

Lucky shook her hand. "Lucky."

"That's a cool name. I can tell we're going to be friends. Red and Lucky. We're going to start some shit, I can feel it."

Everyone laughed and Lucky was immediately at ease. She already liked the woman. Rosebud had been terrifying in a sugar-coated kind of way, but there was something about Red that just clicked for her.

Gwen reached out a hand as well. "Gwen."

"So glad you're here. And is that the groom?"

Ransom grinned at her. "Sure is. It smells great in here."

"By all means, have some pizza. I had a feeling you were going to be hungry for real food. I want you to really be able to taste this cake. I've been experimenting with a new frosting, too. One with ruby cacao."

Lucky perked. "You are definitely speaking my language!"

"Oh, have you had it?" Red asked.

"It's my new favorite thing. Ransom works in chocolate," she said.

Gwen tapped her shoulder and whispered, "I'm going to set the kids up with some pizza. The godmothers, too, while you guys talk. Just don't forget us when it's time for cake."

Lucky laughed. "Of course not."

"No one in here goes without cake," Red promised. "So you were saying Ransom is in chocolate?"

"I own Heart's Desire Chocolate."

"Oh, how marvelous. Do you source your beans from Ecuador, Brazil, or the Ivory Coast? Or a mix?"

"Ecuador. I have farms."

"This is just brilliant." Red beamed. "I thought I was going to have to talk you into this, but you're already there."

Out of the corner of her eye, Lucky saw movement at the table with the godmothers. Roderick had gotten a chair to join them, and Steven had shifted to sit next to him.

Interesting.

She turned her attention back on Red.

"Why don't you have some pizza? Then we'll get started on cake."

"If you have some of the ruby frosting ready to go, I'm good to start there." Lucky grinned.

"Of course! I'll be right back."

All of a sudden, it felt like she and Ransom were alone. She was intensely aware of his presence. If she didn't know better, she'd swear she could feel his touch on her skin, even though he wasn't touching her in the slightest.

He leaned down, and his breath made the shell of her ear tingle. "I was right to think of you with the ruby cacao."

"It's perfect for our fake wedding, isn't it?" she said.

"There won't be anything fake about the memories I'll be savoring with that flavor on my tongue."

She shivered. "You . . . that's not fair."

"What's not fair? Remembering the best night of my life or telling you about it?"

"Both!"

He laughed.

"And it wasn't the best night of your life. Surely, making your first million was better."

"Nope," he said, confidence radiating from him like the rays of the sun. "Not even my first billion."

She pretended she didn't hear it.

Because it didn't matter. This just wasn't going to work. Even if they both wanted it to.

Red came back smiling with several spoonfuls of the cherry blossom–colored frosting.

Lucky accepted hers gratefully and much to her everlasting chagrin, as soon as the sugary spread was on her tongue, she flashed back to the night before.

To when she was alone with Ransom and the ruby chocolate on his fingers had been in her mouth and then . . .

Then.

She'd gotten as close to heaven as she believed she ever would. It wasn't just about the orgasm, it was about the connection. Lucky wouldn't lie, the orgasm was really, really good. Only, there was more.

Lucky had been connected to Ransom in a way she'd never felt with another person. She'd remember it every time she tasted this chocolate.

That made the slight sour undertones of the chocolate that much sharper.

She looked up at Ransom to see he watched her. His blue eyes were as stormy as a churning sea, and something hot and forbidden passed between them. It was the jolt of the memory they shared like an electric spark.

"I think I can say without a shadow of a doubt that this is the frosting we'd like, no matter what we choose for the cake," Ransom said.

"Fantastic! Let me just run back and get those samples. I have some for everyone."

"No worries, Red! Grammy is here!" A voice called out from the back of the shop.

Grammy was nothing like what Lucky had expected. She was tall, solid, and she looked as strong as a lumberjack. She wore a red flannel shirt with the sleeves rolled up past her elbows and underneath a band T-shirt that Lucky couldn't quite make out. With them, she had on torn jeans and shiny red Doc Martens boots.

Her hair was shock white but had streaks of green, purple, and blue at each temple. Her eyes were a strange amber color, and Lucky found herself both in awe and entranced by the woman.

Lucky hadn't even noticed that Grammy carried a massive tray of cake, she'd been so enraptured by the woman. There was something otherworldly about her. Something that made Lucky want to paint her.

She hadn't felt this in so long, that urge to create. To pluck a scene from her mind and create it on canvas with oil and brush.

"Are you all right, child?" Grammy asked her.

"You're not at all what I expected."

"I get that a lot."

"If you have time after the wedding, I'd love to paint your portrait. I'm an artist," she said, tripping over her words.

At least it was only her words and not her feet.

Grammy smiled. "Well, I can say that would be a new experience. Sure. I'd love to. But first, there must be cake."

She put the platter down and handed cake all around for everyone to try. There were all the old mainstays like chocolate, vanilla, and carrot, but there were also new and unexplored concoctions. Like rosewater, chai, lemon, and maple-bacon. Lucky also tried pistachio, pumpkin, and clove. Each bit of cake was better than the last, and they were all so delicious.

Gwen was the first to speak. "They're all delicious, but if you want to go with the ruby frosting, I think a lemon cake would be the contrast."

Ransom agreed. "I could eat that forever."

"Be careful what you wish for," Bluebonnet reminded him.

Red grinned. "My mouth is watering just thinking about it. I can whip up a few samples. Maybe with the chocolate, too."

"Or, what if we did chocolate macarons with the ruby filling?" Gwen suggested.

"That is absolutely brilliant!" Grammy nodded. "Would you like to come by when you have some free time? The godmothers mentioned you might be interested in managing the shop, or maybe taking it over. I'd like an opportunity to get to know you better. Let you get to know us. Maybe bake together."

"And brew some lavender lemonade," Red added.

"I'd love that. Thank you."

Lucky was pleased to see that things were falling in line for Gwen.

"Darlings, I do believe our work here is done," Petty said.

"Yes, we're tired. I do need to get home to my stories," Jonquil said.

"Mm-hmm," Bluebonnet agreed.

"You gotta power up to fairy godmother," Brittany said knowingly.

Jonquil patted her on the head and tapped the tip of her nose. "Yes, we do."

"All this meddling wearing you out?" Lucky teased.

"Too right." Petty didn't even try to deny it. "Plus, we need to make sure your things are moved up to the castle for tonight, since we need to repair the ceiling."

"The ceiling?" Gwen asked.

"It's a long story." Lucky sighed.

"Can we go to the park, Mama?"

"Yes, Mama. Can we?" Steven asked.

"How about if Ransom and I take the kids to the fountain? I hear there's a really big frog that's actually a prince," Roderick said.

The kids' eyes widened and they were on the edge of their seats.

Ransom scooped Brittany up, and Roderick helped Steven to climb on his shoulders. "Please, Mom?" Roderick asked.

"I suppose if you really want to." Then to the kids, she said, "You two behave, okay? Don't ask to do things you know that I wouldn't let you do."

"Wow, she's pretty specific about the rules. I guess you kids are pretty smart, huh?" Roderick asked.

"Calling me smart doesn't make you not a . . . butthead," Brittany said.

Lucky noticed it was progress. She wasn't calling him an asshole. Baby steps, she supposed.

Gwen cast her a quick glance and Lucky nodded.

"Have a good time. Let's meet back at the castle for dinner when it gets dark," Gwen said. "Or sooner if you're tuckered out."

"Thanks, Mom."

Roderick led the charge out the door, and Ransom flashed Lucky a wink. "See you later, wifey."

She rolled her eyes and snorted before turning to Grammy and Red. "You guys do know this isn't a real wedding."

Grammy and Red gave her the same answer Rosebud had. "Just because it's not a real wedding . . ." Red began.

"Doesn't mean you shouldn't have a real and delicious cake," Grammy finished. "A good tip from an old lady like me. Always take the cake. Every opportunity."

"This is exactly what I've been telling her!" Gwen cried. "Listen, I need to know what happened with the ceiling."

Lucky blushed so hard she thought her face was going to break.

"I think we can all figure it out," Grammy said.

"Well. Out with it."

"We did everything but," Lucky blurted. "Um, with a full finish." She coughed.

"And?" Gwen prompted.

"The freaking floor collapsed and the bed dropped like an anchor down into the living room. It took a full five minutes before the bed itself collapsed. And Ransom slept on the couch."

"That's not the worst that could've happened."

"That's kind of bad. What's the worst, if that's not it?" Red asked.

"I'm cursed. I have worse than bad luck. Every time Ransom and I have tried to . . . have relations, bad things have always ensued. Leeches. A pack of feral hogs. Mutant wasps. A tornado. Oh, and after he kissed me, possessed cherries."

"Tell me more about the cherries!" Grammy said excitedly.

"The cherry tree in the godmothers' backyard was bare-assed, but for a single bloom. Until we kissed under the tree and the whole tree erupted in blooms that turned into kaiju fruit."

"Well, dumplin', I don't know how to tell you this, but that's wonderful." Grammy clapped her hands together.

"It is?" Red and Gwen asked at the same time.

"Why, yes. You know Ever After is . . ." She paused, seeming to look for the right word. "Special."

"Uh-huh." Lucky waited for her to continue.

"Ever After has a special relationship with love. Sometimes, the most unexpected things happen here when love is true and strong."

"You don't believe that, do you?" Gwen asked.

"Of course, I do. And our Lucky saw it for herself. She saw the force of love bring life into the world. What a gift to see that with your own eyes."

"One of the cherries gave Ransom a concussion," Lucky said.

"What? You didn't tell me about all of this," Gwen interjected.

"Well, no one said love doesn't hurt." Grammy winked. "Although, one thing that all my years on this earth have taught me is that you must take love whenever it comes to you. It's always worth it."

"Leeches and feral pigs, too?" Lucky asked.

"Definitely."

"It's all fine and good for me, because my *un*luck is always with me. He doesn't have to carry that burden and I don't think it's fair of me to ask him to. Especially since we don't get the best parts," Lucky said.

"What do you mean by the best parts?" Red put her chin in her hands.

"Sex."

"But you said you . . ." Red trailed off.

"Penetration. They can't even attempt it or bad things

happen. The last time they got close, well . . ." Gwen sighed heavily. "It's something that's followed Ransom a long time. The press made a huge deal about it."

"The press?" Red ended on a vocal note high enough for dogs to hear.

Grammy winced and pressed a finger against her ear and shook her head. "So what happened? You can tell us, child."

"He missed."

"Oh no," Red said.

"Oh yes," Lucky replied. "Yes, we fought about it and I said something in anger. I called him The Boy Who Missed, and the rest of the student body picked it up and . . . that is, as they say, history."

"And he still wants to be with you? Lucky. That's amazing," Red said. "When people find out what kind of baggage I've got, they usually run screaming in the other direction."

"We won't," Gwen rushed to reassure her.

"We promise." Lucky already felt a kind of steadfast loyalty to Red. She just knew that they were going to be friends for a long time.

"Don't make promises you can't keep," Red said softly.

"I said the same thing to Ransom." She bit her lip and then put another piece of cake in her mouth. "The turd of it is, I mean it. I don't think there's anything you could tell me that would make me not want to be your friend. Weirdmaste, dude. The freaky curse in me acknowledges the freaky baggage in you."

"We'll see if you feel that way after the wedding," Grammy said.

"That sounds ominous. You're not going to shit in the cake or anything, are you?" Gwen asked.

Grammy spat out her coffee. "Lands no, child. Where would you get such an idea?"

"Well, you were saying after the wedding like something scary was going to happen. What else could it be?"

"In time, darlings. In time." Red nodded. "So what are you going to do with your free afternoon? Do you want to bake?"

"I would love to bake!" Gwen said. "How does the bride-to-be feel about baking?"

"I don't know. I've never been able to do it. I tried once and I set the kitchen on fire. I could paint and watch you?"

Grammy put her arm around Lucky. "You can do anything you want to do. You are the mistress of your own fate. At least in Ever After."

"I know! Let's make those cupcakes and maybe Lucky could put her art on the frosting?" Red suggested.

"That's a fabulous idea! I think you'd love it," Gwen encouraged.

"I don't know. What if I mess it up?" Lucky really wanted to try baking with Gwen and their new friends. It was something a lot of people took for granted, but Lucky couldn't get near a stove without something going horribly, heinously wrong.

"You just eat it," Grammy said, as if it were the simplest answer in the world.

So that afternoon, Lucky Fujiki decided to step out of her self-imposed *un*luck bubble and tried baking with her friends.

She only set herself on fire once.

It occurred to Lucky that even though she was a walking disaster, Gwen, Grammy, and Red wanted her there anyway.

# Chapter 11

"Princes do *not* turn into frogs," Steven insisted.

"Duh, not by themselves. Don't you read? They're bad; then they are punished so they learn a lesson. Then a princess comes and kisses them, becaaaauuuussee, we all know kisses are true love, and—" Brittany stopped to pick up a pebble from the path.

"Kisses are not true love. You don't know anything, Brittany!" Steven yelled.

"You're so dumb."

"I'll tell Mom you called me dumb."

"I'll tell Mom you *are* dumb."

"No, you." Steven crossed his arms over his chest and looked up at Ransom. "Girls, am I right? Sheesh."

Ransom, for his part, was thoroughly entertained by the kids' shenanigans.

"Little man, I hate to break it to you, but girls are fantastic," Ransom replied.

"Well, I guess you would say that. You get Aunt Lucky. I guess that's okay. But come on." He looked up to Roderick, possibly for some backup. The poor kid sounded so frustrated.

Brittany wore a stern look that was all Gwen, and Ransom could tell that she was just waiting for them to team up against her.

"I just don't get why the princes always get the ugly curses. They get turned into frogs, they have to run all over heck's half acre trying to save princesses, who probably should've just did what their parents told them and then they wouldn't be in that situation. It's not fair."

Roderick nodded along, but then he said something that surprised Ransom. "Sometimes, when princes save the princess, they're really being saved, too."

Steven was skeptical. "Huh. I don't see it."

Brittany put her hand in Roderick's after that. "I like the stories where the princesses save themselves. Then they get to be with whoever they love."

"I like those stories, too," Roderick replied.

"Do you like those stories?" Steven asked Ransom. "My dad thinks they're all dumb."

"I do like them. My favorite stories are the ones with the Happily Ever After."

"Why? My dad says they're all pretend."

Brittany snorted but didn't say anything else.

"I don't think that's true. Listen, little man. I'm not going to tell you that your dad is wrong, but don't let anyone convince you that bad things are easier to believe in than the good."

Two fat raccoons waddled across their path and stopped to look at them.

Brittany did her best to contain a squeal, but failed miserably.

The raccoons seemed to cringe, but waited.

Brittany fumbled in her pocket and pulled out a bit of cake.

Ransom tried not to snort. Pockets stuffed with cake. Poor Gwen had her hands full with these little darlings.

Ransom couldn't help but imagine that if he and Lucky were to ever have children, they'd be full of the dickens, too.

Roderick whispered, "Uh, I don't think they're supposed

to feed wild animals. Isn't that a rule? Don't give kids to bears, or something?"

"This is Ever After, Roderick. These animals are unlike any you'll find anywhere else. I bet they'll take the cake straight from their little hands." But still, he decided better to be safe than sorry. "Hey, Brittany. Just hold it out for them and let them choose how close to get, okay? Don't touch."

"I know," she called back.

All enmity between her and her brother was gone as she patiently showed him how to hold out his hand. How to sit down quietly and wait for the animals to come to them.

"Uh, you guys. Don't try this anywhere outside of Ever After, either," Ransom called.

"Okay, Uncle Ransom," Steven answered.

*Uncle. Ransom.* His heart twisted on itself.

He wasn't unfamiliar with love. He wasn't afraid of it. Not like some men who pretended they didn't have feelings because it was unmanly or something equally ignorant. No, he was completely comfortable with emotions and admitting he had them.

What he was unfamiliar with was the concept of where he fit into a family. When he'd been orphaned, he'd lost that sense of self and how he fit into something bigger. Ransom had the godmothers and they loved him incredibly well. They were the best thing that had ever happened to him, aside from Lucky.

Though, there wasn't a bigger family unit.

One of the games he played as a kid was imagining himself as part of a big family, with cousins and siblings and those people you saw on holidays but couldn't quite remember how they were related to you.

Ransom had never felt like someone's son. Someone's brother. Someone's cousin.

Someone's uncle.

He knew in that moment, no matter what happened with

Lucky, he was now and forever Brittany and Steven's Uncle Ransom.

"That just gotcha right in the nuts, didn't it?" Roderick asked.

His friend knew him too well.

"Yeah, it did."

"I kinda like the small humans, too."

The raccoons had approached and had each taken a handful of the crumbly cake out of the kids' hands and one had come back to grab another. Then, they waddled off toward the forest.

Steven got up to follow them, but Brittany patiently explained why they shouldn't follow them.

"Maybe we'll see them at the fountain. Do you remember how to get there?" he asked.

"The path!" They darted forward, but then stopped and waited for Ransom to tell them they could go.

He nodded. "They really are good kids."

"I guess their mom is okay, too. She's dealing with a lot, huh."

"Yeah, and she's still here to support Lucky."

"Why doesn't she get a fairy godmother? Also, any idea when mine is going to be off the injured list?" Roderick asked.

"I don't know, my friend. You're going to have to ask Petty about that. She might know."

Roderick seemed to consider it for a moment. "Nah, probably better not. What with all the matchmaking."

"I think that's a godmother's bread and butter."

"I could use some of those godmother cookies, though."

"Man, I can barely see the kids. Those little legs sure do move fast."

"I know, right?"

They picked up the pace to keep time with the kids and they made it to the fountain in no time at all.

The mermaid fountain babbled and gurgled happily while

the kids chased each other around the perimeter. There was no sign of the raccoons, but Ransom figured they'd done their duty.

Suddenly, Brittany shrieked with glee. "I found him!"

Ransom looked over to see the roundest, fattest, angriest toad he'd ever seen in real life perched precariously on one of the mermaid's shoulders.

"It's the prince!" she squealed.

"It's not a prince. It's a dumb, old toad," Steven argued.

Ransom raised a brow.

Steven held out his hands as if to say, but it *is* dumb.

Ransom just shook his head and Steven did an impression of a glower, but his little shoulders sagged.

The frog made a sound that might've been a "ribbett" on a smaller creature, but this one sounded like the doorbell to the underworld.

It made Steven giggle like a loon and when he stopped giggling, the frog would do it again.

Ransom sat down on the edge of the fountain and acknowledged the frog. "Hey, buddy."

It blorped at him, and Steven and Brittany were both infected with the giggles.

"What's going on? I want to play," Roderick said, and joined them.

Brittany approached the frog carefully. "If you sit still, Mr. Frog, I'll give you a kiss."

Ransom wouldn't have thought that frogs had eyebrows, but this one seemed to arch a brow with doubtful invitation.

Hell, maybe he really was a prince waiting for someone to break the spell.

Steven grabbed his sister's arm. "What are you doing? You'll get warts."

"That's just a story. I will not."

"You *will*."

"If I do, our fairy godmother will fix me right up," she said with confidence.

Brittany leaned over slowly, and just as she was about to smooch the frog on his giant, bulbous head, Steven poked him in the hind parts with a stick and the frog launched himself into the air.

Brittany screamed as she fell into the fountain and the frog landed on her head.

"Oh, I'm going to get you." She sat up slowly, purposefully. She exhaled with a huff. "I'm sorry for my brother's rudeness, your majesty. It's too bad we can't actually put him in the dungeon."

The frog made a sound that might have been agreement.

Brittany picked him up gently and kissed his head before setting him on the edge of the fountain.

"Didn't work, huh?" Roderick asked.

"Nah, I didn't think it would, but I had to try."

"That's very brave."

Brittany beamed at him. "I guess I like you. Lots of boys can't tell when girls are brave, or strong, but I think you can. That doesn't mean you can marry my mom, though."

Roderick held up his hand. "Wouldn't dream of it. We could be friends, though."

"Not the sleeping over friends, though."

Ransom coughed and choked.

Roderick cleared his throat. "No, Brittany. Just regular friends. Like you and me."

"Okay. That's good." She stood up. "Now, Steven is going to pay."

Steven shrieked and ran into the bushes with a sopping wet Brittany on his trail.

"Stay where I can see you, you guys!" Ransom called.

"You're kind of good with these kids. All responsible and dad-like," Roderick said. "Is that what you want? Do you want the whole two-point-five kids and a dog and a . . . frog?"

"Yeah, I do."

"And you want it with Lucky, don't you?" Roderick asked.

"I don't know. I've always loved her."

"But . . ." Roderick prompted.

"But what if our children had whatever she has?"

"That's assuming you actually get to have penetrative sex. Ever. I don't know that I would risk it. Feral hogs? How does that even . . ."

"All of that is worth it for me. I don't care about that. I'm signing up to deal with that. Any little humans we decide to make, they're not choosing that. We're choosing it for them. Is that a risk we can take? If it's not, can we adopt? Some people are immune to Lucky's misfortune. Like Gwen. But what if they're not? Do I want this relationship more than I want a family?"

"You have a family, Ransom."

"Yes, I do. I didn't mean it that way. I just meant children. I want to be a father."

"I think you'd be good at it. For what it's worth, I think Lucky would be a good mother, if that's something she wants. I've watched how she puts everyone else around her first."

"I don't think she's ever let herself consider it." Ransom considered for a long moment. He thought about telling him about the quest, but ultimately decided against it. "What about you, Roderick? You've never mentioned if you want kids, or if you've even thought about it."

"I guess I've always thought I'd have them. Like, I'd meet someone, get married, and that would be the natural progression. I've never thought about whether I wanted it or not."

"Maybe you should."

"Oh, not you, too. I thought we were past that. I'm not about to run around and get involved with a woman fresh out of a relationship and her kids. Even if I like her kids."

Ransom held up his hands. "It's just that the godmothers are never wrong. That's all."

"That takes all the mystery out of it, doesn't it?"

"I don't think so. It's like a road trip. I know where I'm going to end up, but I don't know what's going to happen on the way there."

"We should talk about the press junket."

Ransom saw Brittany and Steven both covered in mud making their way back to the fountain. They each had toads in their hands the size of the one they'd just molested. The animals didn't struggle and allowed themselves to be transported.

"Guys! I said no touching."

"I asked him if I could pick him up and he let me!" Brittany said.

"We wanted to introduce them to the other frog in the fountain. Maybe they can be friends," Steven said.

By all that was holy.

He sighed and sank down in the park bench, and Roderick sat beside him.

"Okay, put them in the fountain, but if they decide to hop off, you let them."

"Yes, Uncle Ransom," they said in practiced unison.

"Press. Junket," Roderick reminded him.

"I know. I know. I'm dreading the damn thing."

"I know you are. Which is why I don't understand why you won't agree to the waiver."

"Because we had a hard enough time getting the press to agree to come to the middle of Missouri. The main reason they want to be here is to ask me about what happened. If they can't ask the questions they've been dying to know the answers to, why would they come?"

"Oh, I don't know. Because you're a billionaire getting married in a kitschy little tourist town?"

"Maybe I just want to get it over with."

Roderick's phone buzzed. He pulled it out and his face was a stone mask. "They were going to do it anyway, I suppose."

"Has it started?"

"Yeah." Roderick passed him the phone.

The headline read: THE BOY WHO MISSED TO WED.

He scrubbed a hand over his face.

He briefly considered buying the gossip rag outlet and selling it off for scrap. He could do it a thousand times over. Except he wasn't that kind of man, he didn't want to be.

Not even in moments like this.

He had to keep proving to himself he was more than The Boy Who Missed.

It was a mistake. An accident. It had clung to him like the stench of an unwashed gym sock almost his entire adult life.

He'd done so many things.

He was so many things.

He was more than this.

Except the press didn't want to talk about the schools he'd built, or the medical research he'd funded, the acres and acres of rain forest he saved, or how he paid workers' tuition and that of their immediate families. No, that didn't matter.

The only thing that mattered to them was that he'd had a mishap that happened more regularly than people might think.

So why him? Why did it stay with him?

His only answer was that there was something else wrong with him. Some other, underlying cause or unworthiness.

The same unworthiness he'd felt his whole life.

That's why it made him so angry. That's why he retaliated. He needed to prove he was more. He needed to prove that he could. He wasn't helpless. He wasn't a failure.

Ransom repeated his accomplishments over and over to himself, a litany and an armor, but somehow, those sharp little arrows always managed to get through.

His own phone buzzed and he checked it with a sigh.

It was Bluebonnet with an update.

"The junket is tomorrow," he said aloud.

"You know what they wouldn't be expecting?" Roderick asked with a cheerful grin. "If after it started, we locked the doors and junk-punched each of them in turn. We could give the kids boxing gloves and just let them go for it."

Ransom didn't want to laugh at that, but the visual was just too good. He cackled.

"You could buy them all a thousand times over. I would, if I were you."

"Yeah, I'm going to destroy an entire business and put people out of work and hurt families because I got my feelings hurt. No."

"You did it with the bank."

"Not quite. They're still in business. Just not with me. They have plenty of other capital to work with."

Roderick nodded. "See? You are so much more than that. Don't doubt yourself, Ransom. You've come too far. What is the saying? Wolves don't concern themselves with the opinions of sheep?"

"I've never wanted to be a wolf."

Roderick sighed. "Listen, fucker. I'm trying to give you a pep talk and you're not making it easy. You have a problem for every solution."

Ransom laughed again. "Yeah, you're right. My bad."

"I think I know what the fairy godmothers feel like. We should buy them some chocolate or something." Roderick scrubbed a hand over his face and blinked.

"Did you get everything set up for Gwen? For her to get her stuff, I mean?"

"Yeah, the movers will be there tomorrow and they'll put everything in storage for her. We arranged for the husband to be there, too, so he can't say she took anything that wasn't hers. He hasn't even asked about the kids. I don't understand it."

"Sometimes people aren't aware of what they have."

"Pot and kettle, maybe?" Roderick nodded at him.

"I know what I have. It's just sometimes I forget that I deserve it," Ransom confessed.

"Honestly? Screw *deserve*. Lots of people get things they don't deserve. Whether it be bad or good. You don't have to earn your right to be happy."

He turned to look at Roderick and saw him now in a new light.

"This is why you're my assistant and my best friend."

"Damn straight."

"Damn straight," Brittany suddenly yelled.

"No, don't do that. I just got your mom not to hate me," Roderick pleaded.

Brittany giggled and Roderick ran over to chase her around the fountain and when he caught her, he tickled her sides and made her howl with laughter.

"Save me, Uncle Ransom."

"I thought princesses were supposed to save themselves," Steven supplied helpfully.

Ransom got up and snatched Steven up, swinging him around under his arm.

"Princes too."

And just maybe, that was something Ransom had forgotten.

# Chapter 12

The castle spires rose high atop the Enchanted Forest and as the sun set on Ever After, it came to life with a flurry of activity. Torches and candles were lit, the royal orchestra played, and townspeople could be seen making their way up the path from the town below in the fading light.

Bernadette from the coffee shop, Rosebud from the dress shop, Red, Grammy, Hansel from the lumberyard with his carpenter's tools, his sister Gretel from the apothecary, and even several frogs who hopped from the fountain and waited patiently for the sun to finish its arc across the horizon.

As Petunia Blossom watched from the ramparts, she was very glad she'd ushered her charges to the castle before the great migration for the town meeting tonight in the Once Upon a Time Ballroom.

"When is Fortune going to get here? I don't know how much longer we can keep this secret from Lucky," Bluebonnet fretted.

"She should be here soon. She texted to say she was fighting with them at the rental counter about extra insurance," Jonquil said, and fluttered her wings.

"I have a feeling, sisters." Petty waved her wand and small, floating candles lit the way through the dark forest to guide their friends to the castle.

"Me too. I thought it was just an angry tummy from eating too many cherries," Jonquil agreed.

"We simply need to take extra steps tonight is all," Bluebonnet said.

"We're so close, but time is of the essence. We need a game plan to insulate us for the normies, and to insulate them from us," Petty said.

"Wasn't that something we should've had planned out before we invited them here?" Jonquil asked.

"Well, yes. I got a little ahead of myself." Petty pushed her spectacles up on her nose and sniffed. "Speaking of, is Ransom and Lucky's room ready yet?"

"They've just finished," Bluebonnet said. "Do you think we have enough magic to fix our floor? We could always hire Hansel, but I'd really like to just fix it."

"I did it before we left," Jonquil said.

"Lovely. What about Mama's tea set?" Bluebonnet asked. "I was just devastated to see it in so many pieces."

"Of course. Everything is back as it should be, but I am feeling a little run-down," Jonquil confessed.

"We must get you some tea right away," Bluebonnet said.

"Hugs!" Petty cried, and pulled Jonquil close.

Bluebonnet slipped into the hug and they held one another tight.

Energy flowed through Petty, but she directed it all to Jonquil freely and with no intent of holding anything in reserve.

"We're so happy to see you three getting along," Lucky said from the doorway.

"Oh, I'm sorry, darling. We haven't gotten you settled in your rooms yet," Petty said.

"We can make time for godmother hugs," Ransom said. "We have to stock up and save them for later."

Ransom and Lucky both joined in the hug and in moments, Petty's magic welled up in her like lava. She hadn't felt this good in centuries. In fact, if she was correct, the lines on her face were smoothing away.

She'd have to stop that, but she didn't want to let go of the hug. Not just yet.

It wasn't because of the power-up, even though that was a lovely bonus, but it was because it was nice to be in the moment with her family.

That's what all of her charges were—family.

For Petty, that was her sacred cow.

Then she giggled, because if her sisters knew she'd just called them cows, they'd hex her into next week.

More love filled her and radiated outward. Petty felt like she was about to go supernova, she was so full of hope and light.

She'd missed these feelings.

Petty loved her sisters, obviously, but she'd forgotten what it felt like to be grateful for them. To be present in a moment with love and not just habit.

This was what they were all missing.

The hug tightened and Petty knew everyone was feeling something magical.

The goodness welled up between them until they were surrounded in a sparkling ball of pure, golden light. Then it shot up into the sky and exploded overhead in a starburst of fireworks. Some of the embers fell down around them like hot glitter.

Lucky broke the hug. "I'm so sorry! I shouldn't have . . . I thought you were immune to my bad luck. I—"

"Hush now!" Jonquil demanded before Ransom could speak. "We are. This is amazing."

"What it is are explosives gone wrong. What if this had hurt you?"

"Pish. That's not it at all. It was a beautiful moment. There is absolutely nothing wrong with you, Lucky."

"We almost caught fire," she said.

"Nothing of the sort, but we have a town meeting tonight

to discuss publicity details. Nothing that either of you needs to worry your lovely little heads about. So we're banishing you to your wing of the castle until morning." Petty started to usher them to the door.

"We can help," Ransom offered.

"All we need you two to do is look pretty. Plus, I'm sure you're exhausted after your fittings, cake tasting, and playing with those two darling troublemakers all afternoon," Bluebonnet reassured them.

Petty led them through the castle and to their honeymoon suite. Philip had done wonders with the castle in the short time he'd had to get it ready.

The double doors leading to the suite were framed by marble pillars covered in real ivy, and the doors were made of light wood and had heavy, black iron-banded accents. When the doors opened, it smelled of jasmine and vanilla.

A giant king-size bed with royal-blue velvet drapes and more pillows than a Bed Bath & Beyond stood as the centerpiece of the room. White marble columns also bore ivy and jasmine.

A fireplace crackled with pine logs, and the room was just chilly enough to enjoy the warm fire. Pillows had been spread out on the lush rug, along with a plate of cheeses, chocolate strawberries, and champagne chilling in an ornate silver bucket.

There was a balcony with a Roman bath hot tub, it seemed as if you could swim to the edge of the world.

Dress forms stood with Lucky's wedding dress, and all the other clothes she'd need for the wedding activities. A white box with rosebud ribbon waited on the dresser, and Petty had a feeling whatever was in that box was lacy.

The room was absolutely stunning.

"I definitely have to give Phillip props on this," Petty said.

"Holy shit," Lucky replied. "This is a lot. I can't wait to show Gwen and the kids."

"The kids are going to love that hot tub," Ransom said.

"The kids? Me, I'm going to love that hot tub," Bluebonnet said. Then she straightened and smoothed the gingham of her skirt. "Well, later. We have work to do."

"Godmothers?" Lucky asked in a sweet tone.

"Yes, dearling?" Jonquil replied.

"There's only one bed."

"Quite so," Petty said, not seeing the problem.

"We're not actually getting married. You remember that, right?" Lucky said.

"You should've thought about that before you 'not actually-ed' right through our ceiling. You're grown-ups. Figure it out. This was the best Phillip could do before next week. The other finished rooms are going to be filled with press. They need to believe this," Petty said.

"We'll be in the Once Upon a Time Ballroom if you need us. That's in the opposite wing," Bluebonnet advised.

Lucky looked back and forth between the godmothers and Ransom shrugged.

"Come along, sisters. We have work to do." Jonquil led them from the room.

As they made their way down to the ballroom, Petty reminded herself to seal the ballroom in case Lucky did need something from them, their secret wouldn't be revealed until she was ready.

"Pets, here's your notebook," Jonquil said, handing her the brightly colored pink organizer covered with washi tape and stickers.

Ah yes, Pets would be quite lost without her magic journal to keep track of all her "projects." She opened to Juniper, her granddaughter's page, and saw that things were still progressing well and she was right on the path she was supposed to be on.

"Petunia," Phillip said as he joined them on the stairs. "Everyone is ready in the ballroom."

"Fantastic news." She turned to look at him, but what she saw gave her pause. "Oh dear, you look awful. A little—"

"By all that's holy, Petunia, if you say green around the gills, I'll end you," Phillip grumbled.

Jonquil snickered and Bluebonnet did her best, but she cackled.

"Green is just your color," Bluebonnet snorted.

"Thanks a lot, witches."

Petunia narrowed her eyes. "What did you call me?"

He cleared his throat but stood his ground. "Listen, I've more than paid for my crime. I know what I did was wrong, and not just because you turned me into a frog."

Petunia decided to give him a pass. He was right. Maybe she should add him to her client list. Not that he'd ever agree to such a thing, but what Prince Phillip Charming didn't know wouldn't hurt him. At least, in this instance.

"I know you have, darling. And honestly, if I could undo it, I would have hundreds of years ago. It's not my fault you can't find True Love's Kiss."

He sighed. "I know, but I'm still very frustrated, and completely disgusted by your sweet little old lady act. It's weird, Petunia."

"I am a sweet little old lady, Phillip. I was seducing men in apple orchards before you were born."

"Petty!" Jonquil gasped.

"Well, we were." Bluebonnet clasped her hands together primly.

"Ah, the days of nymph-hood." Petty wondered briefly if she'd ever fall in love again. She couldn't imagine any man being the right one to fit into their little family unit, but as fairy godmothers their lives were long.

Much too long to be spent without loving another person in that all-consuming passion kind of way.

Phillip snapped his fingers. "Hey, back to the problem at hand, ladies."

"Yes, your majesty?" Petty asked.

He narrowed his eyes. "Don't use the title. It means less than nothing these days. I'm prince of the shit pond, and that's about it. Anyway—"

"It's a very nice fountain," Bluebonnet interrupted.

*"Anyway,"* Phillip said again. "Everyone is here. Shall we get started?"

"That's just where we were headed," Petty assured him.

They made their way into the Once Upon a Time Ballroom and once Petty was inside, she nodded to her sisters and they performed the magic that would seal them off from prying eyes and ears.

Petty stood behind the podium and looked at all of her friends and neighbors each in turn. She was heartened to see how the community had come together and been willing to do whatever it took to not only make this wedding happen, but to help one another. They'd all been open to everyone's ideas to save and rebuild their town.

She was so proud of them.

Petty held her wand up like a microphone. "Friends! Thank you all for being here tonight. We're putting our plan in motion to save Ever After and bring new life and vitality to our sweet, little haven. I know change is hard. It's hard for all of us. But even though we're fairy-tale creatures, the same applies to us as it does to all things. Adapt or die."

A few people in the crowd laughed at her blunt words, and for some, it was a nervous titter. Others nodded along.

"Tomorrow, we're going to be in close proximity to humans that we absolutely cannot trust with our secrets. Later this week, I hope to meet with each of you and discuss developing a security protocol personalized to your gifts and your stories. For now, our wands are sufficiently powered up to do a blanket protection spell. But keep your magic to backrooms in your shops, with your drapes closed," Petty advised.

"Members of the press will be arriving first thing in the

morning. Make sure our woodland friends know to stay off the roads," she added. "This is going to be new for us, having so many normies in close proximity."

"I was reading the press releases so far, and I'm not happy," Bernadette said from the back of the room. "They're already dragging Ransom's name through the mud. I think you should give them warts."

"Or turn them all into frogs," Phillip added helpfully.

Rosebud snorted indelicately. In fact, she sounded like a full-grown sow with her face in a pile of slops. "And what good would that do us? How about you make the releases disappear?"

Grammy growled. "No one messes with our Ransom."

"Guys, guys. This is fantastic, but listen. It's part of his journey. We need to let it be."

"I don't like letting it be," Grammy said.

"Yes, dear." Jonquil spoke into her wand and it reverberated off the walls, startling them all. "But now look at you."

Grammy narrowed her eyes.

Bluebonnet rushed to play peacemaker. "It's just . . . it's part of a lesson he has to learn for the love thing to work out. That's all."

"So what's next?" Hansel said from the far back. "We've got this wedding, but now what?"

"News of the wedding has already given us several bookings. We've got four more right after this one!" Jonquil said. "It's working!"

"We've made up these flyers," Petty said, and released what looked to be a flock of white birds. Except they were folded slips of paper that flapped on enchanted wings to each person. "We're Fairy Godmothers, Inc. wedding planners. So we'll funnel all the happy couples through our business and we'll coordinate each wedding. We'll use our magic to keep the process smooth, and they'll go to each one of you in turn.

We are looking to hire some outside help, but it's time for some new blood in Ever After."

"Like Gwen?" Red asked.

"Like Gwen. We'll introduce them to magic when the time is right," Bluebonnet said.

The double doors to the ballroom were suddenly flung open and there stood Fortune Fujiki, every inch a globe-trotting dream.

She was a tiny woman, but her presence made her seem six feet tall. Of course, part of that could've been the ridiculously high heels that she made look effortless. She was wrapped in a faux-fox fur jacket and had on Gucci sunglasses that were practically too big for her face, but somehow, she made them work.

"I can see you started without me," Fortune said.

"If one wasn't late, one wouldn't be left out," Jonquil informed her.

Fortune waved it off and sauntered into the room as if she hadn't just interrupted a town meeting. "Where's Lucky?"

"She's resting. We're trying to get tomorrow sorted."

"Oh. That." Fortune looked around and found herself some refreshments. "Do carry on."

"As I was saying . . ." Petty trailed off. "What was I saying?"

"I do believe we were going check in on our magic wells," Jonquil prompted.

"Oh yes. Quite." Petty adjusted her glasses. "So far, I've noticed that our wands are powered up and we're able to do much more magic than we have in some time."

"My ovens produced double batches of everything I put in," Red said. "It's not the quad we're used to, but it's progress."

"When I take a tree from the forest, the saplings have started to grow back. It's not the endless supply we had, but it's something," Hansel said.

"Something interesting happened to me! As you know, I grow coffee beans in my back yard. For every coffee bean I harvest, I've been gifted a cacao bean as well," Bernadette said.

"Any negative responses?" Petunia asked.

A woman dressed in all black stood up. She had high cheekbones and thin lips, and was possessed of a cold kind of beauty. Her name was Ravenna, and once upon a time, she'd been an evil queen. Now, she was content to spend her days managing The First Bank of Ever After.

"The wells of magic in the bank vaults are up to three percent," Ravenna said.

"Only three?" Phillip asked.

"What did you expect? We use magic for everything. It's a miracle we're up at all instead of barely breaking even as we had been for the last few years," Ravenna replied.

"This is great news. So we only need a thousand more weddings?" Phillip said scornfully.

"Do you have a better idea?" Ravenna eyed him. "You know, it takes a lot of magic to maintain your curse."

Petty could see where this was going. "That's neither here nor there, Ravenna. Thank you for the report, and for taking such good care of the vaults."

Petty wanted to be sure to remind everyone, including Ravenna, that she wasn't wicked queening anymore. She was part of the town, she was a neighbor and a friend, just like everyone else.

Ravenna's ruby-red lips curled into a sharp smile. "Thank you, Petunia."

"Next on the agenda we have the blessing," Bluebonnet said, reading from Petty's notebook in an attempt to keep everyone on task.

"Thank goodness!" Grammy said. "We haven't done that in some time and these old bones are tired."

"Everyone, join hands," Petunia said.

Everyone gathered in a circle and linked hands. When Petty could feel that everyone was connected, she began to whisper the words of the ancient prayer that kept them bound to one another, to magic, and to the gifts of Ever After.

It was a gift of rejuvenation and cleansing that worked from the inside out. Just as the spell reached its full glorious peak, all of the occupants in the room were levitated several feet off the floor as a whirlwind made of light spun them into euphoria.

It was something holy. Something beautiful.

Just as Petty and her sisters freed their wings and lifted up off the floor to join the bliss, Fortune cried out. Petty's head spun all the way around on her shoulders like a demented owl and saw something she'd hoped never to see.

Lucky, standing in the doorway, her mouth hanging open and fear scrawled across her face.

"Damn," Petty whispered.

Lucky ran.

# Chapter 13

Lucky knew things were different in Ever After, but she hadn't realized how different.

The godmothers had kept this secret about themselves for the whole of her life.

That was when she realized Ransom knew, too. She'd asked him if he knew something she didn't and he'd said she'd find out.

This had to be what he'd been talking about.

Holy shitlords! Were they actually fairies? They'd been on and on about being fairy godmothers. She'd seen wings with her own eyes!

Lucky ran down the various twists and turns in the castle halls until she found her way to the kitchen.

She needed sugar. She'd read that sugar helped with the symptoms of shock.

And she was an emotional eater. Whenever she was upset, sweets were her comfort.

Lucky heard Petty call out her name, but she didn't want to talk to her. Not yet. She needed to center herself. To stuff her face in silence.

Only she heard her mother's voice, too. "Lucky, wait."

Her mother knew, too.

Everyone knew but Lucky.

Assholes.

On the plus side, maybe . . . just maybe all of her problems really *were* a curse. If she was cursed, none of this was her fault. If it wasn't her fault, she wasn't unworthy.

"Please!" Fortune called out.

It was the *please* that got her.

She slowed her steps, which happened to be a boon, because suddenly, the hallway ended in galley stairs, and she hopped down them to find herself in a massive, industrial-size kitchen. Lucky found a box of pastries on one of the tables and sat down and promptly shoved one in her mouth.

Petty, Bluebonnet, Jonquil, and her mother all followed soon after.

"You sure can move fast for being a klutz," Fortune wheezed.

"Nice, Mom."

"Oh, hush. Come here." Fortune wrapped an arm around her daughter. "This is all my fault. I asked them to wait until I was here."

Around her strawberry pastry, she said, "That accounts for this week, but what about the rest of my life? Didn't trust me?"

Petty looked like she'd been slapped.

Jonquil wilted.

Bluebonnet sniffed and wiped away a tear.

"No, my little lucky charm. I wanted you to have a normal life," Fortune said softly.

"Well, I haven't, have I? Everywhere I go, I'm a pariah. Now I find out all of the people I love most have been lying to me."

Fortune pressed her lips together. "When you're ready, we can talk."

"I'm so mad at you right now, Ma. But if you all don't tell me everything, I don't know how I'll ever not be mad. So just tell me."

"Lucky," Petty began, "you were born in Ever After."

She looked up to meet her godmother's eyes. This woman she'd known since birth. She could see the nostalgia, the pride, and even the love in her eyes.

That was no balm, it only made it worse. Her eyes teared up.

"Oh, sweetie. No, listen—"

"Petty. I need to tell this. There's more to the story I've kept from you, too. I'm sorry, but I felt it was for the best," Fortune said.

"Oh!" Bluebonnet gasped. Then she put her chin in her hands as she leaned on the table. "Then tell us your story, Fortune."

"I was very young when I met Lucky's father. He wasn't at all suitable. My parents had allowed the friendship but told me it could never be anything more."

"I thought Dad was just a ship in the night," Lucky said. Then she shoved another pastry in her mouth.

Petty got her a glass of milk.

Bluebonnet handed her a napkin.

And Jonquil, bless her, handed her a cupcake.

"That's what he ended up being, yes." Fortune nodded, but she took Lucky's hand, the one not holding the cupcake. "But for a brief period of time, we loved each other very much."

"So where is it that you met?"

"Not too far from here. His parents had a summer house on the Lake of the Ozarks. My family lived deep in the woods, but me, I couldn't stay away from the summer people. I loved the boats, the food, and I was especially intrigued by the boys. I was out exploring and your father was with his friends in some old tree house they'd built as kids. It was love at first sight. We began spending every minute together. We both started sneaking out and meeting in that treehouse. We would talk for hours about everything. He wanted to be an architect. I think what changed everything for me was when he asked me what *I* wanted to be."

"What did you want to be, Ma?"

Lucky's mother had never told her of her hopes and dreams before Lucky. She'd always acted as if she'd gotten everything she ever wanted. She didn't know much about her grandparents, either. Only that the women in their family were named after virtues or gifts they wanted for their children.

"Human." Fortune's words fell on the group like a bomb.

"What?" Petty gasped.

"Excuse me? What . . . *holy shit*. Am I not human? Is that my problem?" Lucky took a long swallow of the milk. "I think I need a brandy."

"No, honey. You're completely and utterly human, and so am I. Now."

"This is too much. I know there's more, but I honestly don't know if I can take it," Lucky said.

"Another cupcake will calm your nerves, dear." Jonquil whipped another one up from thin air and handed it to her.

Lucky inspected it and realized it was exactly what she'd been craving. Red velvet with cream cheese frosting. "Maybe this magic stuff isn't so bad."

Jonquil patted her shoulder.

"Your father and I fell in love, as I said. It was all very star-crossed and tragic. We made love and I became pregnant with you. My family made me choose. If I stayed with them, I couldn't have you. If I had you, I couldn't stay with them."

"That's awful!" Lucky cried.

"Wait, wait. It's not their fault. It's just the way of things. The physical world doesn't do well in the spiritual, and vice versa. I was born a kitsune. Fox spirit. We're allowed to take human form, but we cannot keep it and stay a fox spirit."

"Oh, Fortune," Bluebonnet said. "I can't imagine being faced with that choice."

"I couldn't give you up, Lucky. So I said goodbye to my parents, my family, and my magic. I didn't know what to do, or how to exist in the human world. When I went to tell your dad about you, he'd already gone home. I cried, and I walked and cried, and I walked until a kindly fox led me here to Ever After, and to the godmothers. Petunia was the first one to see your beautiful face." Fortune squeezed her hand. "I stayed here for a year, and I tried to contact James, but he said he simply couldn't be a father. He had college to worry about. So I did what I could and I was determined to give you a normal, human life. I thought I was protecting you."

Lucky hadn't realized how strong her mother was. Or what kinds of choices she'd had to make.

"Your mother, Ma. You haven't seen her in all this time?"

"I haven't set eyes on her since I chose to be your mother. I know she understood. Sometimes, even though I can't see her, or speak to her, I feel her presence. I know she checks up on us every now and then. My father, too. They would've been the best grandparents. I'm so sorry you won't get to know them."

Lucky looked up at Petty. "That's what I want. I want my grandparents to come to the wedding. I want to meet them. I want my mother to see her family."

Fortune kissed the top of Lucky's head. "If only it were so easy, we would've done it long ago."

"I should've asked why it was so easy for you to accept the idea of magic. If only you'd told us years ago, we could've tried to help you," Jonquil said. "Ever After is magic. Your kitsune family would be welcome here."

"The kitsune have slipped so far away from the human world, I don't know if I would be able to see them," Fortune said.

"Is this why I'm like this?" Lucky asked.

"Like what?" Fortune asked.

"Cursed?"

"Whatever has happened with you, it's not a curse. I was sure I used up all of your luck birthing you. Your delivery was hard because I was so young and you were determined to be born your own way. I named you Lucky in hopes of giving your luck back."

"We thought that maybe because Lucky was born here, that living in the outside world was what put her out of alignment, but now, I'm not so sure," Petty said.

"Can't you fix this? You're magic. You can break my curse!" Lucky cried. Only when she looked into Petty's eyes, she knew the answer was no. All the hope that had flared inside of her was snuffed to ash. "Why not?"

"I think I understand now," Petty said. "It's part of you. It's just who you are."

Bluebonnet nodded. "Kitsune are forces of mischief and chaos. They are not bad or good, they just are. Since your mother gave up her magic to have you, these things that happen around you, they're just part of your heritage."

Those words tore Lucky's heart in half.

"So, there's no cure?"

"You don't need a cure for being who you are. There is nothing wrong with you," Fortune said. "The right person will love you anyway."

"It's not about if he loves me anyway. I know he does. It's about whether or not I can deal with how loving me hurts him. Yesterday, we fell through the floor. What's it going to be tomorrow, if we keep going down this path?"

"I know you may not believe me," Fortune began. "But I do believe that will work itself out."

"Yeah, after an escaped lion from the zoo eats him in some kind of freak accident," Lucky said, and dropped her head into her arms on the table.

"This is Ever After," Bluebonnet said. It's simply a law of the universe that if you have a fairy godmother, and you're not a shit, you get a Happily Ever After."

Lucky slid back up into sitting position. "Well, he's in the doghouse at the moment anyway. How long has he known about magic?"

"Well, always," Petty confessed. "He was just a little orphan when he came to us with no one in the world. He didn't trust us. Didn't believe a word, so we had to prove it to him."

"I'm really hurt he didn't tell me. I understand he promised you not to, which I admire. I just . . ." She grit her teeth.

"It's okay to have complicated feelings about all of this," Petty said. "I was sure you hated us. Or worse, were scared of us. You ran away. That was the worst feeling in the world."

She hugged Petty. "I'm sorry you thought I was scared of you. I love you and I know you love me, but I was in a bit of shock. It explains some things, though. I was sure I saw a family of mice checking on us in the attic. I saw animals sewing dresses, and that damned bird made fun of me. He said caw. And chirp. Next time I see him, he's getting a 'tweet tweet, motherfucker.'"

Lucky stopped and looked up with wide eyes. "Oh, oh no. Everyone here . . . all these fairy tales are real. Gwen is going to shit. I mean, you have to let me tell her if she's going to live here."

"Of course, we'll take care of Gwen," Bluebonnet reassured her. "In fact, I do believe that even though she doesn't actually have a fairy godmother, we've decided to take on her case."

"Even if she doesn't want to be with Roderick?" Lucky asked.

"Roderick, Broderick, Schmoderick." Petty waved her hand. "That will take care of itself."

Lucky began to arch a brow, then another shocked thought crossed her mind. "Red. Grammy. Holy shit, I thought that was just the fairy-tale tourist thing you were trying to . . . wow. Is Grammy a werewolf?"

"What? There's no such . . ." Fortune trailed off. "Are you serious? You have my child in a community with a werewolf?"

"These things happen. It bit her when she was saving Red. She goes out to the country during that time of the month. That's why they want to move." Jonquil said this last to Lucky. "So Gwen is doing them a favor."

"This is so much to process. I can't decide if I'm scared shitless or I think it's really cool, or both. It's kind of nice not being the only freak," Lucky said.

"You're not a freak. You're unique," Fortune said.

"You're my mom. You're supposed to say that," Lucky replied. "You didn't see how when Ransom kissed me, we made mutant fruit."

"What?" Fortune did a double take.

"Oh no. Lucky, that was so good. That tree bloomed because of love. That wasn't a bad thing at all," Bluebonnet said. "It was a gift."

"Uh-huh. Did it smash Ransom in the face because of love?"

"Totally," Jonquil said.

"Lucky, it's true I am your mother, but you know that I am absolutely not that kind of mom." Fortune pursed her lips.

This was true. That's not who Fortune had ever been. Lucky remembered showing her mother her first attempts at drawing and painting and her mother had complimented her lines, but pointed out every flaw. Not with malice, but with suggestions on how to work on her craft . . . how to *make* it her craft. Lucky wouldn't be the artist she was today without her mother's honest critique.

Still, it would be nice if once in a while she got a "good job." Although, she supposed that's what the godmothers were for.

"I have another question," Lucky said.

"I'm sure you have many." Fortune squeezed her hand again.

"The frog in the fountain. Is he really a prince? And if so, who turned him into a frog and why? I need details. Fairy-tale drama might just be a drug, because I'm addicted."

Both Jonquil and Bluebonnet looked at Petty.

Petty blushed. "Why are you looking at me?"

"Oh, you know very well why." Bluebonnet eyed her, but then smiled. "You tell it."

Petty adjusted her glasses. "Well, it is a rather famous story, so I suppose you should know all about it. Once upon a time, a long time ago, in a land right here, there was a prince.

He was a very handsome prince. Everything they tell you a prince should be. Tall, strong, lovely manners, an educated mind, a well-honed body, and hair that looked as if it had been spun from gold."

"She does have a way with words," Jonquil said.

"This prince had taken to courting. It was rumored that he'd fallen in love with a young fairy who'd yet to leave for the fairy godmother training academy, although she'd been accepted."

"Oh, Petty!" It was obvious Fortune could see where this was going.

Lucky had no clue and was dying to hear the rest of this sordid tale.

"The problem with this rumor, however, was that more than one young, pretty fairy fit these parameters."

Jonquil snickered.

Lucky felt a surge of something that made her cringe. She didn't know exactly how this was going to turn out, but she was sure it was going to be awful.

"As we came to discover, Bluebonnet and I, we realized he'd been courting us both. Kissing us both. And"—Petty coughed—"us both."

Lucky gasped.

"I cried when we found out. I thought I was going to marry Prince Charming." Bluebonnet sighed.

"I, being the eldest, had already received my wand. I hadn't quite learned what to do with it yet, but as you know, I simply couldn't let that kind of thing stand. I decided he needed to learn a lesson about love. So I cursed Phillip Charming to be a frog by day to pay for his sins and to be a man by night so he could continue to suffer for them."

"That's how she earned her nickname: Petty." Jonquil nodded emphatically.

"Bah," Petty waved a hand.

"He had it coming." Lucky was supportive.

"So yes, the frog in the fountain is none other than our gracious host," Jonquil said.

"Oh, that Phillip Charming! Oh my God!" Lucky cackled. "How long has it been?"

"I stopped counting, really. I would change him back if I could. He has suffered enough. But just as I was telling him today, it's not my fault no one loves him." Petty put a hand over her mouth. "I didn't mean that, exactly. I meant that no one's kiss has been True Love. That's all that will break the spell," Petty said.

"That's the only thing that breaks any spell, isn't it?" Bluebonnet said.

Lucky knew they'd said that her bad luck wasn't a spell, it wasn't a curse, but she didn't believe them. She had an easier time believing she was descended from fox ghosts or spirits or whatever than she did believing she wasn't cursed.

Because if Lucky surrendered, if she believed that this was simply who she was, that meant she'd never be free of her *un*luck.

She'd never be able to be with the person she loved without hurting them.

No, it was time to be honest with herself. It wasn't some vague idea of some future person. It was Ransom.

If just being who she was brought strife to his life, she'd never be able to live with herself.

That's how she'd break the spell. It wasn't his love she needed to break the spell, but hers. She had to love him enough to let him go.

# Chapter 14

It was late when Lucky returned to their room. Or early, rather.

"Is everything okay?" Ransom eased himself up to sitting position.

"I'm sorry, I didn't mean to wake you. We've got a few hours before we have to be up, if you wanted to sleep more."

She had dark, puffy circles under her eyes like she'd been crying and just the way she moved, it seemed as if the weight of the world was on her narrow shoulders. Ransom would do anything to take that burden from her.

"Come lay down with me," he said. "No pressure. No strings. Just come rest."

"That's the problem, though. I want pressure. I want strings, but we can't have them."

"Let's not worry about that right now. Let me be your friend. Tell me what happened?" he said, and held the blanket up for her.

It took her only a moment to shed her jeans and crawl in bed beside him in her underwear and T-shirt.

Ransom tucked her against him and stroked her hair until she was ready to talk.

"So . . . my mom is here."

He waited for her to go on.

"And I know."

"What do you know?"

"I *know*. About magic. About the godmothers. About everything."

He closed his eyes and took a deep breath. "I wanted to tell you."

"Thank you for not lying to me, even though you couldn't tell me." She turned into him, her head resting against his chest. Her fingers played across his arm. "I found out something else, too."

The tone of her voice caused the hairs on the back of his neck to prickle. Whatever came next wasn't going to be good.

"You know how I thought I was cursed? I'm not," she whispered forlornly.

"Why is that a bad thing?"

"This is just who I am. What I am. I will never be anything but this."

He remembered what the godmothers had told him about loving Lucky for who she was, as she was. Not trying to save her. Or fix her.

That was when it punched him in the face like a wrecking ball. Plenty of inconvenient things happened to Lucky, but actual Bad Things, the kind with the capital letter, didn't. They happened to the people around her.

The godmothers had been incredibly right, and oh-so-wrong at the same time. There was no curse to break, no luck to find. There was only love.

So in a sense, just loving her for herself was enough.

*If* the other person was steadfast, brave, all the things a hero should be in a fairy tale. As much as he wanted to be that kind of hero, Ransom didn't know if he was.

He held her more tightly. "There's nothing wrong with what you are, Lucky."

"I don't know what to do."

"The same thing you've been doing. Living your life. Creating art. Spending your time with the people you love. That doesn't need to change."

"I had this hope that one day I'd find out that I was a under a spell or something. Someday, someone would break that curse and I'd be free. I didn't realize until just now that even as an adult, I'd counted on that. That idea was this hope in the back of my mind and when things were hard, and it was laugh or cry, I'd choose to laugh because I knew someday, it wouldn't be like this anymore. Only there is no someday."

He kissed the top of her head. "You don't know what tomorrow is going to bring."

"I know what today is going to bring. That God-awful press junket."

"It's going to be fine. We'll smile, talk about how we met, where we're going on our honeymoon and some bullshit about future plans with two-point-five kids, a vacation home, and a couple show dogs."

"That sounds absolutely awful. Except for the vacation home."

"You don't like dogs?"

"I love them, but I'm not going to ask them to do something I wouldn't do."

He could feel her grin against his chest.

"Since we're here, we should probably actually hash out some details."

"We have a prenup; we're going to honeymoon in space; you've named a chocolate bar after me that's ruby cacao, honey, and ginger; we haven't made any plans beyond that; and we are going to live Happily Ever After."

"Honeymoon in space, huh?"

"Yeah, so they can't follow us. Doesn't that zillionaire have a tourist rocket or something?"

He laughed. "How about Monaco?"

"Yes, how about it?" she teased.

"Have you been? Do you want to go? We could go there on our date after the wedding."

"You can't just take me to Monaco on our first date."

"Why not? Who is there to tell us no?"

"It's a pretty dream. One I'd say yes to if it comes within reach."

"I'm offering it to you now," he said. "Say yes."

"Let's make a deal. If nothing bad happens to you between now and our wedding, I'll go with you to Monaco. I'll go with you anywhere you want me to."

"Why do you think something bad is going to happen to me?"

"I guess I keep waiting for the other to drop. You know, like we fell through the floor? Although, the godmothers told me that the cherry tree was actually a good thing. The part where you got whomped in the face was a legit accident, but I don't know."

"I'm not worried about it. It was just a cherry."

"I don't want to leave this room. I want to stay here and sleep for three days, eat room service, and soak in that ridiculous hot tub."

"We can do that, but after the press junket. Remember, the whole reason we agreed to this was to help the godmothers and Ever After."

"I know. It feels like I've aged a century in the last few days. It's weird how you can look back at a version of yourself that wasn't even that long ago and think of her as a sweet summer child, you know?"

He knew exactly what she meant.

"When was the last time you did something that you truly loved?" Ransom asked her.

"What do you mean? Like . . . painting? Or?"

He shrugged. "I don't know. Just something for the pure joy of doing it. Not for any specified outcome."

"I don't know. I love painting, but I haven't been really moved to create for a long time. I wanted to paint Grammy. There's something so pure and powerful about her. She's elemental and beautiful."

"Me too."

"What, really? You want to paint Grammy?"

He grinned. "Totally. Who wouldn't?" Then his expression grew serious. "I love Heart's Desire. I thought it was my heart's desire to make chocolate. Don't get me wrong, I'm proud of what I've built, but I don't have the same passion for it as I did when I first started. I mean, I was in a garage with a heat lamp and cacao beans like Jack and the Chocolate Stalk. All my friends made fun of me for spending my last few dollars on beans, but here I am." Ransom shook his head. "That was how I met Roderick, actually. He believed in me."

"That's important. The person who was with you before you had anything, who believed in your dream as much as you did. That matters."

"Yeah, that's why I pay him a lot of damn money. That, and he worked just as hard as I did to help me build the company."

"I don't think he much cares for me," Lucky said.

"He doesn't know you. He's just protective. The same way Gwen is protective of you," Ransom replied.

The sun had gotten higher in the sky, and the light that shone in was warm and bright.

"So much for sleep," Lucky said as she blinked. "It'll be a miracle and a half if I make it through this."

"I think the godmothers are sending someone to help you with your makeup."

"I'm pretty sure my wedding dress would fit in these bags under my eyes."

"You're right about that," Ransom couldn't help but agree.

She slapped his arm. "Jerk."

He remembered what Steven had said to Brittany and decided to try it. "No, you."

"What are we, twelve?"

He took a deep breath. "I was worried about you last night."

"I'm sorry. I didn't mean to, I was just trying to wrap my head around all of this."

"Thanks for not being too pissed at me for not telling you."

"I told the godmothers I admired that you kept your word and I value that in a person. I just hated that it was me who got left out in the dark, alone. It feels like everyone knows but me."

"Gwen doesn't know. The kids suspect, I think."

"Roderick knows?"

"Ish."

"Knows-ish? What does that mean?"

"I told him when Bluebonnet came to bribe me with cookies to marry you."

"You accepted a bribe? I'm so shocked." She laughed. "Wait, why was it okay to tell Roderick but not me?"

"The godmothers made me promise specifically."

She exhaled and wilted, her slight weight resting more fully against him. Ransom felt as if he'd been entrusted with something delicate and precious. Infinitely breakable. Even though he knew Lucky was stronger than that. She wasn't breakable at all. In fact, she had to be one of the strongest people he knew.

"We should get moving. Especially if we want to eat before hair and makeup get here. Luckily, that will just be Petty and magic wand, but still."

"I need some protein. If I never eat another pastry . . ."

"Don't lie to yourself, my girl. If a cart bearing any kind of pastry came rolling through those doors right now, you'd still cram them in your face."

"Just the thought," she began. "Wait, no. You're right. I'm a glutton for punishment, I guess."

"Me too," he agreed, and rolled over to press her down onto the bed.

"You're actually insane." She laughed. "Did you forget the part where you said no strings?"

"Did you forget the part where you told me you wanted strings?" He brushed her hair out of her face and rubbed his thumb across her bottom lip. "So precious."

"There aren't any cherry trees here."

Ransom pretended to look around. "Hmm. Nope, I don't see any leeches, but there might be some in the bathtub."

"No feral hogs."

"I've actually checked for wasps' nests, so I think we're safe on that count."

"The one thing we haven't checked for is tornados, but I don't think Ever After gets those," Lucky said.

"We could always fall through the floor. I wonder where we'd end up? Would it be one of the ballrooms? On the prince's head? Oh, that's what would happen. We'd fall straight through the floor and land on the prince, just like the house on the Wicked Witch."

"That's not funny." Except Lucky giggled.

"Perhaps just a kiss?"

"Okay. Just a kiss, but remember, if you get explosive diarrhea at the junket or something, you brought it on yourself."

"I hadn't even thought of that. I better not kiss you. Just in case." He pulled back from her and rolled his eyes.

"Or projectile vomiting," she added helpfully.

"What else?" he asked. "Get it all out."

"I don't know. Scabies. That could happen." Lucky grinned.

"Shh. I'm going to kiss you now. For Luck." He dipped his lips to hers and she tasted like cinnamon and vanilla. All things good and safe.

She tasted like home.

If the whole goddamn castle fell down around their ears at this moment, it wouldn't matter. Cherries the size of planets could be barreling toward him and he didn't have a single, solitary, flying shit of a damn to give about it.

She reached up to cup his face. "Oh, Ransom. Why is it like this between us?"

"Maybe the godmothers were right. Maybe we're meant to be."

"Kiss me again before there's an earthquake or something."

He obliged her, kissing Lucky like there was no tomorrow.

Like there was no trio of fairy godmothers barging through the door to get them stuffed into the roles they were supposed to play.

"Rise and shine, my little dumplings!" Jonquil called out as they fluttered inside the room, fairy wings out and proud.

"Why, you slugabeds, you should've—" Bluebonnet gasped. "Sisters, I think they're busy."

"You know," Ransom drawled. "For all of the matchmaking and shoving us together, I would think you'd have thought to knock."

Petty cleared her throat. "Well, it was obvious we were getting nowhere, so we gave up."

"That is the worst lie you've ever told, Godmother," Ransom admonished.

Petty tittered. "It's a whopper, I'll give you that. Although, it's nowhere near the worst."

"Oh, really?" Lucky sat up. "I need to hear this story."

"After we've got you ready." Petty peered at Lucky. "Land sakes, child. Did you get any sleep last night?"

"No, not a wink," Lucky confessed.

"You awful man." Jonquil tapped Ransom on the shoulder with her wand. "You knew you both had to be up early."

"Me? I didn't do anything. I was asleep."

"A likely story," Bluebonnet teased.

"Don't you have a potion or something that can give me eight hours of sleep in an eight-ounce jar?"

"Hmm. Intriguing idea, but no." Petty wriggled her nose and her spectacles bounced around for a moment before settling in their proper place. "I think I might have a makeup charm that should do the trick. At least until after the junket."

"Now, don't be nervous, but the Once Upon a Time Ballroom is quite packed with press," Bluebonnet warned. "They've all been given refreshments that have been graced with a little extra something to make them amenable."

"That was kind of you, Bon-Bon," Ransom said.

"We shall assume that you've already seen some of the headlines," Jonquil said, stoic.

"I have and I've put it out of my mind."

"What? What press?" Lucky asked.

"Don't worry about it. It doesn't matter. We've got to get ready," Ransom said.

"No, is this about the thing from uni?" Lucky demanded. She didn't wait for an answer before continuing. "I swear by the sky above and the earth below if just one of them says anything about that I'm going to . . . going to . . ."

Ransom could tell Lucky was about to pop like an overfed tick.

"Going to what, dear? Let it out here, instead of all over them. If you want to have a tantrum, it's fine," Bluebonnet encouraged.

"I'm going to hug each and every one of them as long as they can stand it. I'll rub my bad luck all over them like the stench of an unwashed turtle tank. They. Will. Pay."

"Lucky, it's not that serious," Ransom reassured her.

Except for him, it actually was. This was the gauntlet he was afraid to face, but he didn't want her to know that. He didn't want her to know how bad this name still cut him. He knew she'd feel badly, she'd take the blame and the guilt onto her own shoulders, and Ransom knew there was no one to blame.

What had happened between them and the fallout was no one's fault. They were naïve kids who'd yet to really experience the world or know who they were. They'd yet to learn communication skills and develop mature empathy.

It had been an unfortunate, utterly humiliating accident.

Which was honestly what he feared would happen at the junket: an unfortunate, yet still utterly humiliating accident.

# Chapter 15

As they stood outside waiting for the doors to open, Ransom was sure he was going to be sick. Lucky's joke about projectile vomiting might not have been a joke at all.

At least then he'd get a new nickname.

He'd be The Boy Who Puked. A step up?

The grown-ass, adult man who ralphed all over the . . .

Yes, he *was* an adult. He was a million years, a million miles, and a billion dollars away from the kid that he'd been.

Plus, if he puked, he could just have his fairy godmothers erase the tapes and their memories.

It would be fine.

It was all fine.

Lucky slipped her hand into his and squeezed.

The air was easier to breathe, the lights were a little less harsh, and his heartbeat found a steady rhythm.

He squeezed back and they walked into the ballroom to face his tormentors.

With Lucky's hand still in his, he remembered to hold his chin high, to keep his back straight, and to look each person whose gaze he caught in the eye, and he refused to be the one who looked away first.

Hundreds of lights flashed in their faces, and they were led to a wide table with two chairs, two microphones, and two glasses of water.

He couldn't help but think it looked like they were about

to go on trial, and he realized he wasn't wrong. They were on trial in the court of public opinion. If they were exonerated, Ever After would have a booming wedding business.

If not, they might still. Ransom had heard it said by many a marketing professional that all publicity was good publicity, but he wasn't so sure of that.

Another wave of relief washed over him when he saw Roderick with a microphone obviously playing emcee. Ransom, with his backup forces surrounding him, was ready for battle.

He pulled out Lucky's chair and waited for her to be seated before taking his own seat. As he sat down next to her, he realized he hadn't told her how beautiful she looked in the green sundress Rosebud had made for her. She looked every bit the happy bride.

Except for the ring. Damn it. They'd forgotten a ring.

*Gorgeous*, he mouthed.

Lucky blushed and suddenly the cameras started flashing again. She crossed her arms primly in front of her and said into the microphone, "No, you."

Ransom found he was the one who blushed.

Another wave of flashes started, and many of the sea of faces before them were hopeful and entranced. Lucky had won them over with two words. Himself too.

"Welcome to the engagement junket for world-renowned painter Lucky Fujiki and the founder of Heart's Desire Chocolate, Ransom Payne. We have a few rules here in Ever After. Like all fairy tales. Don't stray from the path or the big, bad wolf will eat you." Roderick laughed. "No, actually, we'll just have security escort you out, and your employer will get a bill for your stay here at Charming's B and B, as well as a suit for damages as outlined in the contracts you all signed to be here today. We ask that you respect their time and their answers. Don't speak over each other, give respect to your fellow journalists. This is a joyous occasion, so let's keep it that way."

Roderick looked to the couple. "Are you ready?"

Lucky gave him a nod.

Roderick pointed to the first man who had his hand in the air. His name tag indicated his name was Melvin James.

"We all want to know, how did you meet?"

"At university. That was in the press release, move along," Roderick answered for them, then pointed at a woman in the front.

"Why did you decide on Valentine's Day? Isn't it a cliché?" She had her pen at the ready and waited patiently for Ransom's answer.

"I suppose that as there is some truth in any fairy tale, there's a reason some things are cliché. What better way to dedicate my life to the woman I love than on the holiday where Americans celebrate love and chocolate?" Ransom said.

"It's all so fast," another said. "This wedding seems like it came together pretty quickly. Do you have other news you might like to share with the world? Will there be an heir to your chocolate empire soon?"

"No!" Lucky blurted out. "Definitely not. We're just excited to start our lives together."

"Everyone is dying to know about the prenup!" A man toward the back said with unabashed glee.

"The usual," Ransom said in a bored tone. "She gets everything."

Some laughs echoed through the room.

"No, but really," the man prompted.

"What, you want a copy of the thing?" Then he laughed. "Some things are private."

"What does it cost to get married in Ever After?" A woman with glasses in the third row asked.

"It's different for every couple, depending on how extravagant their tastes are. We opted for something simple. We're just happy our family and our friends can be here with us.

It's budget-friendly," Lucky said, sounding like a marketing sound bite.

"Isn't everything budget-friendly when you're a billionaire?" the woman asked as a follow-up.

"I suppose it is, but these amazing women behind me who own Fairy Godmothers, Inc. are our godmothers. Because we're both their godchildren, they wanted to pay for the wedding. Just look at those faces."

Ransom turned around to look and saw Petunia push her spectacles up on her nose and flash a demure expression.

"As if we'd bankrupt the dears when all we want is for them to celebrate with us on the happiest day of our lives," Lucky chastised.

The woman seemed to accept the answer, but then her eyes narrowed. "A follow-up question—"

Roderick cut her off. "You've already had a follow-up. If there's time after everyone else has asked their question, we'll come back to you."

"Why isn't Lucky wearing a ring?" she shouted, even after Roderick had told her not to.

Roderick nodded and two men in the back came up to escort the woman out. She tried to stop and wait at the doors for the answer, but Roderick motioned for the men to remove her.

"Bodily, if she refuses to go," he said into the microphone. "The rules were clear before we began."

Once the door was secured, Roderick nodded to the crowd. Melvin spoke up. "Well, where is the ring?"

"We're nontraditional that way. I didn't want one," Lucky said. "As a painter, I'm always working with harsh chemicals and I like my hands to be unencumbered so I can really feel the spirit of my work. I feel jewelry interferes with my process."

Some of the people in the crowd were nodding in understanding, but it was obvious from other people's expressions that it didn't sound romantic to them.

Ransom cleared his throat. "I'm gifting her an art gallery instead."

"Where? When will it open?" someone asked.

"We'll be sure to let you know once my wife decides," he said.

So far, things weren't ideal, but they weren't bad, either. He could tell Melvin James was going to be a problem. Something about the guy was familiar. Ransom couldn't quite place him, though.

"Where's the honeymoon?" a man in the far-left corner asked.

Ransom turned to look at Lucky and their eyes met. He could tell she didn't want to divulge their getaway spot, either. It would be their first date, after all.

"We'll let you know when we get back." He flashed them all a toothy grin.

"Can we hold you to that?" a woman in the back who'd been quiet until now asked. "Will you give us some pictures to run?"

Ransom didn't find that to be an unreasonable request. "Sure. Give Roderick your information and we'll be in touch."

"Honestly," Melvin began. "I don't think anyone here really cares about the wedding. We want to know about The Boy Who Missed."

Time stopped for Ransom.

When he had nightmares, he didn't have the kind where he was in front of his school naked. That had already happened to him.

His naked body wasn't what was vulnerable. It was his naked embarrassment, and ultimately the part where the mishap had cemented in his mind that he wasn't good enough.

This was the dragon he had to slay.

If he ran away again, it would still be there in the shadows waiting to pounce on him and tear his carefully constructed armor to shreds.

Roderick said, "I do believe the instructions were clear—"

Ransom held up a hand to stay his friend. "It's okay. We knew that they were going to ask anyway. I have nothing to hide."

Lucky squeezed his thigh gently under the table.

Having her near him and knowing that she believed in him made him believe he could actually face this.

"No, this is stupid," Lucky said. "I mean, really? This happened years and years ago. It was a college misadventure. There are plenty of people in the public eye who do stupid things in college and you don't hound them the way you've hounded Ransom."

"It's the horror story we all fear," one of the reporters in the back said. "It's the train wreck we can't look away from."

"He's a person. Why can't you just stop?" Lucky said.

Melvin snickered. "Maybe if he hadn't gone into chocolate, it wouldn't be so funny."

"What are you, twelve?" Lucky rolled her eyes. "They don't deserve our time."

"No, they don't. But you know what? I'll speak about it. I'm not hiding from it. Like you said, this happened years and years ago. I was a kid. We both were. Now, we're adults. Successful adults."

A clamor washed over the crowd and everyone had questions. Whereas they'd been fairly restrained asking about the wedding, they were practically frothing on one another to get their piece of the story.

"Is it true you won't do business with anyone who still banks with the first bank that refused your startup loan?"

"Yes," he admitted. "Why would I do business with someone who mocked me? Let them make their money with people they respect. Just as I do."

"Tell us the story. Tell us how it happened."

"That I will not do. That's a private moment that belongs to me and my future wife. I wouldn't disrespect her like that.

But obviously, it wasn't the worst thing that could ever happen to us because we're still going to spend the rest of our lives together."

Ransom wasn't sure what he'd expected from that, but it wasn't the reaction he got. Many of the women put their hands to their lips or over their hearts as if it were the most romantic thing they'd ever heard.

Some of the men did, too.

Melvin James was the only one who not only didn't seem fazed, but had a rather nasty glint in his eye.

Regardless, Ransom realized that with Lucky by his side, he might've actually slain this dragon.

"One more question for Lucky, if you have the time," Melvin said.

Lucky raised her brow and indicated for him to ask his question.

"Do you know a Nancy Slade?"

Ransom caught a movement out of the corner of his eye and looked over to see Gwen and an expression of horror bloom on her face.

"No, I don't believe so. Should I?"

"I've been doing some digging into your life, Lucky. Do you know what I found?"

"If I knew what you'd found, I wouldn't be sitting here waiting for you to take your shot at embarrassing me since you weren't able to embarrass Ransom."

Roderick coughed and the rest of the members of the press laughed. It seemed that she'd won them all over.

Except Melvin.

"I found that wherever you go, disaster follows. People remember you because the most ridiculous disasters follow you around. Nancy Slade said after she met you that her entire life crashed around her ears. From having her identity stolen, to termites that devoured her home in the matter of a day, to her investments tanking."

"That sounds like she had a run of bad luck. It happens to all of us," Ransom said.

"I talked to people who went to school with you both. A tornado hit the motel where you two stayed. Only tore the roof off of one room."

"You're ridiculous," Lucky said. "Do you think I'm some kind of witch who controls the weather?"

"A woman who was majoring in Equine Management said after you and Ransom spent time in the barn that feral hogs ransacked the place," Melvin continued.

"Again, do you think I'm the Bacon Whisperer?"

The room tittered.

One woman said, "It sounds like poor Lucky has had a run of bad luck. Why are you bullying her? This guy is why we can't have nice things."

Ransom could feel Lucky bristle. Waves of heat came from her, and he knew exactly what she felt. The shame of being targeted. Of being put on display.

Well, he wouldn't stand for it.

"Roderick?"

Roderick took the cue. He knew what to do.

Lucky had other ideas. She stood up. "You've hurt my feelings, Mr. James."

The reporter arched a brow. "Seriously?"

"Yes, seriously. What, you think I'm supposed to just suck it up and tolerate being mistreated because I'm in the public eye? No, I won't stand for it, but neither do I want to be on bad terms with the press. I know you all are just trying to do your jobs. You need stories that are interesting and engaging to keep readers in this age of digital media. It's a battle. I understand. Can't we call a truce? We have, after all, offered to give you all pictures of our honeymoon. I'd say we've been more than generous. Can't you do the same?"

Melvin James snorted. It was obvious he thought all of this was a bunch of crap, but the rest of the room didn't.

"Come on, James. What the hell?" a guy said.

"You give us all a bad name."

"You're being a dick."

Melvin was silent for a long moment. Finally, he said, "Okay. Bygones?"

Lucky flashed him her biggest, most genuine smile. Ransom knew better than to trust it. He wasn't the only one who got his sense of right, wrong, and eternal vengeance from Petty.

"Prove it. Give me a hug," she stepped around from behind the table.

"Are you serious?" Melvin asked with disdain.

"As a heart attack, my friend." That smile was still in place.

One of the guys who'd seemed to have become Lucky's champion spoke up again. "Who turns down hugging a beautiful woman?"

Lucky flashed him a smile. "You're too kind."

Melvin allowed her to hug him, and she held on tight. She even kissed his cheek, leaving a smudge of pink lipstick.

"Thank you so much. I feel so much better about all of this." Lucky walked back to her chair and took a long sip of water, and she grabbed Ransom's hand under the table.

"I think that's all for today," Roderick said. "I have some special passes for a few of you whom we'd like to offer exclusive coverage of the wedding."

That hadn't been part of the plan, but Roderick had a savage business acumen.

Excitement rippled through the crowd and Roderick dealt with them, keeping them distracted. Gwen pounced on Ransom and Lucky to guide them toward the exit and back to their room to decompress before the rest of the day's activities.

As soon as they were in an isolated passage, Gwen said, "I had no idea PTA Nancy would ever connect meeting you with her misfortune."

"It doesn't matter. He sounds crazy." Concern creased her features. "They all do."

"How did he find out we were at the motel?" Ransom asked.

"Bad luck, I guess." Lucky exhaled heavily.

"Hey, it doesn't matter," he said.

"How can you say that?"

"Because we survived it. Honestly, I thought it was going to be worse." Ransom took her hand. "I wouldn't have made it through that without you."

"You wouldn't have been in that situation without me. So I guess it's only fair." Although, she did squeeze his hand back.

"Take the compliment," Gwen said.

"Yeah, listen to your friend. She gives good advice."

"Just what I need. You two ganging up on me."

"Do you not know how amazing you are? I mean, obviously you don't. But I'm going to tell you all about it," Gwen promised.

"I know! The way she handled the crowd? She was honest and forthright, just edgy enough to be amusing without being outright mean."

"Oh, I was outright mean, and when everything in that guy's life goes to shit, hopefully he'll have lost his job at the paper where he works by the time he realizes it was me." Lucky scowled. "I just couldn't sit there and watch him take swipes at you."

"You did that to defend me?"

"I'm sorry, I shouldn't have. Now that I think about it, I probably deserve my bad luck. Good people don't wish bad things on others."

"I guess I'm not a good person," Gwen said. "Because I think he'll get exactly what he has coming."

"That's not for me to decide, though. Is it?" Lucky slumped.

"You didn't decide. I fully believe that whatever it is that you have is a gift. It does what it wants to. There are so many of us who are close to you who are just fine. Me, the kids, the godmothers, Ransom is fine, too, except when you try to have sex." She cringed. "Sorry, probably shouldn't have brought that up."

"You know what, I don't care. It's going to be in the papers anyway." It suddenly dawned on him that it *wasn't* a big deal. Not anymore. "I'm done hiding from it. It doesn't define me. Or Lucky."

A surge of hope rushed through him. He realized everything was going to be okay. The godmothers were right—there was nothing love couldn't fix.

His phone buzzed in his pocket. He pulled it out to see an alert from his plant manager in Ecuador.

The dam near his cacao farms had failed. Luckily, only a few people had sustained injuries. There had been no loss of life.

But all of his property, all of his cacao plants, they were completely underwater.

# Chapter 16

Grammy's Goodies had become one of Lucky's favorite places.

She wasn't sure if it was simply because she adored Red and Grammy, the seemingly endless supply of sweets, or if it was because this was the happiest she'd seen Gwen and the kids in a long time.

Lucky was content to just sit at a table in the back while Gwen practiced rolling out dough and the kids practiced using the cookie cutters.

Brittany's favorite was the castle.

Steven's was the dragon.

They made less of a mess with the frosting than Lucky would've thought. They were very mindful of the mess their mama would have to clean up.

"You're quiet this morning," Gwen noticed.

"I'm just enjoying the peace. This is my happy place, hanging out with you guys." She accepted the dragon cookie with the glitter-sprinkled wings Steven handed her gratefully. "Oh, a healthy breakfast." Lucky took a bite.

"It has been a little crazy since Roderick invited half of the press to hang around, but I guess it's been good for all of the businesses. This place got a feature, so I have to definitely up my game."

"I'm sure they were impressed that in a small Missouri town in the middle of nowhere, they were able to get allergen-free vegan cookies. I know I'm impressed." Lucky grinned and ate another bite of cookie.

Gwen smiled and then slapped the ever-loving hell out of the dough. "It's so cathartic. I really love it here."

"I'm glad that they want you to stay." Lucky pressed her lips together. "So, I have to tell you something."

"I already told Mama that Jonquil is my fairy godmother. She didn't believe me, of course." Brittany cut out another castle with the metal form. "I wouldn't, either."

"Wise for your age, punkin' pie." Gwen nodded to her daughter.

"That's the thing," Lucky began.

"Oh, don't tell me you've been slurping the Kool-Aid, too. Lucky. We're adults. That fairy-tale stuff is for kids."

"No, it's for everyone. Remember when I told you I thought I saw mice and birds sewing? You thought you saw it, too!"

"I'm sure it was just low blood sugar," Gwen said. "Everyone in this town takes the fairy-tale shtick much too far."

"I've seen the godmothers fly."

Gwen paused what she was doing with the rolling pin to fix Lucky with a hard stare. "Are you sick? Do you have a flu?"

"I haven't gotten a chance to tell you what I found out from my mother. This is all real, Gwen. I thought it would be easier coming from me, but if you want to stay here, you need to know the truth."

"You're serious about this." Gwen put the rolling pin down.

"Yes." Lucky nodded. "Absolutely."

Gwen wiped her hands on her apron. "Okay, give me the whole spiel. Might as well see how deep the crazy well goes."

"Grammy is busy when the moon is full. Wonder why?"

Gwen laughed, but when she saw that Lucky wasn't laughing, she contained herself. "No, come on. A werewolf?"

"Petunia told me it happened when she was saving Red from a werewolf. It's why they want to move away from town."

"Grammy? I mean, she's cool, but she's not cool enough to be a werewolf."

"You think it's cool? That's kind of terrifying."

"I mean, obviously. But all the best women are."

Lucky nodded in agreement.

"Next. Lay it on me. All of it."

"As I said, Petty, Bluebonnet, and Jonquil are fairies. Fairy godmothers, to be precise. It's obvious who Rosebud Briar is, if you think about it. Phillip Charming, owner of the castle? During the daytime he's a frog that sits in the mermaid fountain."

"I tried to help him. I kissed his head, but he was still just an old frog," Brittany said.

"Don't kiss frogs, Brit. You'll have to do enough of that when you grow up."

Brittany laughed. "I like kissing frogs. They're cute."

"Gross," Steven offered his opinion.

"Anyway, the town runs on magic. Magic is fueled by love. That's why they want to become a premiere wedding destination." Lucky sighed.

"Say I believe you for five seconds. Considering what you've dropped on me, the fact that you're sighing afterward means there's more. What else could you possibly have to tell me? Is your mom the Bride of Frankenstein, or something?"

"Nope. She's a, or she used to be, a kitsune. A fox spirit. She fell in love with my dad and got pregnant with me. She had to choose between giving up her immortality and me. Obvi, here we are. That's why I'm bad luck. It's the last of my mother's magic. It's pure chaos and I can never be cured."

Lucky's eyes watered and her throat was tight after she spoke those last words. Speaking them made them more real somehow. More permanent.

Gwen huffed. "I don't care if you've been dredged up straight from hell. There is nothing wrong with you and I'm tired of you thinking you need to be cured. You are one of the kindest, fiercest, most loving people I've ever known. I wouldn't be half the woman I am today without you."

"What I did to PTA Nancy and Melvin James wasn't at all kind or loving."

"Who said love didn't mean fighting with every weapon in your arsenal? You were protecting me, you were protecting Ransom. You didn't do it to be cruel, or selfish." Gwen reached out and grabbed her hand.

"Are those the lessons you want to be teaching Brittany and Steven?" Lucky asked.

"Hell. Yes. I want them to fight for the people they love. I want them to stand tall for what they believe in, and I want them to fight dirty if they have to. There's a lot of dead bodies on the high road. Everest is packed with them." She gave Lucky a pointed look.

Lucky snorted. "So, you do believe me?"

"You've never lied to me, Lucky. Ever. So even though every word that's come out of your mouth in the last five minutes has been absolutely batshit insane, of course I believe you."

"Good. I'll tell everyone you know."

"Does Ransom know?" Gwen asked. Then her eyes widened. "Does Roderick know?"

She nodded. "I was so pissed Roderick found out before me, but apparently, the godmothers asked Ransom not to say anything and he promised to wait.

"You have to admire a man who keeps his word, even if it means you got left out in the cold."

"Yeah, that was my thinking. I'm still a little mad about it." Lucky ate another cookie.

"Told you so, Mama." Brittany kept cutting out castles from the dough.

"Yes, you did. I'm sorry I didn't believe you."

"That's okay. You do now." She looked up from what she was doing. "See, Aunt Lucky. You're magic, too. I wouldn't have a fairy godmother without you."

"She's my fairy godmother, too!" Steven cried.

"Nuh-uh," Brittany said, smug. "She's just mine."

"Not fair." Steven plopped on the ground and started to cry.

Brittany gave a dramatic sigh worthy of a nighttime soap opera. "I'm sure if you ask Jonquil, she'll be your FG, too. But you have to ask."

He kept crying and Gwen didn't interfere.

"Use your words. That's how you get what you want," Brittany said.

"But?" Gwen prompted.

Brittany sighed again. "But it's okay to cry if you're upset."

Steven sniffed a few times and stopped the roll of tears down his rounded cheeks. "Okay. Will you hold my hand while I ask her?"

"Of course." Brittany had gone back to her task and Steven joined her.

"They're such good kids. Have you talked to Jake?"

"I texted him asking when he'd like to see them and I haven't heard anything back."

"It's good that you're here. You'll have all the support you can handle. So will the kids."

"Roderick's been spending a lot of time with them. They seem to like him now. Probably because he likes to take them to play at the fountain."

Lucky nodded. "It's a pretty magical place."

"Literally, I guess." Gwen looked at the big, hand-carved wooden cuckoo clock on the wall. "Oh! We should get started on this round of cake tasting so you can make your final decisions. Was Ransom going to come?"

"He was supposed to, but he's been dealing with a natural disaster in Ecuador."

"Before you even say it, I am one hundred percent sure that it was not your fault."

"I'm not. I mean, he was cruising along fine until I came back into his life. He tries to kiss me and he gets assaulted by a cherry tree. He does kiss me before a press junket and they bring up his worst memory—"

"A memory they were going to bring up anyway."

"That is directly related to me."

"Lucky, I hate to tell you this, but not everything that happens in the world is a result of you. Things just happen. Good and bad."

"Look at what happened to PTA Nancy. That was a direct result of me."

"Yes, thank you. Want another cookie?" Gwen grinned.

"No, you know what I mean. The dam failed. All of his crops are drowning as we speak."

"Is it really that bad? Has he said anything?"

"We haven't really had time to talk. He had to fly out to survey the damage and meet with insurance adjusters, and he's still paying his employees as if they were working their regular hours until he figures out what he's going to do."

"He's got a lot on his shoulders. Maybe we should just pick the cake," Gwen said. "Take whatever we can off of his plate."

"We should put better things on his plate, Mama. I wanna make Uncle Ransom some cookies," Steven said.

Gwen smiled, but it was a sad sort of smile. "Don't forget, Ransom and Aunt Lucky aren't really getting married."

"I know," Steven said.

"But if it's okay," Ransom said from the doorway, dressed in a finely cut suit and looking every inch the businessman, "I'd love to have the title."

"Make sure that's what you want. I don't want them to get attached to you if you don't want to stay around," Gwen said quietly.

He came in and sat down next to Lucky and gave the kids a big grin when they handed him a plate of their practice cookies.

"Mama said we need to take things off your plate. We wanted to give you a different plate," Brittany said.

"Ah, you guys. Want to have some with me?" Ransom asked them.

"No, we can't. Not if we want cake," Steven replied, his eyes wide with expectation.

Lucky watched him with them. He was so honest and open. He wasn't afraid to be vulnerable with them. Nurturing. Protective.

It stirred longings inside of her that she'd tried to ignore because there was no point in wanting what she couldn't have.

"What kind of cake are we trying first?" Ransom asked the kids.

"I'll get them!" Brittany ran toward the walk-in cooler.

"Thanks for coming back for this. Someday, you're going to make a great groom," Lucky said.

"Thanks for understanding I had to get out ahead of that situation. Someday, you're going to make someone a great bride." He flashed her a grin.

She noticed that his attitude toward her was completely different than it had been these last few days. He sat by her, but his body wasn't angled toward her. He hadn't been in touch with her while he was gone. There was a distance between them now that her logical mind wanted to chalk up to stress, but that little voice deep inside, the one that was never wrong, told her he'd had enough of her disasters.

That he knew what had happened in Ecuador was somehow her fault.

She didn't care about the cake. It tasted like ash in her mouth.

"You did a great job with the ruby cacao frosting. Where did they source the cacao? I think Grammy told me, but I can't remember," Ransom said.

"This is from the Gold Coast, I believe. I have the supplier's number in the back if you're interested?"

"Definitely. I'm going to need to source somewhere. My farms are fucked, not to put too fine a point on it. They don't anticipate the floodwaters going down until they replace the dam. Local government doesn't want to replace the dam. So, you can see my problem."

"How awful. It's quite incredible that no one died," Gwen called out as she headed back to get the number for Ransom.

"It is." He pointed to the lemon cake with the ruby frosting. "This one is my favorite."

"Mine too," Lucky said.

"That was easy. What else do we need to do for the wedding planning? I'm ready to cross things off my list."

"I don't know. Ask Petty and her magic notebook," Lucky said on a sigh.

"Are you okay?" Ransom asked.

What could she say? *I'm upset that you don't want to be close to me after your business was almost single-handedly wiped out?* Yeah, no.

"Fine."

Roderick came through the door just then wearing a grim face. "Have you seen the story that bastard Melvin wrote?"

Lucky's heart sank. "No. What did he do?"

"It's all about you, Lucky."

"At least it's not about Ransom. They're over The Boy Who Missed, and that's what I wanted." She swallowed hard.

"Nancy Slade looks like a lunatic. He did a feature interview with her. Here, read it." He tried to hand Lucky his phone.

"No, I can't look at it. Just sum it up."

Ransom took the phone and paged through the article while Lucky waited on tenterhooks.

"Wow," was all Ransom could manage.

"Will someone please tell me?"

Gwen had returned with the piece of paper with the supplier's number written on it and shoved it at Ransom and, in turn, snatched Roderick's phone out of his hand.

Her eyes kept getting bigger as she read, and her mouth dropped open by additional degrees with each swipe of her finger across the phone's screen.

"Well, you made a convert out of that guy, I guess." Gwen shook her head. "It says here that on his way to the airport his car service was late picking him up. His driver took a turn too fast and they skidded off the road into a ditch. They had to wait for roadside assist to pick them up, but when roadside came, there was only room for one of them in the car. The driver left him."

"I could understand it if he treated his driver like he treated everyone else," Roderick said.

Gwen nodded. "There's more," she said to Lucky. "After he got to the airport, finally, the K-9 unit signaled on his bag for meth. Turns out, his driver was delivering for a Kansas City dealer and they got their bags mixed up in the back of the car. So security took him to a room and strip-searched him. Cavity search and everything. He had to call a lawyer and he was able to prove it wasn't his bag because a police unit went back to where the vehicle was parked and they found the driver with Melvin's bag. His ID was still inside."

"That sounds like good luck to me. I mean, he could've gotten in a lot of trouble," Lucky replied.

"Exactly," Gwen said. "But there's more. So he missed his flight, and he had to pay to rebook. The airline wouldn't comp it. Or give him a voucher for a hotel, so he had to stay in the airport overnight. He finally gets on his plane and his flight gets diverted to St. Louis because someone on board had food poisoning and couldn't stop vomiting. He finally makes it home and on the way home from the airport, they're in an accident with a manure truck. He has to walk the last mile home covered in cow shit. He believes that you are one hundred percent to blame for all of this."

Ransom and Roderick are both snickering.

"I don't think it's funny," Lucky said quietly.

"You're the one who hugged him and kissed his cheek," Ransom reminded her.

"You're right and I shouldn't have. I don't know what I

was thinking. Look at all the harm I caused," Lucky said. "PTA Nancy lost her house."

"How are any of these things your fault, Lucky?"

"I don't know. How were feral pigs my fault? Wasps? Leeches? A tornado." She studied him for a long moment. "A flood."

Ransom opened his mouth to say something, but no sound came out.

"Yeah, that's what I thought."

"Oh no," Gwen said, just as Roderick's and Ransom's phones beeped alerts. Gwen handed Roderick's phone back to him.

"What is it?" Lucky asked.

"Heart's Desire stock just dropped like lemmings off a cliff," Gwen said.

"It seems like the investors and the board think that Melvin's story might be true. I just got a text there's already rumors flying around that what happened in Ecuador is because of Ransom's marriage to Lucky," Roderick said.

Lucky didn't want to look at him. She didn't want to see what she knew would be in his eyes. She supposed it was better to tear the Band-Aid off with a solid rip instead of picking at it. So she met his gaze and she saw all the things in his eyes she'd dreaded.

Regret.

Sorrow.

But ultimately, rejection. He didn't want her now, but deep down, she always knew that was coming.

Ransom's biggest fear had been facing down The Boy Who Missed.

Lucky's had been this moment, right here. This moment where all the dreams he'd encouraged her to hold close were crushed under his heel like so much ash.

# Chapter 17

R ansom Payne knew he was an ass.
He could feel Petty's wrath before the fairy herself could. Granted, she didn't know about what happened in Grammy's Goodies.

Maybe she did already know. Petty knew everything.

He looked over his shoulder.

Pick 'n' Axe Pub was quiet, except for the group of men at a large, round table a few feet from him and Roderick, but that didn't stop him from looking for Petty, Bluebonnet, and Jonquil.

The place was mining themed, and he allowed himself to take it in while still scanning for the imminent wrath of his godmothers about to strike him down.

All of the tables were rough-hewn wood, with hand-carved benches. The lighting was dim, like any good pub. The rocky walls had been painted to look like there were veins of various minerals and precious metals. Of course, now that he thought about it, they might well be the real thing. Quartz candle holders sat in the middle of each table, and strangely enough, they didn't seem out of place.

It smelled of hearty stew, the local specialty they called honey beer, and cedar, with the slight underpinnings of the fire that roared six feet high in the giant fireplace by the bar. They were homey, comforting scents.

He was grateful, however, that there was not live music

this night. Ransom enjoyed the harmonicas and mouth harps that sometimes brought the room to life, but he had too much on his mind to be able to enjoy it.

Roderick sat down at their table with two of the honey beers.

"What is with you tonight? You're acting like a long-tailed cat in a room full of rocking chairs."

Ransom scratched the back of his neck. "Guilt, I suppose. I know Lucky felt bad about what happened today, and I didn't do anything to ease her worries."

"Well, I think you could be forgiven. You have more on your plate than her feelings," Roderick said. "You'll feel better after a pint. Or two."

Ransom wasn't so sure about that. "Also, I'm waiting for my godmother to smite me."

"Is that why you keep looking over your shoulder?"

"Yep." Ransom took a long gulp from his honey beer.

"Worry about that later. Right now, we need to do whatever we can to stop Heart's Desire from hemorrhaging," Roderick said. "I know you want to help your godmothers, but you can't pour from an empty well, and I mean that literally."

"Do you have any ideas?"

"I have you booked on a flight back to Ecuador the day after the rehearsal dinner. You'll be addressing Parliament and the Minister of the Interior to plead your case. You need to call a meeting with the board."

Ransom took another swig and set down his glass. "This is the most ridiculous situation. This is *my* company. What do I have to do to fire the board? Because fuck 'em."

Roderick's eyes widened. "That's one way to go about it. I'll check our charter paperwork. You're talking about taking a company private? You want to do a hostile takeover of your own company?"

"I want to do whatever I have to do to keep other people's opinions out of my life. I didn't want to take Heart's Desire public to begin with, but everything said it was the best long-term strategy."

Roderick nodded. "At the time, it was. You weren't a billionaire when you made that choice. To start with, you need to start buying back shares. The board can remove you as CEO, as it stands, but they can't interfere with your ownership."

"I never liked that option, either."

"Now you can do something about it. Have you thought about a public statement? Making a change like this is going to have all the regulatory bodies up your ass and to the left."

"Well, as you said, I'm hemorrhaging money. It's my money to hemorrhage. I'm going to continue to pay my employees until we find and build a new plant and are able to seed new farms. The board and other investors will try to stop me."

Roderick pulled out his tablet and after a few swipes and nods of his head he said, "Are you absolutely sure this is what you want to do?"

"Yes."

"Okay, we need to get the shareholder stakeholders down to under three hundred. I've e-mailed our portfolio manager and instructed him to buy all that he can."

Roderick studied him hard, and Ransom could tell his friend had something else on his mind.

"Whatever it is, say it. You've got something you're holding back."

Roderick pushed a hand through his hair. "I don't know, man. This is either exactly the right time, or I'm the biggest dick on two feet."

Ransom suddenly knew what Roderick was going to ask him. He wanted to buy the shares, too. He wanted to be a partner in Heart's Desire.

It was something Ransom had promised him long ago when they were working with grow lights in Roderick's garage. He'd sworn that one day, he'd make Roderick his partner. The only reason they hadn't started as partners in Heart's Desire was because of the godmothers. He'd worried about keeping their secrets and now, there was no more reason for that. Roderick had proved himself over and over through the years.

"I think it's exactly the right time," Ransom replied.

"You don't know what I'm going to say."

"Unless I'm mistaken, you're asking to buy shares, too."

Roderick nodded slowly. "I've proved my loyalty. You'll obviously be the majority partner, but I've poured my life into Heart's Desire. I'm willing to do what it takes to save her, and it'll free up more of your capital to buy out the board."

He'd proved himself yet again by asking Ransom's permission to buy the stock. He didn't need it. Roderick was as ruthless as they came; that's what had initially drawn Ransom to him. His acumen and his ruthlessness were wielded like a surgeon's tools.

"Yes, of course. I can't promise either one of us will have more than a pot to piss in and a window to throw it out of when this is over, but yes. And I'm sorry it took so long. It shouldn't have."

"I can only assume it was because of the godmothers. You were worried about keeping their secret."

He nodded. "I talked to them about it not too long ago. I knew it was past time. They said it would work itself out. I suppose it did."

Roderick laughed. "To anyone else in these circumstances, I'd say here's to going to down with the ship." He lifted his beer. "But this is us. Here's to mutiny and taking our ship back and sailing that bitch to a beautiful sea!"

"I can definitely drink to that!" Ransom lifted his beer and clinked their glasses together before guzzling what was left.

A curvy woman with a ridiculous mass of blond hair hanging down her back made her way over to their table carrying a tray with freshly baked brown bread, golden butter, and

two bowls of the hearty stew. As well as full, frothy mugs of
the honey beer.

"Hey, fellas." She set the tray down on their table. "I come
bearing gifts on the house for the groom. Where's your pretty
bride tonight? We'd love to see her."

Her name tag read "Goldi."

Could it be? "Girls' night with the maid of honor, I think.
We've had kind of a tough day."

Goldi nodded. "I heard. I'm sorry. Normies can be awful.
It's why a lot of us weren't sure about this scheme, but we
figured we had to try something."

"So how are you? It's been a long time since softball."

She flashed him a big smile. "I was wondering if you remembered."

"Who could forget the little girl who had to try out all
the bases before she decided she did actually like home base
best?"

She blushed. "How embarrassing."

"Nothing wrong with knowing your own mind," Roderick said.

"Oh, let me introduce you. This is the best man. Roderick."

"Pleased to have you here." A bell clanged from somewhere in the back of the pub. "That's my cue. The bears are
back from the mines. I better fetch their stew. Tell Lucky to
come see me, okay?"

Goldi didn't wait for an answer. Instead, she turned on her
heel and snatched up the tray to carry it to the back.

"This place keeps surprising me. Next thing you know,
you're going to tell me those guys at that table are the seven
dwarves. Do they look short to you?" Roderick squinted as
he looked at them.

Almost as if they knew they were being discussed, all conversation died and they turned to look, in unison, at Roderick and Ransom.

Ransom raised his beer. "Cheers, friends!"

All of them got up from their chairs and when they stood, Ransom realized they were rather short, but they were stocky and looked like small walls of pure muscle. They each grabbed their beers and made their way over to Ransom's table, where they surrounded Ransom and Roderick and sat down.

"Me lads," the one who seemed to be the leader said. He had long dark hair and a matching beard that had been ornately braided and glittered with gold dust. "Ye enjoy'n yer food?"

"Thanks, yes. It's the best beer I've ever had," Ransom said. "We've had a hard couple of days and this is just the stuff."

"Me brothers 'n' me heard about yer problem." He crossed his arms over his chest. "By the way, me name's Doppelbock. This be Wizen, Stout, Lager, Pilsner, and Porter. The little one there be Shandy." He pointed at them all in turn.

The little one he referred to was the biggest of the bunch, with a shock of fire-engine-red hair and rubies in his braided beard. Shandy grinned widely and hooked his thumbs through the straps of his coveralls.

"Anyway, we appreciate what yer doin' to help Ever After. If we can help with yer problem, ye be lettin' us know, eh?"

He wasn't sure exactly what they could do to help in this particular situation, but the fact that they offered meant something. The whole town was behind him. "We will."

Doppelbock patted the table with the flat of his hand three times and winked at them before leading his brothers off.

"Did you notice they were all named after beers?" Roderick asked.

"I did. You know what else I noticed?"

"I'm afraid you're going to tell me."

"I can't bail on this wedding. Whatever it takes, I have to find a way to save this town and save my business."

Roderick sighed. "I figured that's what you were going to say."

"It's the right thing to do."

"Honestly, I thought they were coming over to end my life," Roderick said.

"Yeah, me too."

Suddenly, the one called Stout was standing in front of their table with another loaf of the warm, fresh bread. He was wearing more jewelry than the others with tiny silver hoops lining the shell of his pointy ears and a hoop through his nose.

"By the way, we ain't short. Yer just bloody giants." He put the bread down gruffly.

Roderick, instead of being his usual smart-ass self, said, "My apologies, friend. You've been good to us. I'm new to Ever After and the people who live here. I fully believe you can whoop me whatever size you are."

Stout eyed them both for a long moment before bursting out a deep, riotous belly laugh that seemed to echo up all the way from his toes. "Aye, lad. And I can do it with me wee hand tied behind me back." He patted the table with his palm the same way Doppelbock had. "Yer all right, ye ken?" Stout walked away still laughing.

"I really need to get in the gym," Roderick said.

Ransom cackled. "So you know, I'm going to trot this little gem of a tale out every chance I get until we die."

"You didn't do anything, either."

"Your mouth wrote the check. It's not my ass that has to cash it." Ransom couldn't stop laughing.

"Some best friend you are." Roderick took a bite of the bread and stopped midchew. "This is delicious. It's the best thing I've ever tasted."

Ransom took a bite and he was wowed by the texture, the delicate flavor, the way the bread seemed to almost melt on his tongue. It *was* the best thing he'd ever tasted.

Besides Lucky.

"Oh no," Roderick said. "Don't start that."

"Start what?" He met his friend's gaze.

"You know what. You're mooning over Lucky." Roderick pinched his fingers across the bridge of his nose. "Consider all of the insane things that happened over the last few days, like what just happened now. We met real, living fairy tales. If that can be real, why can't you accept that maybe whatever Lucky has going on is bad for you?"

"How could any of the things that have happened have been her fault? She hasn't done anything."

"Maybe she doesn't have to, you know? You saw her hug Melvin James. You saw her kiss him on the cheek. She admitted to doing the same thing to this Nancy Slade, who I also kind of think had it coming, but that's neither here nor there. You saw the fallout. Why are you the only one who is immune?"

"I'm not. The godmothers are, and before you say it's because they're fairies, I'll tell you that Gwen and the kids are, too. How do you explain that?"

"I can't explain it. All I can do is look at the results of what her presence has done to your life." Roderick held up his hands. "No, wait. I'm not disparaging Lucky. At least, I'm not trying to. I can see that she loves you and supports you. The way she handled that crowd, the way she defended you, she's fierce and she's strong. She's beautiful."

"This isn't talking me out of my feelings for her, if that's what you're trying to do. Those are all stellar qualities."

"Exactly. I admire her. I know she wants the best for you. Which is why it kills me to say that I think you're going to have to choose between the business and Lucky."

"If I love her, that's an easy choice then, isn't it?"

"Is it? Because it's not just you. If her luck, or *un*luck, or whatever you guys are calling it, is causing all of these problems, how long do you think your money will last? How many natural disasters will it take to wipe you out? Quite a few, but it seems like her gift is the one that keeps on giving."

He held up his hand again. "Nope, still not done. I know you don't actually care about the money for yourself. I bet in your mind, you can see yourself setting up house in one of those cute, little, mushroom-capped cottages and maybe helping Gwen in Grammy's Goodies by designing new magic chocolate or whatever the fuck, and it's not a bad daydream. You could have it."

For a moment, Ransom let himself consider it. If it meant being with Lucky, he would take it in a second. In fact, he could go back to the castle right now and tell Lucky he was sorry for being an ass, sorry for being a coward, and beg not only her forgiveness, but paint that exact picture for her that Roderick had drawn in his imagination.

A little bit of Ever After, Happily Ever After.

Why not?

"I can see the hope in your eyes, Ransom. I want you to have every happiness, but I also don't want you to forget who you are."

"Is this where you go into the *Lion King* soliloquy? If it is, I'm going to need another beer."

Roderick narrowed his eyes at him. "No, this is where I remind you that it's not just you. It's not just me, either. It's all the people you employ from your distribution centers, to the farms, to the processing plants, to the staff. They have families, and hopes and dreams. They need the insurance that employment with you provides. They need the other benefits that will educate their children. If you want to trade Heart's Desire for this heart's desire, you can do it. I will support you one hundred percent, but you need to do it now. You need to do it before you lose everything and they do, too."

He thought about his conversation with Lucky the other night. When he'd asked her when was the last time she'd done something simply because she was passionate about it, because he couldn't remember the last time he had.

This was what he was passionate about.

There had to be a way to do both. Ransom refused to accept that it was either Heart's Desire or Lucky.

"You have to choose, Ransom. You can have your heart's
desire, you just have to decide what that is."

He was reminded again about what the godmothers said.
He simply had to love Lucky for herself, with no hope of any
kind of cure, or change. Just herself.

"What would you do?" Ransom asked him.

"Me? I know you won't do what I would do."

"Tell me."

"I know how much you love these people, and this place.
I know you feel the weight of their hope on your back like
a ton of bricks. I'm sorry for reminding you of that other
weight you carry, too. But I wouldn't be your best friend if I
didn't help you stay true not just to who you are, but to the
man I know you want to be."

"And?" Ransom prompted.

"And if I were you, I'd step back from Lucky. At least for
a while. I'd cancel this wedding to appease the investors and
board until I could buy them out and crush them like mos-
quitoes. To help the town, I'd ask my partner, who luckily in
this case is me, to go through the sham wedding with someone in town. The papers would pick it up in a second that
this new couple fell in love with all the wedding planning.
There would be no back scandal to dig into, nothing to upset
profit margins, except send the ones here in Ever After soaring through the roof, and then after I was in a secure place,
then I'd decide what I really wanted. Then I'd make it happen. Everyone wins."

The idea of all of that was anathema. It made him physically ill to think about it. He'd promised Lucky a lot of things.

Things she knew, in the end, he wouldn't be able to give
her. She'd told him herself not to make promises he couldn't
keep.

He didn't want to be in his own skin at the moment. Seeing himself now from her perspective, he wondered why she'd loved him. The fact that he even considered putting his business or anyone else before her . . . damn it, but it was more complicated than that.

The crux of all this was that she knew it.

Ransom was self-aware enough to know that deep down, he didn't think he deserved Lucky, and maybe that was why he wasn't immune to her ill-luck.

He didn't deserve to be.

# Chapter 18

Lucky didn't think she could go through with the rehearsal brunch.

How could she stand with him at an altar practicing to pledge herself to him when she knew he couldn't even stand to be in the same room with her?

She hadn't seen him since Grammy's. He hadn't come back to the room.

Lucky knew he had things on his mind and now wasn't the time to make it about her.

Except some sick part of her wanted to make him say it. Wanted to hear him speak the words that he didn't want to go to Monaco with her anymore.

A bird landed on the open window and began to sing.

She rolled over and pulled the blanket up over her head.

The bird was joined by family and friends, who raised their beautiful song of morning's glory to fill the room.

"Shut up," she grumbled. "I'm wallowing. Go away."

The birds kept singing and someone or something tugged on her blanket.

If she'd been at home, she would've kicked like a mule because it was obviously the demon under her bed that had terrified her as a child. So much so, she had to sleep with her blanket tucked under feet.

Only this was Ever After. It was probably some well-meaning broom come to life trying to help out with the day's festivities.

"I don't wanna." She tugged the blanket back and pulled it up over her head.

The birds continued their chorus and the tug came again.

This time, Lucky shot straight up in bed and glared around the room, looking for the culprit who dared disturb her wallowing.

She didn't see anyone or anything.

Whelp, she decided. Must be the demon. She exhaled heavily. "Bring it on, you bastard. I'll just rub my bad luck all over you, too."

A small squeak answered her and she crawled down to the end of the bed to investigate.

It was the family of little mice she'd seen in the godmothers' house. They were tugging on the blanket with all of their might.

When their eyes met hers, all of their little noses twitched and flicked.

"You guys are incredibly adorable. But it's not going to work." She flopped back on the bed.

The tug came again.

She scowled, narrowed her eyes, and fisted the blanket in both hands before she pulled with all of her might.

The blanket came free, but with it, her fists slammed into her nose and knocked her the rest of the way back.

"Why me?" she mumbled, and lay there like a lump.

A breakfast tray wheeled itself over to her where a pot of steaming coffee waited for her. She poured a cup and took a sip; the warmth of the cup in her hands and the aroma of the freshly ground beans perked her up.

Exploring the tray further, she found cheese, fruit, toast, oatmeal, and bacon. The mice looked up at her balefully. Lucky laughed and shook her head.

"You guys are too cute." She took a saucer and loaded it with a bit of fruit and all of the cheese for her new friends. "Here you go." She put it on the floor for them.

Lucky figured she might as well feed the birds, too. She held up the toast. "Hey, guys. If you want it, come get it. Just please, please don't shit on me."

The birds took turns singing and coming to get bits of toast. Finally, she saw one she recognized and she held out her hand for him. The fat red cardinal landed in the palm of her hand.

"Tweet, tweet, huh?" She raised a brow.

"Eh, fuggedaboutit. Didn't mean to scare youse, though." He cocked his head from side to side.

"Yeah, yeah. Okay." She handed him some toast.

"Thanks, doll. Rosebud will be here any minute with your rehearsal dress. Up, up," he said. "Don't back out now. We're all countin' on youse."

"Bronx, I don't think I can."

He flapped his wings at her and there was a knock on her door.

"Lucky, it's Rosebud."

Bronx didn't wait for her to answer. He and the rest of the birds flew over to open the door.

"Thank you, friends." Rosebud took one look at Lucky and asked, "Why are you still in bed? You haven't even had your breakfast. Where's Ransom?"

Lucky shrugged. "He didn't come back last night."

Another bird sidled up next to Bronx. The fat cardinal bristled and tried to scoot away from him, but he wouldn't stop.

"Hey, man. Whaddya doin'?"

The bird chirped, twittered, and squawked, and Bronx nodded along.

"Yeah, okay. Ladies, he was at Pick 'n' Axe late with the best man. They slept there."

Rosebud scowled. "Go get them, please. We have a full day ahead of us." She turned her attention back to Lucky.

"I have a new dress for you."

Lucky was intrigued by a new dress, but wasn't as thrilled at the prospect since she didn't have anyone to wear it for.

Rosebud seemed to know. "Don't be down in the mouth. When I was a girl, I had an old heifer that made that face whenever I tried to get her to do anything besides eat. You are going to look beautiful in this dress. Problems in paradise notwithstanding. You know, you can dress up for yourself. Feel your power."

"My power? That's the problem."

"No, it's not. I promise to shut up for five seconds if you try it on."

Lucky flopped backward again. "Of course, I'll try it on. I'll do everything the godmothers asked me to. I'm just going to pout about it for a minute."

Rosebud laughed and it was a merry sound. She flopped backward on the bed as well.

"Okay, how does this pouting work? Tell me. Why are we pouting? Because the groom spent the night at Pick 'n' Axe without you?"

"Because he's about to lose his company and it's my fault."

"That's a lot of responsibility, don't you think?" Rosebud took her hand and squeezed. "Did you try to sabotage him?"

"No."

"Then how is it your fault."

"Surely you've heard the stories about me. That I'm bad luck. Natural disasters follow me wherever I go."

"Hmm. Woodland creatures follow me. They do my bidding, mostly. Sometimes I have to bribe them. Especially the tough-talking cardinal. So, does your bad luck do your bidding?"

"Sometimes. When people hurt people I love, I rub my luck on them."

"Did Ransom hurt someone? Did you rub your luck on him?"

"No."

"Then why do you think your luck is responsible?"

"Because the people I did inflict it on are causing him a problem," Lucky admitted.

"Hmm. Sounds like you need to just let nature take its course and not do that anymore."

"You're right, but it makes me so mad. I feel so helpless and that makes me feel not helpless."

"But you didn't like the consequences." She nodded. "I had to learn that myself. You need to make amends, as uncomfortable as it may be."

"Ugh. I don't want to."

"That's the trick, isn't it? Doing the right thing not just because it's right, but because you want to."

"Gross."

"Totally," Rosebud agreed. "Are we ready to get you gorgeous now? Will you come along without a fight?" she teased.

"Yeah."

She allowed Rosebud to shovel her into the new creation and Lucky had to admit, she looked amazing.

The dress wasn't something she'd have chosen for herself. Not at all. It was pink, with tiny bluebell flowers embroidered around the scoop neck, the scalloped sleeves, and across the empire waist. The contrast with her black hair was on point.

Rosebud slipped a comb with blue and pink flowers into the side of Lucky's hair and then presented her with a pair of satin ballet flats with the same embroidery.

When Rosebud was done, Lucky did feel like a princess.

"I feel absolutely gorgeous," Lucky said, looking in the mirror.

"Your mother helped choose the design. She has fabulous taste, I must say."

"Mostly," Lucky agreed.

"Are you ready to face the firing squad?"

"I don't even know where we were doing the vows," Lucky confessed. "I left all of this up to the godmothers."

"Darling, this is going to be wonderful. There's a pumpkin carriage waiting outside the front of the castle. It will take you through a manicured park to a cathedral made entirely of trees. It's stunning and sort of humbling. You'll love it." Rosebud turned away to rummage through the boxes she'd brought with her. "I've almost forgotten the most important part of this ensemble!"

She pulled out a delicate lace shawl. The lace tatting was in the design of the bluebell flowers, and Lucky was afraid to touch it.

"I've never had anything this nice. I'm afraid I'll ruin it."

"Nice things are for wearing and enjoying. If it gets ruined, that's okay. It's meant to be worn, not to sit in a box." She draped it around Lucky's shoulders. "Much like life. It's meant for living."

"Yeah, okay. I see what you did there."

Rosebud kissed her cheek. "Go forth and shine!"

"Will you settle for a slight flickering? I think I can manage that."

"No, I will not. Neither should you." Rosebud shoved her toward the door. "You're going to be late. Do try not to lose a shoe on the stairs down to the carriage. That's not your story."

Lucky cackled. "Well, now that you mention it . . ."

"When the clock strikes noon, the carriage will turn back into a pumpkin!"

"Will it really?"

"No, but don't be late." Rosebud grinned but moved her more forcibly toward the door. "Go, go!"

Lucky allowed her to shuffle her off and she looked down at her dress. It really was a piece of art. No matter what happened, she decided she didn't want to wear any other clothes except what Rosebud made for her.

The halls of the castle seemed too quiet, too bare. She almost felt like she wasn't supposed to be there. Like maybe she'd run into a beast in the halls.

Also not the right story. Not *her* story.

Lucky wondered what she meant by that. Did Rosebud think Lucky was a fairy-tale princess who was going to get her Happily Ever After? As things stood now, that wasn't on the menu.

She tried not to think about it as she ran down the steps toward the carriage, mindful to keep her new shoes on her feet.

The carriage itself was exactly as Rosebud described it. It was large, with a round, metal frame that had been wrapped with ivy and tiny white lights. Much to her delight, the mice sat up on the plush seat with the liveried driver.

She grinned at them and they waved their tiny paws at her in greeting.

Lucky stepped up into the carriage and once she was seated, the team of white horses with pink flowers in their bridles pulled the carriage onto a path at a sedate, yet still high-stepping trot. These horses obviously wanted to strut their stuff.

As a child, Lucky had never been up to the castle. She'd never made it farther than the fountain, so this was a surprise and a delight to discover the grounds. Shrubs that had been cut into mythological animal shapes stood sentry along the wide, manicured path.

The path led them farther and farther from the impressive castle toward a different part of the Enchanted Forest. From the carriage, Lucky could see the cathedral Rosebud had been talking about.

It was majestic and magical. Almost as if she'd stepped

from this world into the next. She supposed that this might actually be the case. Ever After was magical, after all.

Much to her surprise, everyone else was already there and waiting for her.

Her mother was exquisite in a white wrap dress with blue foxes and pink flowers embroidered just on the sleeves. She stood, waiting at the end of a green mossy carpet waiting to walk her down the aisle.

She rather imagined that the godmothers had used magic to get Ransom and Roderick into shape, because they stood up on a green moss-covered platform, resplendent in their wedding attire.

Lucky tried to look away from Ransom. She didn't want to notice how good he looked in his suit. Or the way those breeches fit his incredible ass. The way his Hessian boots made her want to faint like a heroine from some old book.

She looked over at where the godmothers sat, in the first row, with their gossamer wings out and on display, and expressions of warmth and love on their faces.

How could she have even considered not showing up today? She was better than that. Lucky could definitely do better.

Gwen had moved to stand by Fortune, with Brittany and Steven in tow. Gwen's dress was white as well, with delicate yellow flowers embroidered on the sleeves and at the sweetheart neckline.

Brittany was a little fairy princess, wearing fake glittery wings, and a pale-pink and white dress and tiara. From the way they sparkled, they looked like real diamonds.

Steven's outfit matched Ransom's.

Her eyes were drawn back to her fake groom and she found no matter what she did, she couldn't look away.

Everything she ever wanted was wrapped up in this moment. She wanted to run up the aisle and fly into Ransom's arms. She wanted him to tell her everything was okay. That he loved her anyway. He didn't care about anything but the two of them being together.

It was a pretty fantasy.

A childish fantasy.

One that didn't allow for the real world to intrude.

Her mother held out her hand to help her down from the carriage and she stepped down, focusing her full attention on her mother. She reached out to run her fingers over the fox embroidery on her mother's dress.

"It's beautiful. I hope you save it and wear it if I ever do get married," Lucky said.

"I will." Fortune brought her in close to whisper in her ear. "I love you, Lucky Charm. I'm proud of who you are and everything you've accomplished. This day may not be real, but let us celebrate you and the love you give like it is."

Tears pricked her eyes. "Stop it, Ma. I'm going to cry like it's real."

"Me too." Fortune sniffed.

"Stop it," Gwen said. "Or I'm going to cry, too."

"Well, we can't have that," Lucky said. "It'll ruin all of our makeup."

Grammy, dressed in a gray suit with a satin pink bow tie, stepped up to the center of the platform. She was officiating!

"Grammy!" Lucky cried with joy.

"How do you like that? I got Internet-ordained." She adjusted her bow tie with obvious pride.

"I love it!"

Once again, all of this made Lucky wish it was real. She looked up at the cathedral of branches and Lucky decided if she ever did get married, it would be here. She felt safe, cradled, and part of something much bigger and more magical than she could've imagined.

"Okay, places, everyone!" Grammy said, taking charge. "Lucky, when you arrive, it will be much like this. Everyone will be in place. The band will start playing. Brittany and Steven will walk down first, throwing fairy dust. Roderick, you will walk Gwen down the aisle and then you'll take your places on the platform. Fortune, you'll walk Lucky down the aisle and then you'll sit in this first row of chairs. Then we'll begin the service. Let's practice."

Roderick had been up on the platform by Ransom's side, so he quickly moved to Gwen to offer her his arm. She took it hesitantly and then gently pushed Steven and Brittany forward when the band started playing the "Wedding March."

The kids took great delight in throwing the fairy dust, giggling and skipping down the aisle. Lucky loved that no one corrected them or tried to make them be anything but what they were: children enjoying being children.

Gwen and Roderick were next.

Fortune linked their arms and put her hand over Lucky's. Then she led her down the aisle toward Ransom.

Lucky moved slowly, but her brain had completely disengaged. She wasn't even sure her body was moving. It was like she was floating on a cloud and it decided where she would go. She was rattled from her stupor only when her mother let go of her arm and kissed her cheek.

There were two more steps she had to take up the stairs to Ransom, but she couldn't make her feet move.

He reached out to take her hand, and that was exactly what she needed. His touch grounded her, steadied her. His hand was so warm, solid, and real.

When their eyes met, she didn't see any of the regret she'd seen that day at Grammy's, but if she wasn't mistaken, there was sadness there.

Still, he smiled at her and kissed her hand.

Lucky did a quick scan of their surroundings for mutant cherries, wasps, feral hogs, God forbid leeches, and finally, checked the sky for tornadoes.

He snickered and she realized he knew exactly what she was doing.

"Just checking," she whispered.

"We've got it covered," he said.

Grammy, looking very officious, said, "That's very good, but no whispering day of. M'kay?"

She and Ransom laughed together. "Got it," they answered.

Grammy cleared her throat. "Dearly beloved, we're gathered here today . . ."

# Chapter 19

Ransom didn't hear anything else that Grammy said.
He knew that he responded when he was supposed to.
He knew he said the correct things, because the ceremony
progressed until he found himself slipping a golden band on
Lucky's slim finger.

"You may kiss the bride," Grammy said.

He was supposed to kiss her.

He wanted to kiss her.

He just didn't know if he *should* kiss her. This all felt too
complicated.

"Thought you said you had the disasters covered?" she finally whispered.

"We do."

"Then what are you waiting for? Oh my God, this is embarrassing."

He realized everyone was looking at them, waiting for him
to kiss her. Ransom pulled her close and he meant to brush
his lips across hers. Something sweet, romantic. Something
entirely faux-wedding appropriate.

Only that wasn't what happened.

The moment his lips pressed against hers, all thoughts of
sweet romance burned to smoking cinders. She responded,
melting against him and kissing him back with all the fire
that burned between them.

Cheers went up from those present and he broke the kiss.

Immediately sorry for what he'd done. This wasn't fair to either of them. He shouldn't be sending her mixed signals.

Yet, there was nothing mixed about his body's response to her, or his heart.

"That'll make a great promo shot," Petty said. "Be sure to do it just that way on the day of the wedding."

"Yes, wonderful. Who's ready for brunch?" Jonquil asked.

"Everyone is ready for brunch," Roderick answered.

Ransom looked down at Lucky and realized he was still holding her hands. He forced himself to let go.

She didn't say anything, she simply walked toward her mother, who fixed him with a hard glare, that he supposed he'd earned.

Large tables had been spread out and covered with tiny white lights, and the lights reminded him of the carriage.

When he'd caught his first look at her in the carriage, it caused so many feelings to surge in his chest. She was so incredibly beautiful. Ethereal.

"So how did you ensure against the natural disasters that would result from kissing me?" she asked as they were led to the tables that were now laden with all manner of delicious things from fresh fruit, to ceviche, to a create-your-own-omelet station, where all you had to do was imagine the kind of omelet you wanted and it manifested.

"I'm not sure. I asked Petunia, and she said she and the godmothers had it managed."

Lucky didn't say anything. Instead, she moved to the seat with her place card and sat down. Ransom couldn't do anything but follow.

He supposed he should be grateful that she understood. Grateful that she wasn't forcing the issue of what happened between them and why, no matter how pretty a fantasy it was, it had to stay that way.

Except he wasn't. It bothered him that this was what she expected and she was okay with it.

She deserved better.

She deserved an explanation.

She deserved someone who wasn't afraid.

He wished that someone could be him.

Ransom tried to push those thoughts out of his head. He'd done a lot of wishing since he'd come to Ever After. Wishing, hoping, wanting, with no damn follow-through.

"You should paint the cathedral," he said.

"That would be a much better subject of your art than me," Grammy added.

"No, I still need to paint you. I wanted to before, but now that I've gotten to know you, I'm more obsessed than ever," Lucky said to her, eyes alight.

Grammy waved her hand. "Off with that rot."

"I admire you so much. How you saved Red. The way you live on your own terms. Of course, there are your cheekbones, too."

Grammy laughed. "I suppose if you must. If you stay around after the wedding, which I imagine you will be to see your dear Gwen. She seems to be happy here. The kids, too."

Lucky nodded. "I'm happy here, too. I've been giving serious consideration to staying. It's safe here. For me. For the people around me."

"I want you to stay here, kiddo. Everyone adores you. But don't stay because of any other reason than this is where you want to be," Grammy said with a stern nod. "I need to get one of those omelets. Steak on the brain!" She got up from her chair and went over to the other table to acquire her omelet.

Ransom noticed that the godmothers were particularly uninvolved. He looked over to where they were sitting and they each raised a hand and wiggled their fingers in a wave.

He didn't trust it. Not in the slightest.

"Lucky, look at the godmothers."

Lucky looked up from her food and turned her head

toward the godmothers. They waved at her, too. The same little finger wiggle.

"That's suspicious," she said.

"Oh good. I thought it was just me."

"They're plotting like usual. Too bad they can't get it through their heads that you and I aren't meant to be. It'd be a lot less stressful for everyone. Including them."

"This isn't what I wanted," Ransom said.

"I don't want to talk about this now." She took a drink of her mimosa. "Actually, I don't think I want to talk about this ever. It is what it is. You've made your choice."

"Lucky, I . . ." He what? What exactly did he think he was going to say to make this better? There was nothing to say.

"Exactly," she said. "We don't have to have the talk. We don't have to make excuses, or apologies, or talk about what-ifs. They're all useless. Let's just get through this sham for the godmothers and go our separate ways."

"If that's what you want," he said.

"Didn't we just establish I can't have what I want?"

"What do you want, Lucky?"

"Can we not do this here? Please?"

"Then let's do it elsewhere. I think we owe it to ourselves to have some kind of closure."

"Ugh. Closure. Whatever. I don't understand the concept. When a thing is over, it's closed. That's closure. Get over it and move on," Lucky snapped.

"That worked so well for us the first time? Because here we are."

"Fine." She dropped her napkin and stood up.

Gwen, who'd been sitting on the other side of her and talking to Red, turned at Lucky's abrupt movement. "Are you okay," she asked.

Lucky nodded. "Ransom and I need to talk about a few things. Enjoy the brunch. We'll be back in a bit."

Roderick got up, too, but Gwen pointed at him and then at his chair. Much to Ransom's surprise, Roderick sat back down.

Yeah, maybe the godmothers were right about Gwen and Roderick.

"There's a boathouse just down that path where we can talk." Ransom pointed toward a path that led into the trees.

"Fine." She wrapped her shawl around her and walked toward the path.

They walked for a few minutes in silence. "It's just up ahead." He could see the edge of the lake and a pair of swans gliding across the still surface.

"Fine."

She didn't even look at the swans.

The boathouse was actually more like a small marina, and Ransom led her inside to a small lounging area that was boat themed. It sported anchors, fishing nets, and paddles as décor.

"Would you like to sit?" He gestured to the couch that had once been a plush, cushioned bench on a boat.

"Fine." She plopped down on the seat and tightened the wrap of her shawl around her shoulders.

He'd started to think she was using it like some sort of armor.

"Is that all you're going to say is fine?"

"Maybe. You're the one who has things he left unsaid. I don't."

"Honestly, after everything, you're going to tell me that you have nothing else to say to me?"

"What do you expect from me, Ransom?" she cried. "You don't want me. You made it clear. The rest of it doesn't matter."

"It does to me."

"Great. So let's make this all about you. Let's pick all the old wounds, all the old scars open, and you can watch me bleed so you can have closure. FINE."

"Damn it, Lucky."

"No, listen. You wanted to talk this out? Here we go. Remember the junket?"

"As if I could forget."

"I know the junket was the culmination of all of your worst fears. I held your hand. I supported you. I watched you die until you could resurrect yourself and find the man you are in the boy you once were. You found that fear, you faced it. It's over now, right? Those words, that nickname, it's nothing to you."

"I wouldn't say it's nothing, but yes. I did face it. I did conquer it with you by my side. I—"

She held up her hand to stay him. "The culmination of my darkest fear was what happened between us in Grammy's."

Her words sliced straight through him. He'd swear he could feel the blade of them in the marrow of his bones.

"Guess who I had to hold my hand? Guess who I had to tell me it would be okay?"

She was right. He hadn't been there when she'd needed him.

She continued. "And it's fine. It's all fucking fine. I get it. I'm bad luck. I'm a curse. You'll lose everything. Blah, blah. *FINE*."

There was that word again.

"I expected it. Do you remember? I told you not to make promises you couldn't keep. You swore to me that you could. Your feelings were hurt that I doubted you. Yet, here we are." Her lips quivered. "Here I am. Alone. No matter what you have to say about what happened, and I know exactly what you'll say while we're at it, and like I said, I understand. I do. That doesn't change the end result for either of us. I just choose not to bleed for this anymore."

Panic closed around his throat like a vise. He knew he needed to say something, but the words he'd been so ready to spill all over her evaporated. His chance to tell her what he felt slipped through the hourglass, and each granule of sand was a moment he'd never get back. A chance he'd never have again.

He didn't know what else to do. He didn't know the right words to sum everything in his heart. His whole body was a raw nerve and he needed her.

Damn him for being a selfish bastard, but he needed her more than he needed his next breath.

Any thought of consequences fled in the face of losing her.

He grabbed her arms and pulled her closer, and as he did so, the shawl she'd been using to shield herself fell to the ground in a pool of lace and tears.

"Don't cry," he whispered. "Please don't cry."

"I'm not allowed to love you. I'm not allowed to have you. And I can't cry. What can I do, Ransom? Tell me!"

"Kiss me goodbye," he said, knowing full well it wouldn't stop there, but he couldn't stop himself.

"We both know how this ends," she whispered.

"Then walk away from me."

She reached up shaking fingers to cup his face. "You mean like what you're going to do to me? I can't do that."

Even as her words sliced him deep, she arched up on her tiptoes to kiss him.

She wrapped her arms around his neck and he lifted her up so he could taste her at his leisure. Lucky opened beneath him like a flower blooming for the first time, her desire unfurling like the tender leaves of a new bud.

In that moment, Ransom knew that not even rabid dogs could stop him. Wasps, he'd take the stings. Leeches? Fuck 'em. A tornado? He'd just try to make sure that she found her pleasure before the twister touched down and wiped him off the face of the earth.

No, the only thing that would stop him now was if Lucky said no.

This was a culmination of years of desire.

Of polarity that surged between them.

He was a moth, and she was an eternal flame. Ransom had decided he was ready to burn. After he did, there'd be nothing left between them but goodbye.

She knew it, too. Lucky met his kiss with an urgency of her own.

This was heat, passion, and a mournful desperation.

Some part of him knew that this wasn't fair to her. Or to himself. He could tell himself that this was goodbye a hundred thousand times.

Ransom was sure he'd always want her.

He needed to take his time with her. To seduce her, to bring every nerve ending to life so that she could find her bliss over and over again.

Only she wasn't having any of that. "Ransom, we've had years of foreplay. I have plenty of those memories. Give me a new one," she panted in his ear.

"I didn't ask you before," he began. "Because I didn't plan on ever taking it this far. Are you on birth control?"

"Yes," she said.

He kissed her neck. "I haven't been with anyone since I was tested. You?"

"No."

He worked his way back up to her mouth. "Do you still want this? Are you sure?"

"Surer of anything I've ever been in my life," she said.

Ransom eased her down on the overstuffed, plush couch, and she reached up eager hands to tug at the waist of his breeches and freed his cock.

"Oh my God, is this actually happening? Hurry up, before a comet hits the earth and ends us all."

He laughed, because she was right. Every time they'd attempted this, there'd been some catastrophe. Apparently, this time the world was just going to have to end to keep them apart this last time.

Lucky slid out of her panties quickly and dropped them on the ground. "Now, Ransom."

He gently lowered his weight atop her, and she wrapped her slim legs around his hips. Only as he was looking down at her face flushed with desire, he knew it wasn't the universe that would stop him.

Ransom should stop himself.

She'd bared her heart to him, and told him how much this hurt her, yet she was still ready to give him everything.

Everything he didn't deserve.

"What are you waiting for?" she asked breathlessly.

"I don't want you to regret this."

"I told you what I wanted, Ransom. I'm a big girl. I can live with my choices. Can you?"

He let himself drown in the dark depths of her eyes when he slid himself deep inside of her, and when she dug her nails into his back and begged him to take her higher, all he could do was comply.

She held on tightly, almost as if she were afraid to let go. He carried them both on waves of ecstasy until he'd wrung every last drop of pleasure that was to be had from the moment. From the connection.

When Lucky reached her climax, she whispered ever so softly, "I love you."

Those words pushed him over the edge and he spilled, earthquakes rocking his body as he shuddered against her.

He trailed kisses across her face, from her cheeks, to the tip of her nose, to her forehead. She cupped his face and pulled him down to kiss her lips.

It was the tenderest of kisses. Slow, lingering.

When she opened her eyes, she searched his face. Studied

him for a long, solid moment. He didn't want that moment to end, because when it did, this moment out of time had ended.

"Lucky." He said her name like a benediction.

She put her finger to his lips. "You don't have to say anything. We've already said everything that needs to be said."

He eased off of her and adjusted his clothing. His wedding costume.

Ransom didn't understand how the aftermath from something that had been so right could feel so awful.

# Chapter 20

L ucky couldn't believe it.
    She'd had actual sex with Ransom and it had been beyond her wildest dreams.

She didn't regret telling Ransom that she loved him. It wasn't the first time. It wasn't a new feeling. She hadn't said it with any intention or expectation except that she wanted him to know it.

How could she regret it? Love was something that was meant to be given. It welled up in her like a spring, and she wanted him to have it.

Besides, when she thought of him, she didn't want to be bitter. She wanted to remember him with all the love she'd felt for him. She wanted to be able to wish him well when he crossed her mind, as he invariably would.

Ransom hadn't yet moved the rest of his things out of the room, but she knew he would. She promised herself she wouldn't let it hurt her; it was just what had to happen. Of course, that was easier said than done.

The bedroom door creaked open and she shot upright in the bed, hoping against hope it was Ransom, but it wasn't.

It was Gwen.

She was dressed in pajama pants, a T-shirt, and hard-soled slippers. She carried a box of what Lucky was sure was donuts and two coffees. "Jonquil is with the kids," she said by way of explanation. "I thought we could have a quiet morning. *If* you were in bed by yourself. I was fully prepared to make an exit. Although, the godmothers were sure you'd be alone."

Lucky pulled the covers back in invitation, and Gwen put the box and the cups down to leap into the bed and curl up against her.

Lucky exhaled a heavy sigh she hadn't realized she'd been holding and snuggled up to her best friend.

"Your hair smells like apples," she murmured. "And coffee. Why do you always smell like good food?"

"It's to lure you in. I have to do something to make sure you keep me," Gwen teased.

"You do know the way to my heart."

"So tell me."

"Tell you what?" Lucky demurred.

"Everything. Obviously." Gwen stroked her hair. "Unless you're not ready to talk. I understand that."

"It was wonderful."

"It happened? Like . . . IT?"

"Yeah. The world didn't explode. No floods or volcanoes as of yet."

"Wait, clarify. Are we talking metaphorically or literally?"

"Metaphorically, it was comets, and starbursts, and I heard the Hallelujah Chorus on repeat. Literally, no disasters. Although I'm waiting for that shoe to drop."

"I know you've been through a lot." Gwen tightened her embrace, as if to show Lucky that she wasn't going anywhere. "But have you considered maybe this is just something that you get to have?"

"That would be pretty naïve of me, don't you think?"

"I don't think hope is ever naïve. The people who do are sad and weak little goblins. Although, seriously. We're in a fairy-tale town and you can't find the will to believe?"

"I have the will to believe, but after what I did to Melvin and Nancy, I don't deserve it. I haven't earned it."

"Whether you believe you do or don't, it's true."

"Stop with that. We've all read the fairy tales. Is this the part where I get everything I want? No."

"Okay, I'll give you that, but when do we get to that part?"

"Never?"

"I don't like that story and I don't want to read it," Gwen said. "That's a DNF for me."

"Too bad we can't opt out like that."

"You totally can. If you don't like how your story is going, change it. I think you said something similar to me about my marriage to Jake. Didn't you?"

"Maybe, but that's different."

"How so?"

"You're not cursed."

"Neither are you. I tell you what, sometimes when you're on the wrong path and you don't know what to do, it can feel like being cursed."

Lucky hadn't thought of it that way. "Have you heard from Jake yet?"

"No, I know he's getting ready to lay down some legal nonsense. I've contacted every law firm back home, and he got a consultation with each one so none of them can represent me."

"What a crappy thing to do. I know Roderick isn't your favorite person, but I think his degree is business law. If nothing else, he could probably get you a good referral."

"You know, he's not my favorite person, but he's not my least favorite person, either. I'll ask him. The worst he can say is no."

A loud pounding on the door echoed like thunderclaps.

Lucky's gut twisted on itself and nausea rose like waves. This was it. She knew it. It was some kind of bad news.

Gwen hopped up out of bed and padded to the door.

"Someone better be dead. What's wrong with you, pounding on the door this early in the morning like you're the police," Gwen said as she opened the door.

Roderick stood there, his expression grim. "Is he here?"

"Ransom?" she asked.

"The Dalai Lama. Who do you think?" Roderick growled. Then he sighed and scrubbed a hand over his head. "This is awful."

"What's happened?" Lucky asked as she slid out of bed and wrapped a robe around herself.

"Heart's Desire. The board made a move to push him out as CEO. They're trying to buy up falling shares faster than we can. He's going to lose the company."

Lucky was stricken. She put her hand to her chest as she tried to catch her breath and digest the news.

Was this because of what happened between them in the boathouse?

"Didn't he come back with you last night? I thought you two . . ." He splayed his hands. "Whatever. I have to find him."

"Wait, I'll help you look. Maybe the godmothers can help."

"No! You've done enough," Roderick snapped. He sighed again. "I'm sorry, that's not fair. But I told him if he went through with this, this was what was going to happen. The stock ate shit, and after the board saw that story Melvin did on you, it was too easy to blame you for what happened in Ecuador."

Gwen grabbed him by the lapels. "What is wrong with you? Can't you see she already blames herself for everything as it is? And you come in here and dump this on her? If your board lost confidence, that has nothing to do with Lucky. Those are from your own decisions. Stocks tanking? Still not her fault. How dare you."

"No, it's okay. I told you the other shoe would drop," Lucky said quietly.

"I did, too. I warned him. I told him this was too far gone and he needed to make other plans, but he didn't listen to me," Roderick said.

"And he chose his own path. He's an adult. You don't get to drop it all in Lucky's lap."

"You're right, but I need to find him. He's not answering his phone."

"Maybe he's with the godmothers. He might have slept over on the couch," Lucky suggested.

"We'll go with you," Gwen suggested.

Lucky thought that she was probably the last person he wanted to see, but she had to do something and Roderick didn't tell her not to come.

"I'll get dressed." Lucky stepped into the massive walk-in closet to quickly shrug into some clothes and joined them.

This was made of awful. She wouldn't let him lose his company. Lucky wasn't quite sure yet what exactly she could do about it, but she'd figure it out.

Gwen slipped her hand into Lucky's and they set out to find Ransom. If he wasn't at the godmothers', she didn't know what they were going to do.

On the way through the path in the forest, Lucky's phone buzzed with a text. It was Bluebonnet, bless her.

*Ransom is here. Come.*

"You guys, Ransom is there! Bluebonnet just texted me."

"I've got it from here," Roderick said.

"No, Bluebonnet asked me to come."

Roderick didn't say anything, but continued down the path toward the godmothers' house.

Gwen squeezed her hand.

She didn't know what she'd ever do without her best friend. The thought turned sour in her mind, and something told Lucky she was about to lose everything she cared about.

Each step she took seemed heavier than the last one, but she wasn't going to lose faith.

Not even when they walked inside the godmothers' house and it didn't smell like vanilla and cinnamon. Neither Bluebonnet nor Petty had warm, welcoming smiles, and Ransom's eyes were haunted and tired.

"What's happened?" Lucky asked.

Petunia shook her head slowly. "They've all canceled. All of the guests who started booking when we announced the wedding. They saw the story Melvin did and every single one of them has pulled out."

"I refuse to think our plan failed," Bluebonnet said. "Something will happen. Something good. It has to."

Lucky didn't look at Ransom when she went over to comfort Bluebonnet.

"Ransom, I need to speak to you outside," Roderick said.

"Whatever it is, just say it," Ransom sighed.

"The board made a move to take the company. They cited loss of confidence in you as CEO and they're not only trying to push you out, but they're buying up stock as fast as we are."

"So we have to outbid them and get to the shareholders before they do," Ransom said.

"You can't do that here."

"No, I can't. I still have to go to Ecuador. You can, though."

Roderick shook his head slowly and closed his eyes. "Ransom, you have to choose."

"This isn't about her. It's about my godmothers. I'm not going to leave them when they need me most."

Petty put her hand on Ransom's shoulder and squeezed. "That's okay. You go do what you need to do."

Lucky could feel Ransom's eyes on her, but she couldn't bring herself to look at him.

"I still need you on this while I'm in Ecuador."

"Fine. I'll get the chopper to pick us up." Roderick pulled out his phone and stepped outside.

To Petunia, Ransom said, "We'll figure this out. I promise."

"I know we will. I was just so sure this would work." Petunia looked at Lucky and it seemed that her words were more meant for her than anyone else.

She wished she knew the right thing to say. How to explain to her godmother she'd tried her best. "We will figure it out," Lucky reiterated. "We will."

"Anything I can do, I'm here for it," Gwen swore.

"You kids are the absolute best," Petunia said.

"I'm going to go home so Jonquil can be here with you."

"Lucky, why don't you go with her?" Petunia suggested.

Her first thought was that the godmothers didn't want her. This latest catastrophe had been the bridge too far. The one that made them wash their hands of her.

Bluebonnet patted her hand and leaned over to whisper in her ear. "She's going to need you. My wings are tingling. That usually means trouble is on the way."

Relief washed over her. "Okay. I'll be back later to check in on you."

"I'm going to step outside, too. I'll wait for you, Lucky." She nodded toward Ransom and followed Roderick outside.

The godmothers suddenly found work to busy them in the kitchen.

Was she expected to apologize? Well, she wasn't going to. They both knew the risks when they decided to flip fate the bird. Now, here they were. Dealing with the consequences.

"Whatever happens, we have to make sure the godmothers are okay," he said.

That hadn't been anything near what she'd expected him to say, but somehow, it was a relief. It was something normal. Something real.

She nodded. "Of course."

"I'm leaving, but I'll be back as soon as I can. Promise me you won't leave until I get back."

"I can't do that. What if you never come back? Then I can't

leave." She'd meant it to be lighthearted. A little humor in the midst of all the gloom.

It hadn't exactly worked.

She laughed, a nervous and high-pitched sound. "If that will help you do what you need to do, I'll try to wait for you to come back. Is that better?"

"Yeah, it is. Take care of them until I get back."

"I will." She pressed her lips together in a grim line. They tingled, remembering what it felt like to have his lips on hers.

Bluebonnet's wings tingled before a catastrophe, maybe that's what this was. Maybe Lucky's lips tingled.

She decided in that moment that she was done with this self-doubt, self-recrimination. She was tired of feeling this way.

So Lucky decided to leave before Ransom did. She was done watching him walk away. It was her turn.

Of course, he could let her. "Lucky?"

She turned on her heel. "What?"

"I don't blame you."

Lucky thought those were the words she'd wanted to hear, but they weren't. Instead of soothing her, they enraged her. "Good to know. I wasn't there by myself."

"I know that." He shoved his hands in his pockets. "I blame myself."

"Ugh. I'm so done with this. The Blame Game. I'm not playing anymore. Have a safe flight. I hope you save your company."

Lucky lifted her chin and turned away from him to walk out the door. She linked her arm with Gwen's and they walked down the little path toward her cottage.

"It's all going to work out," Gwen reassured her.

Gwen opened the door and they found Jonquil sitting in the rocker as it rocked all on its own, knitting needles in her hands, but with her head tilted back and long, deep snores rattling her tiny body.

Gwen sighed. "I guess someone is sleeping well. That's a plus. I hate to wake her."

"We could let her sleep for a few minutes."

Suddenly, the needles started clacking and Jonquil coughed. "I'm up, I'm up."

"I'm afraid there's been some bad news," Gwen said.

"What's happened?" Jonquil put down her knitting needles.

"After the article that appeared in the paper about me, and because Ransom is about to lose his company, everyone who booked canceled," Lucky summoned the courage to say.

"Everyone?"

"Everyone," Lucky repeated.

Jonquil gathered her things quietly. When she stood, she said, "This may seem like the darkest time, but this is when people show you who they are. All will be well, child."

Lucky didn't understand how she could say that. She desperately wished it made sense to her, because if it did, it meant Lucky understood that kind of hope. It meant she could believe.

Jonquil kissed Lucky's and Gwen's cheeks on the way out the door. "I'm sad I won't see the kiddos today, but I'll get some good time with them when things calm down." Jonquil winked.

Gwen leaned on the counter. "Irish coffee?"

"Make it a double," Lucky said.

Gwen was pulling out the coffee grinder when her phone buzzed. She stopped to check it, and then she shook her head slowly.

"That philandering shitlord," she murmured. "The audacity."

"What's happened?" Lucky asked, unable to swallow past the lump in her throat.

"He's going for full custody."

"Why? I thought you said you couldn't even get a firm

commitment out of him for when he was going to see the kids, and now he wants full custody?"

Gwen looked down at the phone and back up at Lucky. Then back at the phone again.

"It's because of me, isn't it?"

"It's because of what Nancy said about you. He thinks you're a danger to the children."

Lucky didn't know what to say. What to do.

She'd lost everything.

Tears slipped down her cheeks, hot and angry. She wouldn't put Gwen in this position to have to choose between going to war with her husband and keeping her children.

Lucky locked Gwen in a fierce hug before heading for the door.

"You don't have to go. You know I'll fight this."

"You shouldn't have to. Tell the monsters I love them. I'm going to fix this," Lucky swore. "All of it."

# Chapter 21

Lucky didn't actually have the first clue how to fix what she'd broken, except by leaving.

But that wasn't the solution she wanted, so she had to keep looking. Even though she accepted that eventuality might be best for everyone.

Honestly, she thought she should probably seclude herself on some mountaintop or desert island somewhere.

Lucky's first instinct was to ask the godmothers for their opinion, but they had too much on their plates right now. If they'd had a ready-made solution, she was sure she'd have been the first to know.

She considered the nature of choices.

Her mother knew what it meant to make hard choices.

A lot of people never knew out of the thousands of choices they made every day, which one would be the one that dramatically altered the path of their life, so they did the best they could with the information they had and went in blind. Only this lesson has been different for Fortune Fujiki. Her choice had been put to her, a riddle with no answer.

Lucky made her way back up to the castle and to her mother's room.

"Ma?" she asked quietly, easing in through the door.

Her mother sat in the butter-yellow light of the morning sun, drinking her coffee and reading the paper. She made a pretty picture that reminded Lucky of when she was young.

When things were much simpler and all she'd needed was a kiss on her skinned knee.

She supposed she'd skinned her heart this time.

One glance at her daughter, and Fortune asked, "What's happened?"

"Everything, and it's all bad." Lucky shook her head. She didn't know where to start.

"Certainly not everything is bad. Come here and tell Ma all about it." She patted the chair next to her.

Lucky sat down in the chair next to her mother and wilted, an exhausted little flower. "After that stupid article about my luck ran in the paper, Ransom may lose his company, all of the potential customers canceled their bookings with the godmothers, and Gwen's husband is suing her for full custody."

"Okay, you're right. That's all awful. So what are you going to do?"

"I don't know. That's the problem. I don't know what to do." Lucky wanted her mother to hand her a solution wrapped up in a glittery bow. A solution that didn't hurt. A solution that on the other side, she knew for certain everything would be okay.

"Yes, you do," Fortune reminded her gently. "Think about everything that's happened. If Gwen were in your position, what would you tell her to do?"

Lucky considered for a long moment. "I'd tell her that she has to be honest. That if she wanted to help Ransom save his company, she had to talk to the investors. I'd tell her that she had to talk to the godmothers and tell them she's going to come clean."

She sank farther down in her chair. This was not the solution she'd been looking for.

"Don't slump, dear."

"I can't help it. Everyone's future is on my shoulders. That's kinda heavy."

"Not slump? Sure, you can. Just straighten your spine."

"That's not what I'm talking about. I can't tell Ransom's investors the truth. It would ruin what the godmothers are trying to build. They've done so much for me, I can't betray them."

"No one is asking you to betray them. Just as it's not okay for them to ask you to betray yourself."

"They would never!" Lucky was insulted on their behalf.

"Exactly. You need to go back and talk to them. Tell them what you're planning and get their blessing. I have a feeling that they'll be expecting you anyway. Your godmothers know you. Inside and out."

"What about Gwen?"

"If the problem is you, remove yourself. Not forever, just until Gwen can get things figured out. Take yourself out of the equation. You know she'd fight for you. This is you fighting for her."

"I want to be there for her. I don't want her to feel like I abandoned her."

"She's fighting on all fronts right now. Let her focus on her children. Let go a little bit, Lucky."

"I feel like I have to let go of everything that matters," she confessed. "I can't have Gwen and the kids. I can't have Ransom. What do I get, Ma?"

"I'm going to ask you a hard question, Lucky Charm."

"Aren't they all hard?"

"Some are easier than others. You said you've got the weight of the futures of all of your dear ones on your shoulders. It's so heavy it's physically pushing you down. I know it's a lot of responsibility, but isn't it also a tremendous gift?"

"I can't see how."

"Because you're looking at the outcomes that affect you negatively and not what those outcomes will be for them."

"Was there a question in there that wasn't rhetorical?" Lucky grimaced.

"None of it was rhetorical." She took a sip of her coffee and nudged a pastry Lucky's way. "Go on, have a bite."

Lucky didn't have to be told twice. She needed the fortification.

"The people you love are all facing impossible dilemmas. Each of them is locked in a kind of an escape room, but there's no key inside. They're all with you on the outside. Your gift is the ability to unlock their doors. Wouldn't you do that for them at all costs?"

Imagining any of her loved ones in that situation and Lucky knew she would do anything to give them those keys. Looking at it that way made her course of action so much easier.

For a single, selfish moment, she wondered when it was going to be her turn. When someone would save her, but maybe that was the lesson all along. She had to learn how to save herself.

Or maybe there was no lesson at all. Maybe this was just how things were. There was no point in wishing things were different, and later when she was alone in the dark wishing she could play with the monsters, or eat ice cream sodas with the godmothers, or kiss Ransom Payne, she'd remind herself of that.

Like she'd said, wish in one hand . . .

She ate the rest of the pastry slowly. This time, she didn't cram the whole thing in her mouth. Lucky allowed herself to chew each bite thoroughly, to let the buttery crust melt on her tongue.

This was her last breakfast in this phase of her life. Everything was going to change and she didn't know if it was for good or bad, but Lucky was choosing the best lane of a bad lot.

Again, if she framed it the way her mother had, that she was the one with the keys and her friends were locked in puzzle rooms with no hope of getting out, well, she supposed this lane wasn't so bad.

"You're right, Ma. I'm going to unlock their doors," she said finally.

"That's my Lucky Charm."

"I have one more idea."

"Oh?"

"Maybe since Ransom and I aren't getting fake married anymore, maybe you could."

Fortune coughed and spluttered into her napkin. "After the great advice I just gave you, that's the meanest thing you could say to me."

Lucky giggled.

"Ungrateful child," Fortune teased. "Didn't you learn your lesson about fake weddings?"

"No, I mean, for me. Yes, we can't give up on the idea that Ever After could become a premiere wedding destination. I think it could. If this had been my real wedding, aside from the whole having to break up with the groom, it would've been everything I could've dreamed of."

"So your plan?"

"Offer you up to the godmothers as a replacement. When I tell the investors this was all a publicity stunt, then out of the ashes comes an insta love romance where you and whoever was so caught up in the magic of the place that you decided to tie the knot."

"That's the worst idea ever."

"May I pitch it to the godmothers?"

"Pitch is a much better word than your earlier description of 'offering me up to the godmothers' like some kind of sacrifice." Fortune sighed. "Well, of course. Anything for my Lucky Charm. But then we're going to Paris. I'm full up of this fairy-tale nonsense." She looked around the room. "No offense."

Lucky thought about it and maybe it was time for her to have an adventure. For her to go to Paris and spend hours in the Louvre and lose herself just for a little while in the city of lights. What better place to nurse a lonely and broken heart? "Okay, I'll go with you. We'll have an adventure. Maybe Gwen can come with the monsters when things settle down."

Lucky straightened in her chair. Lifted her chin. Squared her shoulders. She could do this. The first thing she had to do was text Gwen. She could do that on the walk back to the godmothers' house.

"These boots were made for walking, I guess. I've been over Ever After's half acre already this morning," she said as she stood.

"Eat another pastry, then. You need the fortification."

Her mother knew her so well.

"Thanks, Ma."

Fortune stood and enveloped her daughter in a fierce hug. She squeezed her daughter tight.

"Can't breathe."

"You don't need to. Mama's got you."

It was then that Lucky realized that maybe she wasn't un-Lucky at all. She had so many people who loved her. Lucky had become so used to feeling bereft, alone, and unworthy. Hopeless.

She was none of those things.

What she'd thought was a burden on her shoulders was nothing of the sort. It was an honor.

A gift.

"Thanks for telling me to do the hard thing, Ma."

Fortune kissed her head. "Go save your loves."

"Before I go to Paris with you, I'm going to have some loose ends to tie up."

Fortune gave her a patient smile. "I can wait. Seems like now that you know the truth, it doesn't bother me so much to be in one spot. Funny how that works."

"See you later, Mama." She hugged her one more time and headed with renewed purpose back the way that she'd come.

Ever After looked different to her now. The trees were greener, the air smelled sweeter. How strange that it felt so good to ultimately break her own heart.

She shook the thought out of her head. Lucky wasn't going

to think of it like that. This was the person she wanted to be. The only one she could face in the mirror. That's what mattered. Sometimes, doing the right thing hurt.

And that was okay.

When she came across the mermaid fountain, a fat frog sat there, eyeing her. She realized she hadn't yet done her civic duty and tried to break his spell.

"Well, come here," she said to him.

He used his massive hind legs to propel himself to the edge of the fountain.

"Why do you hang out here anyway? That lake behind the castle seems like a much happier place for a mighty green boy such as yourself."

The frog made a sound deep in his throat.

"Yeah, I suppose you would need to be visible. You'd probably have to kickbox those swans. I wonder if any of them are lost princesses. You think?"

He looked up at her expectantly and she dropped a smooch on his head.

When nothing happened, instead of feeling like her magic wasn't good enough for anyone, she was proud of herself for fixing something she should've done a long time ago.

"Sorry it took me so long, and sorry it didn't work."

The frog's blorp seemed to say he understood.

She lifted him gently and put him up on the stone mermaid's shoulder. That was when an idea hit her right in the chops.

"You know what? What if we had a carnival instead of offering up my mother as a sacrifice? We could have a frog kissing booth? Get tons of kisses, maybe one of them will be the magic you need?"

Three other, smaller green faces popped up from the outer edge of the fountain. The bigger frog made a sound that Lucky could only describe as a growl and they disappeared again.

"Anyway, I'll tell the godmothers. Thanks, Phillip."

She was nervous about talking to Petty, Bluebonnet, and Jonquil, especially after the rough morning they'd had, but she knew what needed to be done now.

Her mother was right. Her godmothers knew her. They'd helped raise her. They'd taught her to do the right thing. The hard thing. They'd understand.

Lucky walked right by Gwen's house, but didn't stop. She knew Gwen was the weak link. Gwen would talk her out of it, and she couldn't let that happen.

She hurried her steps and found the door to her god-mothers' cottage open, as usual.

Petty was in the kitchen making ice cream sodas. She had four glasses. Her pink day dress was crisp and starched, and she wore a white apron over the frock.

"It's almost like you knew I was coming," she said.

The three all had sadness in their eyes, but they each gave her a warm smile that reassured her of her welcome.

Bluebonnet was the first to speak. "Dear, actually, I was going to have two. Sugar helps me think."

"It doesn't help the rest of us," Jonquil grumbled. "You zip around here like a demented lightning bug."

Bluebonnet tittered.

"See? She's already at two. I can't work in these conditions." Jonquil fretted with her yellow-checkered apron.

"I have to talk to you about something." She let out a heavy breath. "I don't know if any of this is going to work, but I have to try."

Jonquil came over and took her hand, leading her to the table. "Whatever it is, we'll try our best to support you."

Petty gave her one of the ice cream sodas, and they all sat down at the familiar kitchen table where they'd had so many long talks about everything and nothing.

"Did you know I hadn't kissed Phillip?"

"Ew, I should hope not." Petunia slurped her soda.

"As a frog, Petty." Bluebonnet took another drink.

"Oh. Have you now?" Jonquil lifted a curious brow.

"Yes, it didn't do anything, but I had to try. It gave me an idea." Lucky gulped a long drink of her icy treat. "First things first. So this morning was a total donkey kick to the face."

They all nodded in unison.

"I think the only way for us to help Ransom is to come clean. Let him off the hook, so to speak."

The godmothers looked around between themselves and then back at Lucky.

"Have you spoken with him about this?" Petty asked in a measured tone.

"No, and I'm not going to. I think he'd feel like it was a betrayal if the thought so much as dared to cross his mind."

"We've considered as much ourselves, but he's asked us not to meddle further in his business dealings," Jonquil said.

Relief flooded her. "What if there was a better way?"

"We're all ears." Bluebonnet twitched her pointy ears.

Lucky giggled at the sight of Bon-Bon's ears wiggling through her long, unbound hair.

"Oh, that used to make you giggle constantly as a baby. It broke my heart when Fortune asked us to hide our ears and wings from you," Bluebonnet said quietly.

"But you did, because you're the best fairy godmothers anyone could ask for."

The three old dears all puffed up with pride.

"I suppose you could pay Ma back by matchmaking *her* wedding."

"She'd kill us," Petty gasped, but her eyes were bright with mischief.

"Actually, she volunteered. I had this idea about revealing that the wedding was actually a publicity stunt, but all the love in the air was contagious and et cetera and so forth."

"It is. It's like the flu," Jonquil said. "Wash your hands."

How could Lucky have thought they'd be angry with her?

They each listened to everything she had to say. They considered her wants and needs. How hadn't she realized her godmothers were practically saints?

She was more determined now than ever to fix this.

"But this isn't the idea you want to go with?" Petty prompted.

"No, I think we can do better. What if we have a spring carnival? We can invite all of the big wedding magazines, have a bridal fashion show, and instead of having foods like funnel cakes and corn dogs, we have wedding cake samples and the like. We can play up the fairy-tale angle with a frog kissing booth. The prize can be a princess wedding. Crown included, because yeah." Lucky grinned at them.

"That's a brilliant idea!" Jonquil was the first to speak.

Bluebonnet nodded. "We can have carriage rides into the town to keep those nasty autos off our roads. Gondola rides in the lake behind the castle. Archery and hunting stations with Red and Grammy."

"Free ballroom dance lessons. Tours of the wedding wing of the castle. Maybe we can even talk some of the animals from the Enchanted Forest into a free-range petting zoo," Lucky said. "That might be an Evil Queen too far."

"No, no. It's perfect. Ravenna could give Evil Queen lessons. She'd love it. She could teach little girls how to cackle with terrifying glee," Petty said.

"Crushing the patriarchy and building a business." Lucky nodded. "I think we have a winner."

"It's a fantastic idea, Lucky. We're on board," Bluebonnet said. "But are you sure that you want to tell the world the truth? We can do the carnival without saying another word about the wedding."

"No, it needs to be done. I made this mess because of what I did with Nancy and Melvin James. I have to be the one to fix it." She slurped her empty cup. "I think I'm going to need another one of these for what I have to do next."

Petty nodded in support and got up to go make another round.

"It's going to be okay, if you believe it will," Jonquil said.

"I have faith that I'm doing the right thing and that has to be enough," Lucky said. "I'm going to text Roderick and Gwen."

"Wait, did something happen with Gwen?" Petty asked.

"Jake is suing for full custody because of the article about me."

Jonquil narrowed her eyes and actual sparks shot from her hands and ears. "What?"

"Plug her up!" Petty commanded.

Petty grabbed her hands and looked into her eyes, while Bluebonnet stuffed her fingers in her sister's ears.

"Breathe in the calm, exhale the rage. Breathe in the calm and exhale the rage." Petty breathed with her.

Puffs of multicolored smoke issued from Jonquil's nose like a dragon about to breathe actual fire.

"Remember what we talked about?" Petty went through the breathing motions again.

In a moment, Jonquil was herself again.

Petty looked back at her. "I'm the one known for my fury, but this one. She's quiet, but the deadlier of the two. She flunked out of Fairy Godmother Academy the first time because she roasted one of our professors. Literally. He'd been picking on a student two years behind us and Jonquil had just decided it was enough. She had to go to Fairy Anger Management."

"If he touches one hair on those dear little heads . . ."

"He is their father."

"Bah," she said.

"They love him," Bluebonnet reminded her.

"Fine. I don't like it, though."

Jonquil settled back down in her chair.

"I'm glad they have you, Jonquil." Lucky pressed her lips

together tight, as if that could somehow hold back her sorrow at what came next. "They're going to need you. I'm going to take myself out of the equation for a little while. Just to deal with my mess."

"Gwen would never ask you to do that, honey," Petty said.

"I know. Which is why I have to. It's only for a little while. Only until she gets this sorted."

"You could ask us for a wish," Petty offered. "We could grant you three."

For a moment, she considered it.

She could wish away everything that had happened. She could fix it all. It tempted her more than a third ice cream soda.

Lucky remembered that this wasn't about choosing what was easy. It was about choosing what was right.

On this path, she'd found herself. Connected with her mother. Her past.

All of the choices would be wiped away, even those that other people had made. Like Gwen's choice to leave Jake. It wasn't for her to choose a blank slate for them.

"No, Godmother. Thank you for offering, but it's not the right thing."

She texted Roderick.

*Can you send that helicopter back for me?*

Instead of texting back, he called.

"Why would I do that? Are you dying? Is one of the godmothers?" he said, getting right to the point.

"I'm trying to fix this. I've cleared it with the godmothers, and if you'll call a meeting of the investors and the board, I'll tell them all it was a publicity stunt to launch Fairy Godmothers, Inc. Which, in turn, means my bad luck isn't going to hurt the company."

"You'd do that?"

"Of course, I would. I can do it by myself if I have to, but I'd like your help."

"This is crazy enough it just might work, Lucky."

An idea hit her. "I need another favor. Please?"

"You're a needy bit today, aren't you? Since you're trying to help save our company, I'll hear you out."

"It's Gwen. She's in trouble and she needs a shark of a lawyer. Her husband is trying to get full custody of the kids."

"He doesn't even want to take them for the weekend, why would he want to get full custody?"

"This thing with me in the news. He's always hated me and hated our friendship. He got a consultation with every single lawyer in the town where they lived so she couldn't retain anyone."

"Oh, it's like that, is it?"

Something in Roderick's voice had changed. There was an edge of danger, but not for Lucky.

"Can you find her someone?"

"So you know if you're part of the problem, you need to step back. Your first instinct will be to fight me on this, but—"

Lucky knew her instincts had been right. "No, it's done. Or it will be."

"Good. And I don't need to find her someone. You did. I'll eat this guy for breakfast and still want a snack before lunch."

These words comforted Lucky more than she could say.

"By the way, if you need the ammo, he was having an affair with Nancy Slade. That's why I did what I did."

"The chopper will be at the castle in fifteen minutes. Be there."

Now, all she had left to do was text Gwen. Even though it was only a temporary goodbye, it felt like leaving their safe, warm house in the dead of a cold night to throw themselves to the wolves.

# Chapter 22

After Petunia, Jonquil, and Bluebonnet sent Lucky on her way, they looked at one another across the table, ice cream sodas abandoned.

"So, of course, this means war," Jonquil said matter-of-factly.

"Quite," Bluebonnet agreed.

"Let's take a moment here to celebrate our win," Petunia reminded them.

"What was the win? Our poor Ransom. Our poor Lucky. Those poor little babies," Jonquil said. "I can't imagine what Gwen is going through."

"Lucky! She's our win," Petunia said.

"How's that? She's had to tear her life apart," Jonquil said. "She's had to give up everything."

Petunia huffed. "This is just that part of the story. You always forget that they have to suffer through the darkest night before the dawn. *They* have to fight their monsters, Jonquil. We can't do it for them. We can only give them the tools."

Jonquil crossed her arms across her chest and huffed. "I would prefer the magic wand approach."

"I know you would, and you weren't listening when I offered it to Lucky. This was her test. Why must I explain this every time?"

"Oh, right!" Bluebonnet grinned widely. "Remember the

part about staying true to yourself? This is what Lucky is doing. Oh, it really is all going to be okay." Bluebonnet sagged with relief. "Why do I always forget that part, too?"

"It's easy to forget when our little loves suffer. We just want to make it all better for them, but we can't. That's not actually what we're for," Petunia said.

"When did you get so wise?" Bluebonnet asked her.

"When did you start to notice?" Petty teased.

Jonquil snorted.

"You have a special attachment to those babies, don't you?" Bluebonnet asked her.

"Yes," Jonquil grumped.

"Oh, sister. Tell us," Petty prodded excitedly.

"I don't want to. This is mine."

"Please?" Bluebonnet begged. "You're such a crunchy old thing and these babies got you right in the feelings. I must know."

"Ah, I suppose you must get used to disappointment." Jonquil flashed a self-satisfied grin.

"Come now. We love them, too." Petty nudged her sister with the tip of her wand, poking her in the side just enough to tickle her.

Jonquil giggled and then slapped Petty's wand away. "Oh, fine. Brittany knew exactly what I was. She saw straight through the veneers we wear for outsiders. She wasn't scared, or intimidated. She didn't doubt herself at all. She not only believed her own eyes, but this adorable child asked me to be her fairy godmother."

Bluebonnet put her hand over her heart. "You couldn't say no to that."

"Of course, I couldn't. Steven got very upset when she told him I wasn't his fairy godmother. So she told him how to ask me and he did, too."

"That's too precious," Petty said. "Look, we're already

filling the world with more love. Just look at us. I feel much more connected to you two now after all of this."

Bluebonnet feigned clutching her pearls. "Are you saying you didn't love us?"

"Silly goose," Jonquil muttered.

"I know, things had started to lose their color. Of course, I loved you both. Always. You're my sisters, but it wasn't an active, giving love. Even though things went incredibly wrong, this was still a good thing for all of us," Bluebonnet said. "I'm glad Lucky didn't wish it away."

"Fine," Jonquil conceded. "You're right. Me too. We wouldn't have our new charges without all of this."

"What is the update on Roderick's fairy godmother?" Petty asked.

"We can wait to burn that bridge when it's time to cross it," Bluebonnet said.

"Is she upset with us?" Petty raised a brow.

"Oh, more than you know. She doesn't like Gwen at all. She doesn't think they're a good fit," Bluebonnet replied.

"If she wanted to be the one arranging things, she should've arranged for someone to cover her missing shifts, I would think." Jonquil sniffed. "But that's none of my business."

They laughed together, the sound causing the herbs in the flowerboxes to grow and the rest of the plants in the kitchen to perk up as if they'd been drinking the best sunshine.

"I love Lucky's carnival idea. I think it has real potential to be something fun," Bluebonnet said.

"Me too," Jonquil replied. "I think we should plan it, but I also have a feeling that I haven't had in a long time."

"What's that?" Petty cocked her head to the side.

"That everything is going to be okay."

Petty's heart overflowed with love. "I think it will be, too. So you know what that means?"

"It's time for your favorite thing?" Bluebonnet grinned.

"Meddling," the three of them said in unison.

"My plan is to get the key players together. In fact, I think we should trot on down to Pick 'n' Axe for a pint and see if Rosebud, Grammy, and Fortune could meet us there."

"Maybe Ravenna, too. I wonder what she knows about kitsune. Lucky said she wanted all of her family at her wedding. Let's make it happen," Bluebonnet said.

"Wait, wait." Jonquil grabbed her sisters' hands. "Just because it's going to work out doesn't mean that Ransom and Lucky are going to get married."

"Yes, it does," Petty said.

"Rewind. There's still a lot of balls in the air." She cut a sharp look at Bluebonnet. "Don't do it."

Bluebonnet pressed her lips together, but it was no use. "Balls!" she spluttered with a giggle.

"I told you not to do it. I'm serious here."

"Serious is good, but levity is better," Petty said.

"I mean it. Ransom still has to summon his courage to do what needs to be done. First, he has to realize he wants her no matter what; and second, he has to make a grand gesture. I don't think that's going to happen. He's currently"—she put her finger up to check the wind direction—"on his way to Ecuador. What's he going to do from Ecuador?"

"He'll be back. Ransom already knows what he wants. He just has to face it."

"Okay, we'll roll with this, but I don't want to hear any complaining if he doesn't." She shook her head.

"Shall I get The Beast?" Petty asked hopefully.

"No," Jonquil and Bluebonnet said simultaneously.

"You two never want to have any fun," Petty pouted.

"You can take The Beast out if Ransom and Lucky get married on Valentine's Day."

A knock on the door surprised them, and they were never surprised by visitors. They always knew when company was coming. Things were changing in Ever After, and Petty could only have faith they would be for the better.

The sisters looked at one another, each unsure of what to do until Petty sprang to action.

When she opened the door, she saw that it was Rosebud and Grammy.

"We heard that the helicopter took Ransom and now Lucky. What's happened?" Rosebud asked.

"Yes, I thought the rehearsal went quite well. Where did we go wrong?" Grammy asked.

"Just the ladies we wanted to see. Can someone call Ravenna?" Bluebonnet asked.

"Ravenna? Oh, this must be serious." Grammy hooked her thumbs under her suspenders.

"I'll call her," Rosebud offered. She stepped back outside the door and held up a hand while singing a rather dark song.

A shiny black raven landed on her fingers and she whispered into the bird's ear, all the while petting his head. He cawed at her and flew off toward the bank.

"Thanks. I meant with the phone, but that will work, too." Petty shrugged.

"Sometimes the old ways work best." Rosebud stepped back inside.

It wasn't long until a black cloud of smoke manifested on the front steps of the happy little cottage. It formed into the shape of a woman. Ravenna.

Her black and purple hair hung in waves down her back, and she wore a floor-length black dress and a black crown that looked to be made of claws. A perfectly groomed, precisely arched black brow was raised in obvious curiosity.

"You called?" she drawled.

Petty seemed to recall a similar instance the last time they'd all been in the same space. There'd been a royal birth, a missed invitation, and a spinning wheel. . . .

That was neither here nor there, she supposed. It was ancient history for all of them.

Except from the expression on Ravenna's face, she'd forgotten nothing.

At least they didn't have to deal with her sister, Corvaxia. She was still mad that when the huntsman was to have returned with Snow's heart in a box, she'd instead gotten a geoduck. Which apparently was a very large saltwater clam that appeared to be a penis with a shell. So in essence, the huntsman had given her a dick in a box. She had not found it amusing.

"I don't actually have all day?"

"What do you know of kitsune?" Bluebonnet blurted.

"You're not even going to invite me in for one of your famous ice cream sodas?" Ravenna asked.

When no one answered for a long moment, Petty shifted uncomfortably. "Yes, of course. Please come in."

She flashed a large, vulpine smile. "Thank you. I'd hate to have to remind you what happens when I'm left out of invitations."

"Ugh," Rosebud grumbled. "Listen, this is about the whole town. Not just us."

Ravenna gave a dramatic roll of her eyes. "It's always something with you do-gooders, isn't it?"

"I suppose it is," Bluebonnet said happily, and scooted over to make room. "Sit by me."

Both of Ravenna's brows slid almost all the way up into her hairline. "Well, okay, then."

Jonquil hopped on board the welcome train, too. "I'll make you one of our famous sodas. Anyone else?"

No one said anything, and Jonquil made another for herself and one for Ravenna.

Ravenna waited for Jonquil to take the first drink and then tried her own. Her stern features softened into the beginning of a smile. "Okay, I'm appeased. So what is it you want to know? Kitsune?"

Everyone nodded.

"They're fox spirits. They used to walk the mortal world, but since the shift, the dying of the old magics, they retreated from the world. Much like us, but for some reason, crossing the barrier is hard for them unless they're in a human shape, which they can only do a few times. I'm not sure on the number."

"Is there any way to communicate with them?" Petty asked.

"You can give your message to a fox, but there's no guarantee he'll take it to the proper kitsune. He'll give it to the first one he sees." She sipped her soda. "Why all of this interest in them?"

"Never you mind that," Rosebud said.

"If you want me to help, I need to know all of the situation. For instance, if you were to have, say, a kitsune who had surrendered her immortality, I could use her blood to craft a portal. There are other things I could do as well. Like possibly a potion so that the fox spirits could be seen. They're all around us, along with other things. They're simply behind a veil."

"That sounds kind of terrifying, Ravenna. We don't want to set this girl up to meet her family and bring something ugly through. Or you make it so she can see fox spirits, but don't tell her she'll be able to see some kind of monster, too."

"I wouldn't do that. You came to me in good faith. You invited me into your home. You fed me. These are the laws of my people. If you'd said that out of any other wish than to protect your new friends, I'd be gravely insulted."

"As you should be," Jonquil said. "But not everyone knows the rules, Ravenna. If you'd like to be more actively involved in Ever After, we want you, but you need to communicate your needs to us."

"Oh no. This sounds like an intervention. I can't." She shook her head and stood.

"Don't leave. Please?" Petty asked her. "All Lucky wants is to have the family she never met at her wedding. Fortune would give anything to see her family. She traded it all for Lucky."

She cast a quick glance at Rosebud before looking back to Petty. "All right, then."

That's when it hit Petty with a brick. They'd never understood their own story! Rosebud was Ravenna's daughter.

Holy Fairy Dust on toast!

How had she missed it? Rosebud was a carbon copy of Ravenna. Her sweet, rosy lips were Ravenna's if they'd been painted black. The same curve of the cheek, the shape of the chin, the same large, wide eyes. Even the same eyebrows.

Petty couldn't believe she'd missed the eyebrows. They were the stuff of legend.

They weren't so intimidating on Rosebud because she was blond. Except when she furrowed her brow—even though she was all sunshine and light—it put her in mind of Ravenna's ferocity.

She couldn't wait to tell her sisters.

But first things first.

"What do you need from us, and how fast can we make this happen?"

"Wait, wait. I thought the wedding was pretend?" Ravenna asked. "With your groom gone, hasn't it been canceled anyway?"

"That was actually my concern. How are we going to pull off a wedding with no bride and no groom?" Rosebud asked.

"Lucky will be back and so will Ransom. We just have to get them together. Then fate will take its course," Petty said.

Ravenna rolled her eyes. "Oh, will it?"

"Maybe!" Rosebud argued. "How about we defer to the experts on this one? The godmothers have been doing this for a long time. When we need an expert on curses, that's when we'll ask you."

Ravenna growled, but didn't say anything else.

"Oh! Lucky owes me a favor. I can use that to get her in place, I'm sure," Rosebud said.

"Good thinking!" Grammy said. "What do you need me to do?"

"You need to be waiting close enough to know when you should come out and start the ceremony, but far enough away so if things get a bit more . . ."

"Passionate?" Ravenna offered.

"Exactly that," Bluebonnet finished.

"I can do that," Grammy agreed. "I can also spread the word. I'll get everyone else in place."

"Ravenna, do you have time to meet with Fortune today?" Petty asked.

"I suppose, but I need to speak with you. In private."

"It looks like we have a plan, then." Rosebud headed toward the door. "I'll be in touch to finalize plans. I do love a wedding." Rosebud hugged her arms around herself.

Grammy said, "I'll take that as my cue to skedaddle, too."

"This is coming together wonderfully. Thank you, everyone. We couldn't do it without you. Just wait until I tell you all about the spring carnival."

Grammy laughed. "Of course, there's already more shenanigans on the to-do list. Well, I for one can't wait. This has been the most fun I've had in a long time. See ya, kids."

It amused Petty to no end that Grammy called them "kids." Petty was probably a hundred times her age.

After Rosebud and Grammy were gone, Ravenna turned to Petty. "Must they know as well?"

Petty cringed. Of course Ravenna would know she'd figured out her secret. There was no point in pretending she didn't know. "I wish I could promise I won't tell them, but I'm already about to pop like an overfed tick. They're my sisters. I tell them everything."

"Can you at least promise that my secret will not leave this room?"

"Whatever it is, we won't tell a soul," Jonquil swore.

"Promise," Bluebonnet said.

"She must never, ever know." A look of sadness crossed Ravenna's face and she added, "Not ever."

"Far be it from me to meddle—," Petty began, but she was cut off by her sisters' cackling.

"Ooh, that's the damnedest lie I ever did hear out of your mouth, Petunia Blossom," Bluebonnet shrieked with laughter.

"All I'm saying is, maybe you should tell her," Petty finished. "I assume there's much she doesn't know. She thinks you're the villain."

"That keeps her safe," Ravenna answered. "I'm only going to say one more thing about it and I really don't even know why I'm explaining myself to you. I don't need your approval or anyone's."

"No, you don't, but we all need to be understood." Petty almost reached out a hand to Ravenna in support, but decided they weren't quite there yet.

"The spindle was never meant for her."

Petty's mouth dropped open. She had so many questions!

"Nope, that's it. I don't want to speak another word about it. If you really want to build a relationship with me, you'll respect this."

"Of course," Petty promised.

"I'll get to work and do some more research on the kitsune. I know I have a book somewhere that can help us." Ravenna disappeared in a shadow of bats that flew out of the window.

Petty looked out the window and saw that clouds to the west side of Ever After had parted and a new castle rose up behind the darker part of the Enchanted Forest. The Evil Queen had reclaimed her part of Ever After.

Jonquil coughed. "I think it's a good thing; I mean, villains are all the rage now."

"What's the secret?" Bluebonnet demanded.

"You mean you didn't figure it out? Fluff in your brainpan, Bon-Bon?" Jonquil answered.

"Rosebud." Petty conjured a picture of her out of smoke. Then she did the same for an image of Ravenna. "Ravenna. See? They're the same."

"No, they're . . . oh hell."

Bluebonnet slapped a hand to her forehead. "I see where this is going."

"What?" Petty asked, feigning innocence.

"No, absolutely not," Jonquil said in answer.

"I haven't even suggested anything yet." Petty bit her lip.

"Yet, the word is yet. I'm not trifling with Ravenna Black-heart. We just broke the ice with her and it's been how long? No," Jonquil insisted.

"But you know why she's Ravenna Blackheart? Do you?" she sing-songed.

"Aren't we busy enough without risking certain death?" Bluebonnet asked.

"No, you've forgotten our most important lesson," Petty said.

"I'm sure you're going to remind us." Jonquil sighed.

"Love is always worth the risk," Petty said. "Always."

"Better Ravenna than me, I say." Jonquil nodded.

"Why do I let you two talk me into these things? We haven't had a vacation in at least a century. When is it break time?" Bluebonnet pouted. "We've not even finished with Ransom and Lucky."

"We will be. I'm sure the wedding will happen on Valen-tine's Day."

"Wasn't St. Valentine beheaded?" Jonquil asked.

"Hush. Ransom is going to have his epiphany in five, four, three, two . . ."

# Chapter 23

Lucky called Gwen on the ride from the airport to the Heart's Desire headquarters.

She was going to text, but realized that was the coward's way out. If she was going to do this, she needed to actually do it.

"I heard a rumor," Gwen said when she answered the phone. "I heard you got on the chopper this morning. Where did you go?"

"I'm on my way to Heart's Desire's HQ. I spoke with my godmothers and Roderick, and we decided that we're going to tell the investors and the board that the wedding to me was just a publicity stunt that didn't work out."

"Roderick called me. Is this the price that he asked you to pay for his help, because if it is, I don't want it."

"No, not at all. This is me doing what I think is the best thing."

"Because Roderick told you it was the best thing?" Gwen asked.

"What do you mean?"

"He called me and told me how I shouldn't interfere with what you're doing, and I told him to go eat two dicks and not call me in the morning."

Lucky swallowed hard. "Take the help, Gwen. I made this choice, but not on my own. I talked to my mother, to the godmothers."

"You didn't talk to me. You didn't ask me what I thought was best."

"You're right, because I would never put you in that position. I love you, Gwen. I love those kids more than anything. I will not be the weapon he uses against you."

Gwen let out a small sob. "What am I going to do without you?"

"You're not without me. Not at all. This is only temporary. We're going to be old and gray and living next door to each other just like we promised. Best friends. Forever."

"I will absolutely hold you to that promise. Tell me where else you're going. Just so I know you're safe."

"After I fix this part of my Grand Mal Fuckup, I'm going to talk to Nancy."

"She doesn't deserve your apology."

"It's not for her. It's for me. I've spent a lot of time thinking about what I want to do with my life. Who I want to be. So this is a quest, you could say. I'm on a mission to reclaim myself."

"If you'd just said that to start with, I wouldn't have been sitting here chewing my fingernails off with worry."

"Roderick has said he'll help you in any way that he can. Let him. The godmothers, too."

"Any other orders, bossy pants?"

"Yeah, kiss those monsters for me. Tell them I'm on a quest, if they ask. Tell them Aunt Lucky is going to be her own hero."

"I'm going to tell them that Aunt Lucky is our hero, too. Don't stay gone too long, okay? I have Ever After gossip."

"Ooh, tell!"

"Nope, not until you come back," Gwen teased.

"You know I travel for tea."

"Don't we all?" Gwen was quiet for a long moment. "No matter what's going on with me, you know if you need me, you can call."

"I know. I will. I'll be back soon. Promise."

"Good. Or I'll have to come kick your butt."

"I'll see you soon," Lucky said. "Love you."

"Love you more." Then Gwen hung up so she got the last word.

Lucky knew with every fiber of her being that she'd finally set herself on the right path. She found it a strange dichotomy that she was both ready to get all of this off of her chest, but still nervous at the thought of confession.

When the car stopped, and the door opened, she'd never been more grateful to see a familiar face.

Roderick held his hand out to her, looking every inch a corporate shark. That also gave her comfort. If she was swimming with a shark, the other predators couldn't make her prey.

"You ready?"

"Yes and no. I kinda feel like I'm going to throw up."

"Hmm. There will be a man sitting to your left. His name is Anthony Searle. He's the one who orchestrated the take-over, so if you puke, do hit him in the face. If you're able to control the stream."

"So noted."

Roderick put his hand on her back to guide her through the glass doors and toward the elevator. He nodded to the security team, who simply nodded and allowed them to pass. Roderick entered a card into the control panel and hidden numbers lit up. He typed in a code, and the elevator doors closed.

"If you have a chance, do you think you could persuade Gwen to accept my help? I can't exactly follow through on that favor if she won't speak to me."

"I spoke to her on the way here. She was just concerned about me."

"Yes, she thought I'd influenced your decision. That I was cruel to you." Roderick cleared his throat. "I know I was harsh, but outright cruelty wasn't my intention."

No, just cruel enough to get her to do what he wanted.

Only she couldn't be angry at him. She'd already proved she'd go to the same lengths to protect those she loved.

"It's okay. As you know, I've done things myself."

"I'd like us to be friends, Lucky. I don't know what the future holds, but I think it'd be a boon to both of us to have the other in our corners."

"I'd like that."

The elevator stopped and opened into a small anteroom outside of a wall of glass. Four men and three women who looked like they guarded the gates to the afterlife sat in that room, all dressed in what looked to be the same suit.

"Please tell me I don't have to go in alone," she said. "I know I'm supposed to slay a dragon here but . . ."

"I'm running the meeting. I have to go in with you."

"You didn't tell him I was here, did you?"

"Of course not. He'd try and stop you. Look, we've bought up as many shares as we could, but the ones who will sway this in our favor are in this room. Not to add any pressure or anything. I think your confession could persuade them to sell to us instead of Searle."

"It'll be nice to actually be the lucky charm instead of the cooler."

Roderick opened the door for her and Lucky stepped inside the room. It smelled of industrial window cleaner, burnt coffee, and a wisp of chocolate.

He entered right behind her and motioned to a seat behind him, and she sat there, happy to have his body between her and the rest of the room.

"That coffee smells like burning tar. Who did that?" Roderick asked. "You know HQ is only supposed to smell like fresh coffee and chocolate. Ransom leaves for five seconds and this is what you do?"

"Ransom has a bigger problem than burned coffee," Searle said. "He has a drowning cacao farm and a non-majority stock position in a company where the board has what we call a loss of faith in the CEO."

"I know what it's called, Searle. Thank you for that update. Before we get into the business at hand—"

"Where's Payne? Why isn't he addressing the board in this time of crisis?" a woman asked.

"Amanda, he's in Ecuador dealing with the plant. Before anyone says anything, no, we're not cutting our losses. At least as long as Ransom is in charge. You should think about that. He doesn't let anyone who works for him crash and burn. Searle can't say the same thing."

"I wouldn't dream of trying," Searle spoke. "Investing is a risk. So if you lose, you lose. I'm not here to save anyone. We all know the risks."

"As I said, before we get into this today, I've brought someone to speak to you. May I present Lucky Fujiki?"

Lucky swallowed hard and stepped up next to Roderick. She looked around the table and made eye contact with each person, even though Searle looked like he was about to ask her for a gold coin to cross the River Styx.

"I'm Lucky Fujiki and I have a confession to make."

Searle's laughter interrupted her. "Should we be in the same building with this woman? Just sitting close to her we might all get syphilis or something."

Rather than take offense or get angry, Lucky smiled. "No, you don't get syphilis from sitting next to someone. They should've covered that in health class. Speaking to a further lack in your education, your mother should've taught you not to interrupt when other people have the floor. It's not your turn yet."

Searle held up his gnarled hands. "By all means. I surrender."

"Thank you." She looked back to each of the seven people around the table. "I'm afraid that I've not been honest."

Searle laughed dismissively, but she ignored him.

She also ignored the tremble in her belly and her shaking hands. Instead, she made a tour of the room as she spoke.

"Ransom Payne and I share a trio of adorable godmothers. You know that he's an orphan, right? Well, they basically raised him. They're just the loveliest old dears. Petunia, Blue-bonnet, and Jonquil Blossom. They live together in the cutest cottage in the most ridiculous place you can imagine. Ever After, Missouri. The silliest thing, am I right?"

"Yes, Miss Fujiki. That's quite silly," one of the men answered.

"They started a little wedding planning business called Fairy Godmothers, Inc. A place where dreams come true. As you can imagine, a little town like Ever After hasn't ever been on anyone's radar."

"Don't tell me this was some kind of publicity stunt gone wrong. I don't buy it," Searle said.

Lucky wasn't sure what possessed her, but she was tired of Searle's nonsense. The fact that he breathed her air irritated her to start with, but she was doing her best. So she flicked the back of his ear.

"If you insist on interrupting me like a child, I will treat you like a child. May I continue?"

Searle didn't say anything, and she could feel Roderick's amusement echoing off of him in waves.

"Yes, friends. It was a publicity stunt. If your dear old grannies were trying to start a business, wouldn't you do anything they asked you to? They gave Ransom the seed money to start this business. So when they asked us both if we would pretend to get married for some good publicity, of course we said yes."

She continued to walk around the room. "You all can't surely believe that another human being is bad luck? That's superstitious silliness that has no place in an educated brain."

"I don't know. You've got quite the track record," Amanda said.

"I do. Because I'm uncoordinated. That happens to a lot of us."

"How do you explain what happened to that reporter?" someone else asked. "That sounded like a lot of bad luck."

Lucky nodded. "That's what it was. Just bad luck. That had zero to do with me."

"We could believe that if it were only one person. But that taken in conjunction with Nancy Slade?"

"Coincidence. Not to mention, personal anecdotes do not scientific research make. I'll spill some tea. Nancy Slade made her own bed by having an affair with a married man. That might be karma, but not bad luck. And even if you did buy into all of that, it doesn't matter since Ransom and I definitely aren't getting married. If you're worried simply about my proximity to him, you have an option. You can let Ransom buy you out with a golden parachute. He wants his company back. I wouldn't stand in his way."

"Is that a threat?" Searle asked.

"No, not at all. It's just when you see a human being who is as absolutely driven and devoted to a task as Ransom Payne, it would probably be easier to just get out of his way. For the rest of you, I think you've mistaken his kindness for weakness. Yes, Ransom has a very big heart, but he also knows that a company has two main assets. Money and people. He's preserving the assets. In the long run, he's saving money. He's instilling a loyalty in his employees and by retaining them, he's keeping quality standards by making sure he has skilled labor. He's in Ecuador right now fighting for this company and the people who work here, while you've got Searle over here counting his stacks of gold like Scrooge."

She waited for her words to sink in before she spoke again. "I myself recently had to decide who I wanted to be and then make some changes in my behavior. Who do you want to be? Choose your actions accordingly." She turned to look at Roderick for a moment. "And thank you for your time."

Lucky headed toward the door.

"If you'll wait a moment, I'll see you out?" Roderick asked her.

She nodded and waited for him outside the glass doors. She saw him hand out packets of proposals and what looked to be legal papers. Many of the people inside at that table turned to look at her before they put their pens to the papers.

Lucky hoped that meant what she thought it did, that her speech had helped Ransom save his company.

Roderick exited and walked her to the elevator. "I think it worked. We'll get a majority. When we take the company private, Searle will want out, if he doesn't already. You were wonderful in there."

"Thanks. I know I've been kind of on it with asking for favors lately, but could I hitch another ride in the chopper and maybe have the car service for a little longer?"

Roderick raised a brow. "Are you planning on flying to Ecuador to chase him down? You'd have to borrow the jet for that."

Lucky looked down at her feet. "No, that's finished. I need to visit Nancy and Melvin. I was serious when I told you I was going to fix this. I could travel commercial, but I have to get back to Ever After somehow when I'm done."

Roderick laughed. "I'll call the pilot and let him know you have a couple stops to make."

"Thanks, Roderick. For everything."

Roderick opened the elevator for her. "Take care, Lucky."

Once she was back in the car, she gave the driver Nancy Slade's address. Lucky could only hope that she was home, and that the woman would speak to her.

The ride to Nancy's neighborhood didn't take long. She lived in a McMansion cul-de-sac that made Lucky's artistic sensibility try to physically crawl out of her body to avoid looking at it a second more.

As luck would actually have it, Nancy was getting out of

her new Escalade and ushering the kids into the house when Lucky got out of the car.

"Fire!" Nancy screamed as soon as she saw her. "FIRE!"

Lucky held up her hands. "What are you doing? I'm just here to talk. I'm not going to hurt you."

"Fire!" she screamed again.

Her children began looking around, ostensibly for the fire.

"I don't understand. Are you actually on fire?" Lucky searched for signs of smoke or flame.

"No, you awful creature. People don't respond to cries for help, so you yell fire." Nancy directed her kids to go the rest of the way into the house and close the door. "You're lucky I don't call the police."

Was she lucky? She tried not to snicker, because this definitely wasn't the time or the place.

"I came to tell you I'm sorry."

"Did you?" Nancy eyed her like a hawk would a field mouse. "Well, I'm definitely not recanting what I said to that reporter. Every bit of it was true."

"As is the part where you had an affair with my best friend's shitty husband."

To her surprise, Nancy's stance relaxed and she rubbed a hand over her face. "I knew that was wrong before you cursed me. I was sorry for it before then, too."

Lucky was reminded again how she was on the right path.

"Can you take the curse off? I know what I did was wrong, I'm just trying to raise my children and get by."

"I'm trying," Lucky said.

"I know Gwen left him. Is she okay?"

Lucky debated answering. She wasn't sure if this was some kind of ploy to get information for Jake to use against her or what exactly Nancy was up to.

"Can you tell her I'm sorry?"

"I'm discovering the way this works is that you have to do it yourself."

"I was so jealous of her. No matter what she did, what obstacles were thrown in her path, she still had this perfect life."

"The grass is always greener, I guess." Lucky took a deep breath.

Nancy nodded. "I actually miss the PTA meetings with her. Any challenge I had, I could just throw them at her and she'd find a solution. It's boring as hell without her."

"That's the ultimate crime, isn't it? You can be as awful as you like as long as you're not boring."

Nancy snorted. "That's kind of my motto. But hey, I'll apologize to her myself, but can you tell her I'm not with him? That's important to me. He definitely wasn't worth it."

Lucky decided to share a piece of news with her. Maybe she could help. "He decided to go for full custody."

"He *what*? I have a PI on retainer. If I dig up some dirt on him, maybe she'll forgive me."

"She might." Lucky nodded. "Thanks for hearing me out. You know, after the screaming."

"That's what I'd want."

"Maybe after things settle down, you can bring your kids to Ever After. It's a long way for a playdate, but I think they'd have fun."

As a strange, stray thought formed in the back of Lucky's mind, she had to wonder if maybe she was blood-related to her godmothers somehow. She had the strangest sudden urge to meddle.

Nancy would be a *great* project for the godmothers.

Lucky noticed that she'd started seeing the opportunities for love and forgiveness everywhere. She wanted to throw it all around like fairy dust.

Maybe it was actual fairy dust, she didn't know.

Like Petunia said, love was for everyone.

Even the awful Melvin James, who was next on her list of amends.

# Chapter 24

Ransom was in the car on his way from his hotel to meet with the new Minister of the Interior, Elizabeth Serrano, when his phone exploded with texts from the godmothers, Roderick, and Gwen.

*Bluebonnet: Calllll mmmmmeeeeeeee. Naow.*

*Roderick: Call me when you get a chance. Good news.*

*Gwen: Call. Me.*

Ransom smiled to himself at all the different incarnations of the same general message. Bluebonnet had insisted that learning to text was learning another language and she'd thrown herself into it heartily.

He found it completely adorable that even though she now knew how to speak that language that she still called them "texturals."

Ransom knew Roderick had some trick up his sleeve to get the last shares they needed, so he must've pulled it off, which was a frigging miracle. He could walk into this meeting with all the confidence of a man who had complete control over his assets and his company. He could make any promises he chose.

Gwen's text, however, seemed like an admonishment in itself.

They were all going to have to wait until after his meeting with Ms. Serrano.

His car rolled to a stop and a security force opened the

door to greet him. He passed through their security procedures with little trouble. He'd been prepared. He didn't have so much as a pen on him. The only things he carried with him were his phone and his Rolex. The first thing he'd bought himself when he realized he could not only pay rent, but buy a house, pay all of his bills, and still have money left over. It was a bit of a good-luck charm.

Just thinking of it, much like anything else these days, brought Lucky to the front of his mind.

He wondered what it would take to get her out of his head?

Self-induced amnesia? A concussion? Hypnotherapy?

After he was thoroughly searched, scanned, and found safe, he was led to a private dining room, where a table waited for him covered with crisp white linen. He was instructed to sit down and the security forces stood at the entrance and exit.

Serrano entered the room dressed in a white suit, with white heels that made a clipped sound with each step she took. Her white hair was swept up in a bun, and the only contrast was the brown of her sun-kissed skin. She was a force to be reckoned with that radiated power.

Ransom adored her.

He stood as she approached and they air-kissed cheeks.

"Ransom, it's very good to see you, but I am sorry that it's under such circumstances," Elizabeth said in a smooth voice with a rich accent.

"Me as well, Elizabeth."

"Just to get it out of the way before dinner, I'm afraid we don't have the answer you were hoping for."

Ransom refused to let his mind play out the worst scenarios he could imagine. She hadn't spoken yet. He tried to keep an open mind.

"Go on."

"The vote was taken to rebuild the dam and the resolution failed. New information came to us that the building of the dam harmed the ecosystem and this will set that area back to rights. The government, however, is prepared to buy those lands back from you at the price you paid."

No, this wasn't the answer he wanted. He had no idea where he was going to rebuild, how long it would take. There were a lot of moving parts to consider.

"Is it true that you are still paying your workers?" she asked.

"Yes, I plan to keep paying them until I can get them back to work at new farms and at a new processing plant."

"We'll need to see proof from your books, but if that's true, we will allow you to purchase the same amount of land you lost on Cacao Ridge."

It was every chocolatier's dream to get cacao from the Ridge. It was a mostly protected land, and few were ever allowed to purchase land there.

"Also, of course, you must maintain your current environmental standards. Provide low carbon footprint transportation up and down from the Ridge, affordable green housing, and we want your operation to be plastic-free."

"None of that is a problem."

"Not even plastic-free?"

"It was one of my goals for the company. Since I have to start from scratch, I can rebuild however I'd like. I'll be applying for solar panel permits as well."

"This is exactly the response we were hoping for. Lawyers will draw up the contracts and we'll get this pushed through. I anticipate we could have you on course to be operational in six months, if you're willing to spend the money to update the village. While, of course, being mindful of local heritage."

"Choose my advisors and I'll get them hired on right away."

Elizabeth flashed him a big smile. "This is a pet project of mine, Ransom. I've been watching your company very closely since you first opened your doors. I've wanted to bring modernization to these areas, but keep our footprint small.

We needed corporate money to do that. Someone like you who doesn't balk at the initial cash investment and who has the same ideas about stewardship that we do. So, your advisor will be me."

A thrill shot through him at the prospect. "Elizabeth, I can safely say that I'm overjoyed not to have gotten the news I'd hoped for. This is so much better."

"I'll admit, at first I was a little skeptical of a man who takes business advice from his godmothers, but when they're right, they're right."

"They're always right," he admitted.

"Have you told them this?"

"Of course not. They know it."

Elizabeth laughed. "If you won't be terribly insulted, I have another meeting I need to fit in today and don't have time for an actual meal. I wanted to make sure I delivered this news in person, though."

"It was lovely to see you." He stood as she did.

She leaned over to air-kiss his cheek again. "I'll be in touch soon. Stay and enjoy the food. I had them make your favorite."

Ransom sat back down as servers brought out a ridiculously large tray of llapingachos: potato omelets stuffed with cheese and fried crisp, served with various proteins, avocado, and peanut sauce.

As he ate, he thought about his godmothers.

First, he wanted to ask them to learn to make llapingachos with him, and second, the part where they were always right.

If they were always right, what the hell was he doing in Ecuador while Lucky was in Ever After, thinking that he was afraid of her luck?

When he thought about all the people he wanted to tell of his victory, the first person on the list wasn't Roderick.

It was Lucky.

He wanted to share this moment with her.

The win wasn't as sweet without her.

It was a double-edged sword because it had taken almost losing his company to realize how much he loved what he did. How much it still mattered to him. He was still passionate about this behemoth he'd built.

Ransom wanted Lucky, too.

Another realization slapped him in the face with all the force of a brick. Even if Lucky was bad luck, he could've withstood it, if only he'd been brave enough to do it.

After they'd had the best sex of his life, the world had come crashing down around their ears. Instead of standing by her and rebuilding together, he'd run away to hold on to the ashes of a life that was no longer his.

Even if Searle had succeeded in taking his company, the company would've failed and Ransom could've started again. Elizabeth wouldn't have given this opportunity to Searle.

Another epiphany slapped him in the face.

This time, instead of a wrecking ball, it was a brick.

Every single thing that had happened to him had been a blessing in disguise.

When he kissed her under the cherry tree, it had given the godmothers more magic.

When they'd fallen through the floor, it had been the catalyst for Lucky to learn about magic.

When the dam had failed, it had been the answer to a problem.

When his stocks tanked, he'd been able to regain control of his company.

When Searle tried to take his company from him, it reminded him how much he loved what he built.

When the government said they weren't going to reconstruct the dam, he'd been given an opportunity to rebuild and expand his business in a way he'd never dreamed.

If only he'd been a better man.

He didn't deserve her. He knew that. Only instead of sitting on that fact and trying to hatch it like a rotten egg, he was going to change it.

He called Roderick first. He couldn't eat and talk to his godmother at the same time and he was starving.

"So it's good news?" Ransom asked as soon as Roderick answered.

"Almost unanimous buyout. We had to go top tier on all the offers, but we did it. Or rather Lucky did it."

"*What?*"

"Lucky talked to the godmothers, and they decided together to tell the board about the fake wedding. Searle was brutal, but Lucky didn't take any of his shit."

"Did she hug him? Oh no."

"Nothing like that at all. She may have flicked his ear like a little kid once or twice, and I'll admit I found it highly satisfying."

"I don't understand."

"She gave this rousing speech like you were some general off to lead your troops to victory. She really does love you, Ransom. So do your godmothers."

"I didn't want them to do that."

"They knew it. Which is why we didn't tell you until it was done. Tell me there's good news on your end."

"The answer on the dam wasn't what we wanted. It's better."

"How can it be better? Did they find some secret Mayan spice or something no one's known about for a hundred years or what?"

"They're giving us purchase rights on the Ridge."

"Say that again?"

"The Ridge. I've got a proposal I need to show you once I get back stateside. Now that I know our ship isn't the *Titanic*, draw up those papers for partner, my friend."

"This is fantastic news, Ransom. We did it. We won."

"You don't sound as ecstatic as I would've expected."

"I am, I'm just dealing with a little more drama in Ever After."

"Tell me."

"Has Gwen tried to call you?"

"I have a text from her."

"Jake is taking her to court for the kids."

That was the moment he knew that Gwen had found a champion in Roderick. "What do you need?"

"Some time to bury him, and any legal team he's hired, in paperwork and motions until shit sticks to the moon."

"Take it. Obviously."

"You're going back to Ever After, aren't you?"

"My godmothers live there, so it's a strong possibility." Ransom took another bite.

"You know what I mean. You're going back for Lucky, aren't you?"

"I want to, but I have to figure out how to fix this. I left her when she was at her most vulnerable. She told me what happened between us in Grammy's was her worst fear come to life. I can't undo that."

"Ugh, now I feel like crap for being part of that. I was trying to protect you and the company."

"I know. She knows. It might be easier if she could be angry with me. If she didn't understand, but she did. Every step of the way."

Roderick blew out a loud breath. "We're going to have a real wedding, aren't we?"

"If she'll have me. I want the rest of my life with her. When I got the news about the Ridge today, I hate to say that you weren't the first one I wanted to call."

"Why didn't you call her?"

"The things I need to say to her deserve to be said in person."

"You better get on it, then, my friend."

He didn't like the tone in Roderick's voice. "What do you mean?"

"She's trying to give Gwen some distance while she fights this thing. The basis for Jake's case is that Lucky is dangerous to the kids. So she's on this tour of amends before she goes to Paris with her mother."

"You know what? Just when you think you've buried Jake Borders in enough paperwork and motions, you should do at least ten more. I hope he never, for the rest of his life, ever, catches a light interchange green again."

"And this, folks, is why Petty is your godmother."

"It could be worse. I could've wished him to get anal warts."

"Fair," Roderick said.

"I have to call Bluebonnet and Gwen. I'll see you when I get back."

"I'll meet you in Ever After. I can work from the mushroom cottage," he said.

Ransom found it mighty interesting that he hadn't planned on getting a room at the castle. He wanted to stay close to Gwen.

Yes, indeed, the godmothers were always right.

When he realized that, that was when hope bloomed like a delicate flower. If the godmothers were always right, they'd said that he and Lucky would get their Happily Ever After.

They'd get the fairy tale.

He'd been through the dark night, and he failed. He'd been a coward. So Ransom had to own that now, and he had to run a different gauntlet.

He'd surrender his pride and beg if he had to.

Most importantly, he had to prove himself. He'd made her many promises he hadn't been able to keep.

Ransom would put his trust in love. In his godmothers.

Most importantly, he'd put his faith in Lucky.

# Chapter 25

With all of Ransom's resources at her disposal, it hadn't been hard to find Melvin James.

Instead of surprising him like she had Nancy, she'd called him to see if he'd meet with her.

He'd agreed, as long as it was in public and she didn't touch him.

They met at a small café in downtown Springfield.

Lucky found him to be the same unpleasant man she'd met at the junket.

"So what do you want? To tell your side of it?" he asked as soon as she sat down at the table with him.

"In a sense."

"I'm not interested. I don't know how you did it, but you did it on purpose."

"You're right. I did."

He held up a finger and pointed it at her, but he didn't say anything.

"I also wanted to tell you that it was wrong, and I'm sorry."

"You almost ruined my life. Of course, it was wrong."

She wanted to tell him that maybe if he weren't such a jerk, then maybe people wouldn't want to destroy his life. Blaming him for her actions wasn't what she'd come here for.

"That's all I wanted to say. If you don't have anything else you'd like to say to me, I'll be going and leave you in peace." She started to stand up.

"Sit down," he demanded.

"If you don't care about my apology, and don't have anything you'd like to say, what are we supposed to do? Sit here and stare at each other all day long?"

"Questions, girl. I have questions. You're going to answer them. If you're actually sorry."

"I will answer to the best of my ability, if it's my question to answer."

He nodded. "That's fair. You don't have the right to tell other people's stories unless they give you that right."

"You told my story without my permission," she couldn't help but counter.

"No, I told my own story. Are you going to let me ask my questions?"

She signaled the server and ordered a coffee. "Now, I'm going to let you ask your questions," she said to him.

"When did you know you could do that?"

She was tempted to ask if he meant order coffee, but she knew what he wanted to know. "I've always been what you would call clumsy. Things break around me. People sometimes catch my clumsy." She shrugged. "With Nancy, it was a lark. I'd never done it before, but I was so angry at her I wanted to. I wanted to rub bad luck all over her."

"The same with me?"

"Yes," she admitted.

"You and Ransom actually dated in college. Were all of those stories true?"

Lucky nodded. "The Boy Who Missed thing was all my fault. We'd just been trying to get somewhere for so long, and I was so upset, I thought it was me. In those situations, no one wants to be the one who is at fault. It's a self-esteem killer. The words got past my tongue before I could stop myself. It stuck."

"Was your wedding real?"

"No, we just wanted to help our godmothers."

"That's a noble pursuit, I reckon."

"Well, a lesson learned. Bad things done for a good reason are still bad. I've apologized to Nancy, I've done what I could to fix the damage to Ransom's company, and I've said my apologies to you. I'm doing the best that I can."

"I'm afraid it's my turn to confess something. Just like you got us to Ever After on false pretenses, I'm here with a secret of my own."

"Good grief. What could you possibly have to drop on me now?"

"More of a question, really. Are you an only child?"

"Yes."

"Are you Fortune Fujiki's natural-born child, or are you adopted?"

The importance of what he asked her slammed into her.

"Oh, please no," she murmured.

"I don't like it either, honestly. But we should know."

"My mother said my father's name was James."

"Melvin." He pointed to himself. "James."

"No."

"Probably."

"Let's not and say we didn't?" Lucky offered.

"Fine by me," he said.

Only, they both sat there for a long time in heavy silence until the server brought Lucky's coffee.

"Thank you," she said.

"When I saw your mother at the junket, I got the shock of my life. I never expected to see her again."

"So I've been told."

"I tried to find her a few years after I got married and had other children."

"That's all well and good, but if you thought I was your daughter, why did you write that story?"

"I knew if we got to this part of the conversation, you'd

ask me that. I still don't have an answer. I think I was jealous that you grew up fine without me and you didn't need me."

"You're not supposed to be jealous of your children. You're supposed to want good for them."

"I know that. I feel awful. It's why I've been such a jackass. I hope you can forgive me."

"Words are easy. It's actions that matter."

"I'd like to come back to Ever After and maybe have lunch with you and your mother and we could all talk about where to go from here."

"You're mean when you get your feelings hurt," Lucky blurted.

"Runs in the family, it seems."

There was no way on earth that this man in front of her could be her father. Her father's name was James, it wasn't Melvin James.

Melvin.

No.

Except the way he looked at her had changed. There was something in the tilt to his head.

"How's your mother been?"

How would her mother feel about all of this? Lucky wondered briefly if this was a ploy to get revenge on her for the bad luck, but she didn't think so.

"If you really think you're my father, let me hug you again."

He looked stricken, but he nodded. He stood up and held open his arms.

Lucky hugged him and remembered her wish to her godmothers. She'd wanted all of her family at her wedding.

She released him and he sat down again, looking around the room in a panic.

"I think you're fine, but I appreciate your willingness to face certain doom to prove you believe what you told me."

"Ask your mother."

"I will." It was possible that her mother hadn't recognized him. He didn't look anything like the way her mother had described her father and if he'd told her that his name was James, she wouldn't have made the connection.

"Did she by chance come with you?"

"No, she's waiting for me to get back so we can go to Paris. After all of this, we need a vacation."

"I can see why you would." He nodded slowly. "Tell me more about your childhood. Did your mother ever marry?"

"No, my mother had no interest in marriage. Or relationships more than casual. She had to leave her family to have me."

"But you did get along okay? You had everything you needed?"

"I did. I spent a lot of summers in Ever After with my godmothers. It's a great place to be a kid. It was magical for me. I'm very lucky."

For the first time, she actually believed it. She believed her name wasn't a curse.

She wasn't a curse.

"I'm sorry, but I have to go. We have each other's numbers to stay in touch."

"I meant what I said. Ask your mother if I can call her."

"I will."

"Another hug?"

"You're a glutton for punishment, huh?"

"You bet."

She allowed the hug, and it was a little less awkward this time. A little more like something she might even look forward to. Someday. She made a quick exit. This was not what she'd been expecting, yet it was exactly what she asked for.

On the way back to Ever After, Lucky felt as if she'd been reborn. She'd scrubbed all of the old barnacles off, the things that clung to her like fear and shame. She'd been able to shed them after she'd faced them.

Lucky had needed to take this journey.

She'd found herself.

She'd saved herself.

Lucky Fujiki was ready to live her life.

Whatever came, good or bad, she knew now she was ready to deal with it. Ready to be open, vulnerable, and she wasn't afraid to love or be loved.

She'd wanted that love to be with Ransom, but she'd faced that fear, too. Even if he didn't feel the same way about her as she felt about him, that wasn't the end of the world.

Losing him was no longer her worst fear.

If he didn't love her, it didn't change her worth.

"Welcome to the rest of your life," Lucky whispered to herself as the castle came into view.

Castles. Plural.

One white and one black.

A lot had happened since she'd been gone for an afternoon.

As soon as she landed, she ran from the helipad to her mother's room to find her much as she'd left her.

She was still sitting in the morning sun, eating. This time, it was tacos from this place she loved in Texas. Her arm was bandaged.

"What happened?"

"Oh, I had an interesting lunch with an evil queen. It was all very exciting. How did your errands go? You look like a completely new woman."

"I feel like one. I had some realizations while I was making amends."

"Oh? Is there to be a wedding after all, then?"

"No, of course not. That would be ridiculous."

"No more ridiculous than seven dwarves named after beers. Or a werewolf who bakes," Fortune said casually.

"Or a father who came to his long-lost daughter's press junket."

Fortune spat out her water. "Excuse me? What did you say?"

"Oh, I believe you heard me."

"Yes, I heard you, daughter of mine. The problem is, I'm not understanding. Those words strung together in that particular way make zero sense to me. It's all road noise."

"Melvin James. The one who wrote that awful story about me?"

"Why, that grifter! That man is not your father. I would know."

"I didn't think he looked anything like the way you described him; you said his name was James, not Melvin, although I'd go by James, too, if my name was Melvin. He said he looked for us after he got married. He said his wife knows about you and me. He asked me to give you his number."

"Yes, give it to me right now. Then when he tries to extort money out of us, we'll have him caught red-handed."

Lucky gave her the number, and Fortune typed it into her phone and then put the phone down. Then picked it up. Then put it down once again.

"Ma, if you want to call him, I can wait."

"I do not want to call him. I don't know if I'm more furious that it could be him, or that someone would try to use this to hurt us. Either way, I'm livid."

"I figured we could just start packing for Paris."

"Oh, honey. I know you don't want to go to Paris."

"Yes, I do." Lucky put her hands on her hips.

"Maybe you do want to go," Fortune conceded. "You don't want to go right now. Your heart is here in Ever After."

"It is, Ma. It's with you, too. I want a trip with my mother." Lucky smiled. "It seems like I'm getting everything I asked for. So let's get packed."

Gwen rushed through the door with the kids right behind her.

"Oh no, what could I do?" Fortune said in a mocking voice. "Oh well, she's here. Might as well hug her."

Brittany wrapped herself around Lucky's left leg, and Steven chose her right. Gwen hugged her tight.

"You're back!"

"When I said this was temporary, we both knew I meant longer than the afternoon," Lucky said.

"Maybe you did, but I decided it was long enough," Gwen said.

She looked to her mother. "I thought you were the one who told me to take myself out of the equation."

"Mm-hmm. That was until I saw that Roderick had taken on her case. Nancy agreed to be a witness for Gwen after your visit."

"That's amazing," Lucky cried. "I almost can't believe it."

"Me either," Gwen said. "She called and offered her apology, her support. We talked for a long time. I guess I'm supposed to be mad at her, but I'm not. Not anymore. I don't want to fight a death match over a man who doesn't love me. That's canceled. If he wants to see the kids, I'll let him. I mean, I want him to want to be a dad, but this punitive behavior . . . the kids deserve better than that, too."

"They do. They're the best monsters in the world." She hauled Steven up into her arms and smooched his cheek. "The sugariest!"

Steven giggled and smooched her cheek back. "No, you."

Almost everything had started to work out exactly as she'd hoped.

Did that mean she and Ransom would, too?

Even though she loved him, he hadn't believed in her. He hadn't trusted her, and while she understood why, she really did, Lucky had come to believe she deserved better than that.

She wanted Ransom, but she didn't want any half measures. She wanted someone who was either all in or nothing at all.

She wanted the fairy tale.

She wanted the Happily Ever After.

If Ransom couldn't get with the program, it was time for her to move on.

That didn't mean she'd stop loving him. Lucky believed that real love was forever. It could grow and change in so many ways, and the root system was still there, nourished in the fertile soil of the heart.

So yes, she'd always love Ransom Payne.

But Lucky was ready for a mature love that would last her all the days of her life. Not only was she ready for a real partner, but she was also ready to *be* a real partner.

She refused to settle for anything less.

# Chapter 26

Ransom Payne, CEO, billionaire, and grown man, had come home to his godmothers' house to ask their advice on how to fix his relationship with Lucky.

"What do I do?" he said to the circle of three women sitting at their kitchen table.

"Well, Ransom. It's good that you took that first step and admitted that you were absolutely, unequivocally, patently wrong," Bluebonnet said.

"Should we take this to mean"—Petty faked a gasp—"that you want us to"—she faked another for effect—"meddle?"

"Hmmmmm?" Jonquil added for good measure.

"Yes, Godmothers. Yes, meddle. Do whatever you want. I just want to win Lucky back."

"Good." Petty clapped her hands together. "We roll ready to fight."

"Wait, I don't want to fight," Ransom said, panicked.

Bluebonnet patted his hand. "It's just a saying, dear."

"So you three have a plan? Will you clue me in on it?"

"Hmm. You know how these things go, Ransom. Sometimes, you have to ask for what you want," Jonquil said.

"I did ask. I asked for advice."

"Advice is usually rather useless. It's either unsolicited, which is the very worst, or you do ask for it, and what you're looking for is someone to tell you what you want to hear. Let's cut out the middle man. What do you want to hear?" Petty asked.

"I want to hear that she'll forgive me. I want to hear that she still loves me. I want to hear that . . . I want to hear . . ." He was startled by the direction of his own thoughts. "I want to hear that she'll spend the rest of her life with me. I want to hear that she'll marry me tomorrow. I want the freaking cliché. That's what I want."

"You know the extent of our powers, dearest. We can't make her love you. Other than that, make a wish," Bluebonnet said.

"I've never had to make a wish before, why do I have to start now?"

"Because it amuses us. Because we said so. Because we want to make you dance like a puppet on a string. Does it matter?" Jonquil asked.

"Why are you so sassy? Did Bluebonnet put starch in your girdle again?" Ransom asked.

"I will thank you not to mention my girdle." Jonquil wrinkled her nose.

"Ransom, certain magics require certain things. You know this. Ask for the action you want us to perform, please. Just so we're up to godmother code," Petty explained.

"There's a code? Next thing you know, you'll be telling me there are fairy godmother inspectors and—"

"We don't have time to explain the OFG to you at the moment," Bluebonnet replied.

"OFG? I'm lost."

"Original Fairy Gangster. Get with the program, Uncle Ransom," Brittany called to him from the front room, where she played with a potions set Jonquil had made for her.

"My apologies. Fairy Gangster." He grinned. "Fine, I wish for Lucky to meet me at the cathedral just like we'd planned."

Jonquil nodded. "Yes, that should do it."

The fairy godmothers raised their wands, but instead of launching their magic into the air, they opened a window for the obese cardinal that pecked on the glass.

"Shouldn'tve eaten that last piece of pizza. I'm dyin' here." He landed on the sill and wheezed.

"When you've caught your breath, you can tell Rosebud she needs to cash in that favor tomorrow," Petty said.

"Hold on, woman. I'm still wheezin' like I'm dyin'. Gimme a minute, will ya?" The cardinal huffed and puffed, his little ball of a body expanding and retracting dramatically with every breath.

"Bronx. Time is of the essence. So. Rosebud. Favor. Tomorrow, she needs to redeem that favor to get Lucky to the cathedral at the arranged time."

"Gotchyouse." He wheezed a few more times before lifting off into the air.

"Is this the part where you use the poppets, Petty?" Bluebonnet asked.

"No, of course not. That was a joke," Petty said.

"Poppets? What?" Ransom asked.

"Never you mind that," Petty said. "Have you thought about what you're going to say?"

"Yeah."

"Well?" Jonquil prompted.

"I don't want to practice too much. If I do, it might sound rehearsed."

"Sometimes rehearsed is good. Why don't you give us a little preview?" Bluebonnet asked gently.

"Basically it adds up to this. I got my company back and the first person I wanted to tell was her. It didn't matter to me as much without her. I made her a lot of promises I didn't keep because I wasn't worthy. I was scared, but I'm not scared anymore and I hope she'll take one more chance on me and spend the rest of her life with me. Starting with the date I asked to take her on after the wedding."

Bluebonnet sighed. "You're going on a date after your wedding? That's so romantic."

Jonquil sniffed. "I suppose it's okay. Where were you planning on taking her?"

"Monaco."

"Well, that could be nice." Jonquil looked at him pointedly.

Ransom laughed. "Jonquil, would you like to come on our honeymoon with us?"

"Well, when you put it that way." She crossed her arms over her chest and huffed.

"If Lucky says yes to marrying me, I know she'll say yes to having you come with us. Family is the most important thing to both of us," Ransom said.

"Lucky did say she wanted her whole family at her wedding, so why not the honeymoon," Bluebonnet chirped.

"Stop, you silly old goats. You know very well why we're not following them on their honeymoon. They need the room-room to do the boom-boom," Petty said with a titter.

"If you could never say that again, Pets, that would be wonderful," Ransom said.

"Bam bam?" Bluebonnet offered.

"Furgeling?" Jonquil tried.

"Bandicooting?" Petty said.

"Oh God, please stop," Ransom begged.

"The hibbety-dibbety-do?" Bluebonnet cackled.

"Good one, Bon-Bon," Petty praised.

"Kill me. Kill me now," Ransom said when Roderick walked in the front door.

"I thought we were getting the girl? Why does he want to die?" Roderick asked.

"He thinks we're too old to know about the hurkey-jurkey." Petty grinned.

"The rumpy-pumpy, you mean?" Roderick offered. "Or would that be playing Tetris?"

"Polishing the porpoise?" Jonquil questioned.

"I'm going upstairs to hang myself," Ransom said conversationally.

"Oh, you mean where you MOVED THE FURNITURE?" Petty cackled.

"Is that what they're calling it these days?" Roderick asked.

"You're all the absolute worst," Ransom said, but from the expression on his face, it was obvious he didn't believe a word of it.

"So, you're really going to ask her this way?" Roderick asked. "You're going to get everyone dressed up for the wedding, but you're not going to ask the bride until she gets there? That seems"—Roderick paused to find the right words—"like a bad idea."

"I think it's perfect," Petty said.

"How is putting her on the spot like that perfect?"

"She's not on the spot," Petty explained. "Ransom is. His biggest fear was having people mock him. Humiliation, basically. He's giving her the keys to his fear, his pain, his vulnerability. He's trusting her with all the things he didn't before. You'll see."

"I'm glad it makes sense to you." Roderick peered around the godmothers in the kitchen.

"Are you looking for something?"

Roderick cleared his throat. "Just checking to see if anyone was drinking sodas. If they were, I wouldn't mind one."

"We've converted him!" Jonquil cried with glee.

"That's how it starts. It's the sodas, and next thing you know, you're dressed up in breeches and getting married behind a castle. It's how they get you."

"Not me," Roderick said. "I just want some ice cream."

"It's a gateway drug, I'm telling you." Ransom shrugged. "Don't say I didn't warn you."

"Oh, we have news on that front, Mr. Roderick. Your FG is on the mend. She's asked us not to meddle. She doesn't like Gwen."

"What do you mean, she doesn't like Gwen? No, I won't

tolerate it. She hasn't even met Gwen. She's not paid attention to me all this time and wants to drop in now? No."

"That's what I said," Jonquil replied. "If she wanted to be involved, she should've made sure her cases were covered."

"I mean, not that Gwen and I are like that. I just respect her. I like her," Roderick said.

"Mm-hmm," Bluebonnet said agreeably. "Because you're not supposed to like and respect the person you fall in love with. I see."

"Here we go." Ransom laughed. "At least it's not me anymore."

"If I surrender, will I get ice cream?" Roderick asked.

"Maybe." Petty tied a clean, crisp apron over her pink and yellow dress, then grabbed her trusty ice cream scoop and brandished it like a sword. "Sodas all around?"

"Definitely," Ransom agreed.

There was nothing for him to do now but wait until tomorrow. Wait until Lucky showed up at the cathedral and decided whether or not to take a chance on him.

Whether she said yes or not, Ransom would know he'd faced his fears and surrendered utterly and completely to the love he had for this woman.

The godmothers were right again.

It was worth it, it was always worth it.

Another knock sounded on the door and Gwen walked in. "Did the kids wander over again?"

"I'm over here, Mama. I'm playing magic potions."

"You have to tell me when you come over, and you have to ask the godmothers. They might be busy. Like now," she corrected Brittany.

"They're busy planning Lucky's wedding. Shhh."

"What?" Gwen said.

Everyone stopped and looked at Gwen with sheepish smiles.

"We weren't going to call you until tomorrow. Can you keep a secret?" Petty asked.

"Oh, I don't know if this is a good idea. Ransom, you can't just . . ."

"She'll understand the gesture," Ransom said. "At least, I think she will."

"The gesture is a proposal," she said, as if he didn't know that.

"Yes, and I want her to say yes. It's the real thing, but doing it this way, it has significance. I promise. I just need you to show up in your dress, just like we planned," Ransom said.

Roderick squeezed her arm. "Please."

"Oh, fine. But this better make her happier than a bee in clover."

"Want me to make a vow to you as well, Gwen?" Ransom asked.

"What? No, that's dumb."

"Is it?" Petty asked. "I think you should, Ransom."

Ransom dropped down to one knee and held out his hand.

"No, I'm not holding your hand."

"Yes, you are, Mama. I want to keep Uncle Ransom," Steven said from behind her.

"I want to keep you, too, little man."

"Oh, fine." Gwen put her hand in his.

Ransom looked for the right words. "Gwen Borders?"

"Yes?" she rolled her eyes.

"Would you do me the honor of granting me the forever title of Uncle Ransom to your children? I swear by the sky above and the ground below I will love and protect those children, you, and if I'm lucky, your best friend for all the days of my life. You will never doubt my devotion, my loyalty, or my honor. I do so swear."

Gwen sniffed, teary. "You jerk. Get up."

"Not until I get an answer."

"Say yes, Mama," the kids cried.

"Maybe he does do okay on improv after all," Roderick said with a grin.

"Yes, jerk face."

"Hey, it's like you're my actual sister. You call me jerk face and everything." He hugged Gwen to him. "I really do love you all."

"God, I can't take it. Too many feelings." She sniffed again.

"Family is everything, Gwen." Petty joined the hug. "Welcome to this one."

"Aww," Bluebonnet cooed, and joined in.

Jonquil eyed Roderick. "Might as well. We're here."

The kids tangled themselves around Ransom's legs and he realized he had a family. It didn't look like the family he'd longed for as a child, but it was much better.

This was a family built on the bonds of love, hope, and a little bit of redemption. Blood was fine, but it wasn't what mattered in the end. It was in the moments like these when the call to arms sounded, and it was in those precious moments after, when it was only those named family who answered.

Ransom realized this was part of Happily Ever After, too. It wasn't just about the prince and princess riding off into the sunset. It was the journey after, when they got into the same carriage and decided together which path to take and who to take with them.

"Oh," he said out loud as the next epiphany hit him so hard his ears rang.

"What, dear?" Petty asked.

"Why does it do that? When we have epiphanies, why is it like getting my clock cleaned with a gong?"

Bluebonnet nodded sympathetically. "Yes, especially if they come one right after another. Makes a body dizzy."

Petty set the ice cream soda in front of him. "What did you discover?"

He looked around at all the faces in front of him and Ransom realized he wasn't scared to share his vulnerability or fear with them because again, this was family.

"I'd thought being a coward made me unworthy of Lucky, but as we were sitting here talking, I was thinking about family. About how the bonds of this one are love, hope, and a little bit of redemption."

"And?" Bluebonnet prompted, almost like she'd been waiting for this.

Maybe she had been.

"It's okay to be afraid. Fear is normal. If I didn't think being afraid made anyone else unworthy, then I'm not unworthy for being afraid, either."

Gwen and Roderick exchanged glances.

"The final lesson is learned," Jonquil said. "We're so proud of you."

"Yes, Ransom. We don't know what Lucky's answer will be tomorrow, but we do know that you've learned the lessons you need. You're running the gauntlet," Petty said.

"Wait, what do you mean you don't know what she's going to say? I thought you said we get Happily Ever After?"

"You do." Bluebonnet grinned. "We just don't know if that starts tomorrow or not. It depends on what Lucky says."

The godmothers all cackled and for a moment, Ransom thought they sounded a bit like wicked witches.

"I heard that," Petty said, and fixed him with a pointed look.

"I didn't say anything." Except he grinned.

"Drink your ice cream, Casanova." Petty handed him the ice cream soda. "You need fortification for tomorrow."

"Yes, everyone should get to bed early tonight," Jonquil said. "Especially the two little sprites I see on the floor. Clean up your potions, Brittany. Steven, if you help her, I'll give you a piece of candied ginger."

"Mama says I shouldn't do things for candy," Steven said.

"Do them because you want to, and then the candy is an unexpected treat," Jonquil said.

"But how is it unexpected if I'm expecting it?" Steven's brow furrowed.

"An interesting conundrum that I think we shall have to have many long conversations trying to figure it out."

"Love you, Blossoms." Steven kissed his hand and blew the kisses toward the trio of fairy godmothers.

"Oh, I think I like being 'Blossoms' as much as I like being the OFG," Petty said.

"I'm going to hold you to your promise, Ransom."

"You won't need to," he swore.

# Chapter 27

Lucky had never cared about Valentine's Day one way or another. She'd gotten her fair share of cards and candies in school. She'd sent her fair share, too.

She didn't complain that it was a commercialized holiday designed to make people spend more money on flowers than they needed to. In fact, people like that who did complain irritated her. Why couldn't they just let people have things that made them happy?

Valentine's Day wasn't her favorite holiday, but she didn't have anything against people who loved it. Lucky thought any excuse to put more love out into the world had to be a good thing.

All of that changed today.

This would've been her fake wedding day. It would've been a moment to treasure because of why they'd decided to do it.

All of the love of their godmothers.

Only it wasn't happening now and Lucky was grateful for that. She couldn't pretend she was happy when she wasn't. She couldn't pretend the words she spoke didn't mean something to her.

From now on, every Valentine's Day, she'd always remember it was the day she was supposed to fake marry the love of her life.

Lucky had chosen not to be bitter. She'd chosen to look for happiness wherever she could find it. She knew that the pain she felt about this day would fade to something bittersweet, and when she was old and gray, it would only be sweet. It would be a story she'd tell her grandchildren.

But for right now, enough was enough. Lucky was ready to put some space between herself and Ever After. Space from Ransom and everything that had happened.

Even though the kids had asked Lucky to stay, she'd decided she was going with her mother to Paris. She would miss them desperately, but she needed a break.

She would tell them goodbye this time.

No, not goodbye. See you later.

Goodbye sounded so final. So sad. See you later was all about the good things to come, and that's how Lucky had chosen to look at life.

She would live in the moment and not worry about what the future held, aside from choosing to expect good things.

Her mother had been recalcitrant about packing and was taking her dear, sweet time.

"Ma, neither one of us is getting any younger." Lucky shoved some of her clothing into a bag, not paying much mind how it went in and not caring how it would look when it came out again.

"Speak for yourself. I'm now friends with an Evil Queen. I bet she has one hell of an anti-aging regimen."

"You think you're funny." She looked under the bed to make sure none of her belongings had migrated under there during her stay.

"I know I'm funny. You get it from me." Fortune grinned. "Why are you in such a rush? Paris isn't going anywhere anytime soon. We'll get there when we get there."

"I just feel like there's something going on that I don't know about. I don't like it and I want to get going before anyone can spring anything on me, or talk me out of having my adventure."

Fortune cocked her head. "How can someone talk you

out of something you really want to do? Not my headstrong Lucky Charm."

"Okay, you're way too cheerful. What are you up to?"

"Nothing. Why do you think I'm up to something?" Fortune fidgeted in her chair.

"Because you definitely are."

"Pish."

"Aha! Aunt Petty says that all the time. You never say it unless you're trying to avoid my wrath."

"Your wrath? Little Miss is getting too big for her britches."

"Listen, Ma. Just this one time, can you just let it be?" If ever she needed a time for her mother to understand, it was this one.

"I'm afraid there's more involved than just me."

A knock sounded on the door and Fortune motioned for the person to enter. It was Rosebud.

Rosebud, to whom she'd agreed to grant a favor.

"No," she said before Rosebud could ask.

"Yes," Rosebud said gently. "It's a small thing, really."

"You said it wouldn't be anything I didn't agree with morally, and I'm sure that whatever this is, it goes against my religion."

Rosebud gave her a kind smile. "How can love go against any religion? If it does, you need to find a new one."

"You know what today was supposed to be," Lucky said, as if that were an argument in itself.

"The groom asks that you meet him under the cathedral of trees. That you wear the dress I made for you."

Lucky's nose tingled like she'd been hit with a homerun baseball. She hated that tingle that squirmed up her face until her eyes watered and the tears fell whether she'd given them permission to or not.

She didn't want to face him. Not yet. Lucky needed to give her broken heart time to heal before it was ready to go another round with anyone. Let alone talking this to death with Ransom.

Rosebud put her hand on Lucky's shoulder. "This is my favor, and then your debt will be paid in full. Wear the dress. Meet him."

"Lucky! Get your bottom in gear or I will never, ever forgive you."

"Ma! Whose side are you on?"

"Yours, dumb-dumb. Always. Move it." Fortune nudged her forward.

Lucky found herself being shoveled into the beautiful dress that had appeared like a poltergeist, because she'd thought for sure she'd sent it back to Rosebud's shop.

Her mother fussed with her hair, while Rosebud painted a pale lipstick on her lips.

"I didn't agree to the lipstick," Lucky protested. "I didn't agree to any of this."

"Just go with it. If you want to leave right after you see him and give him a piece of your mind, and some of mine, we can do that. For right now, just go and see what he has to say."

"What could he possibly say?" Lucky asked.

"I understand now why the godmothers are so frustrated all of the time. Context clues. You're a bright girl." Fortune stared at her daughter intently, obviously waiting for the light to come on, but it didn't happen.

Lucky just stared at her blankly.

Rosebud led her to the mirror and the family of mice who'd been visiting her emerged dressed in tiny gray suits.

"Will you carry them?" Rosebud handed her a basket.

It slowly began to dawn on Lucky that this was not what she'd been expecting. They were trying to dress her up in all of her wedding fineries.

She accepted the basket with the mice and absentmindedly looked for cheese or something to give them.

Rosebud came to her rescue and gave them each a dandelion puff to hold, though the smallest mice gnawed on the ends of their puffs.

Fortune had quietly slipped on the white dress she'd worn to the rehearsal brunch, the one with the embroidered foxes on the sleeves.

The foxes began to twist and move, looking like a family of foxes chasing one another's tails in a happy swirl around the sleeves and when Lucky looked up into her mother's face, she saw that tears had gathered in her eyes.

"This is your family. They're here for your wedding, if you choose to get married."

Lucky reached out a shaking hand to touch the sleeves, and the embroidered foxes curled around her fingers and moved to her wrists and up her arms, where they settled against her skin with a warm, somehow-familiar touch.

She knew they were talking and while she didn't know the language they spoke, she knew what the words meant.

Love.

Hope.

Family.

"Thank you," she said to the foxes, to her mother, to Rosebud, and to the mice.

Gratitude filled her.

"Will you go, now? Will you listen to what he has to say?" Rosebud asked.

"I was always going to go. I love him."

"Yes, but don't forget, loving someone doesn't mean they're good for you. You make the choice your heart wants," Fortune said.

Lucky's bottom lip quivered. "That's what you did. How did it turn out for you?"

"My Lucky Charm, it was the best choice I ever made. I'm your mother."

Fat tears rolled down her cheeks. "I'm not going to make it. I'm going to dissolve into a puddle of tears before I get there."

One of the mice blew on his dandelion puff, sending the tufts right into Lucky's face, and she laughed.

"Thank you," Rosebud said to the tiny, helpful mouse.

"You'll walk me? Oh, where's Gwen?"

"You'll see," her mother promised.

Lucky let the two women lead her down to the carriage and she held the basket up so the mice could see where the carriage took them.

Bronx, after much huffing and puffing in a vain attempt to keep up with them, landed on the carriage and was content to ride along. It seemed everyone was going to be there.

As the cathedral of trees came into view, Lucky saw Ransom waiting for her in his wedding attire at the beginning of the green mossy carpet that led up to the altar.

Was this actually real?

Holy hell, she was going to end up the worst kind of cliché. She didn't care. Lucky Fujiki might just end up a Valentine's Day bride after all.

It was the grand gesture of all grand gestures, but she knew she couldn't let herself be caught up in the showmanship of it all. Although it would be a lie if Lucky said she wasn't a little bit enraptured by the ritual of it all.

She remembered saying that if she ever got married, her fake wedding had been perfect and this would be exactly what she wanted.

Her breath caught in her throat as the carriage rolled to a stop and Ransom held out his hand to her to help her from the carriage.

She paused, unsure if she should step down. Would he think it was an automatic yes if she did?

*No pressure*, he mouthed.

She tilted her head back and forth. *Kind of*, she mouthed back. Instead of stepping down, she stood in the carriage and waited for what he would say.

"Smart. She can make those horses run if she doesn't like what he has to say," the tall black-haired woman in a clawed crown said from the front.

It was a good strategy, if she needed it.

Or if she didn't faint first. She couldn't catch her breath and her heart fluttered like the wings of a butterfly in a rapid tattoo.

*Are you ready?* he mouthed.

She snorted. "I'm listening," she said aloud.

"I didn't say what I should've when I should have and I thought that made me unworthy of you. I was afraid."

Ransom held her gaze and his expression was open, honest, and she could see from the tic in his jaw that he was more than a little nervous.

"It's okay to be scared." She swallowed hard. "I was, too."

He nodded. "It is, but the way I handled it wasn't."

"You don't have to marry me to apologize!" she blurted. Lucky wanted him to want her for herself, not as a grand gesture to assuage wounded pride.

The crowd laughed.

"I'm getting there. Will you let me get this out?" he teased.

She nodded her head and clasped the basket in her hands as tightly as she dared.

"You were afraid, too. You were facing your darkest fears and when I should've supported you, when I should've been a man who deserves the kind of faith I'd already asked you to put in me, I failed you. And myself. I didn't know how to fix it. Instead, I let you believe that you were the one who needed fixing. You don't. You never did."

Ransom paused and studied her for a long moment before continuing. "I know you put more stock in actions than words, but I have the words, too. We've given them to each other before."

He sank down to one knee and even though everyone had to have known it was coming, they all gave a collective gasp.

"You know my biggest fear was being The Boy Who Missed for the rest of my life. Being mocked. Being less. Those aren't my fears any longer. My biggest fear is that I'll have to spend the rest of my life without you. I love you, Lucky. I don't have shining armor, but I can promise you Happily Ever After."

"I told him to say that," Bluebonnet whispered loudly.

He held up an open velvet box with an intricately crafted gold band nestled in the center.

Emotions washed over her in wave after wave. She drowned in the surge and she couldn't come up for air long enough to speak.

When she didn't say anything, he spoke again. "That is, if you say you'll marry me."

This was everything she'd ever wanted, exactly the way she wanted it. Lucky reached out to grab it with both hands. "Yes, Ransom. Yes!"

Someone took the basket of mice from her hands and she realized it was Gwen and she handed the basket to Brittany.

The kids walked down the stretch of the mossy carpet, and the mice blew the dandelion tufts that erupted and multiplied as they drifted across the guests.

Ransom slid the ring on her finger and she looked up into the depths of his blue eyes to discover he was absolutely right. He could offer her Happily Ever After because it sparkled like a promise in the oceanic depths of his gaze.

She cupped his face and pulled him down to kiss her.

The crowd cheered.

"I love you," Lucky whispered against his lips.

"In my day, we got married before the kissing," Grammy said from her place on the altar with a wink.

So much love welled in her heart, it was like an eternal spring that overflowed and the world around them erupted in flowers and vegetation. Life was everywhere, thriving on the love of those who had come together to celebrate and cherish it.

Luckily for them all, there wasn't a mutant cherry in sight.

Only two hearts who had chosen to beat as one, eager to begin their new journey. The one the storybooks called Happily Ever After.

# Just a Smidge More Meddling

Petty cried as she waved Lucky and Ransom off to Monaco on their first date. Honeymoon. Whatever they wanted to call it was fine with her.

All that mattered to Petty was that her charges had found their way to each other and they were currently skipping down the primrose path of Happily Ever After.

"Another job well done, I say," Bluebonnet said, sniffing. She tucked a delicate lace handkerchief up to her nose. "Weddings always make me cry."

"Did you know that we have bookings again?" Jonquil asked, swiping her finger over her iPad notifications. "Look at this, it's ridiculous. We're not going to need that carnival Lucky suggested."

"I still like the carnival idea," Bluebonnet said.

Petty leaned over her sister's shoulder and pushed her glasses back up on her nose. "Huh. Looks like people found us anyway once I removed the cloaking from Ever After. Just goes to show you that some things are meant to be and they will find a way."

"Oh, girls. Have I got a story for you. I was reading through the applications to hire some help at Fairy Godmothers, Inc. You know, planning for the best. This one is a doozy."

"Do tell," Jonquil encouraged.

She pulled up the résumé on her tablet of one Zuri Davis.

"Zuri has been a wedding planner for several years—"

"How many? A couple is two. Several can be three, four, five?" Jonquil asked.

"Bah, we don't care about that. She needs our help."

"Thought you were tired of helping?" Jonquil needled her.

"Hush. Listen. Zuri fell in love with the groom in the last wedding she helped plan. Unbeknownst to her, of course. It did not have the cute ending like that one movie. Her whole life is in flames. She needs a place to recover. A place to hide from the fallout, at least for a little bit anyway."

"What she needs, girls, is Fairy Godmothers, Inc.!" Petty cried.

They all agreed, and that was how failed wedding planner Zuri Davis acquired herself not one, but three fairy godmothers with a strong penchant for meddling, and a story she'd retell her children night after night until they, too, dreamed of their own Happily Ever After.

TELL THE WORLD THIS BOOK WAS

GOOD   BAD   SO-SO

Can't get enough of Petty, Jonquil, and Bluebonnet?

Keep reading for a sneak peek at more adventures
from these mischievous matchmakers
in *Ever After,*
coming soon
from
Saranna DeWylde
and
Zebra Books.

Petunia "Petty" Blossom was currently fluttering around the boardroom of Fairy Godmothers, Inc., making quite the sparkly mess. Glittery fairy dust followed in her wake as she zipped from one project to the next like an overcaffeinated bumblebee with too many luscious blooms to choose from.

Of course, it was Gwen's fault for bringing them so many of her decadent espresso brownies.

*Oh, bless that child.* Petty made herself a mental note to shake some fairy dust into Gwen's coffee. She needed to get things moving so Gwen and Roderick would be a done deal before Roderick's MIA fairy godmother could show up and thwart her lovely plans.

"Petunia!" Bluebonnet's voice startled her and Petty dropped out of the air and landed firmly on her rounded bottom.

She rubbed her rump. "I don't know why they call it extra padding. I don't feel padded at all."

"Never mind that, sister. I see that look in your eye. What are you up to?"

Petunia widened her eyes and blinked slowly. "Whatever do you mean?"

Bluebonnet squinted at her. "I've known you for too long. You're wearing your meddling face."

"Of course I am. That's what we do." Except Petunia and her sisters had all agreed they'd be leaving Roderick and

Gwen alone to find their way when they were ready. Petty just didn't think she could risk Roderick's FG messing up their plans. His FG hadn't seen the whole thread. (Actually, she hadn't seen much of anything since she'd fallen off her broom and with magic stores low, it had taken her several years to heal.)

Jonquil popped her head in the door. "Did I hear the sounds of meddling in the morning? I brought coffee from Bernadette's!"

"Oh!" Bluebonnet clapped. "Bernadette's cappuccino always pairs well with meddling."

Petty spread her wings and used them to lift herself off the floor. She also zapped her bottom with her wand because she wasn't about to deal with a bruise.

"We also have a fresh batch of espresso brownies from Grammy's Goodies. Gwen made them," Petunia said. "Also, I need you each to eat at least one or extra hijinks may ensue. You know what it's like when I'm on the caffeine."

Bluebonnet and Jonquil were quick to come to her aid and each grabbed several brownies from the pretty red box.

"Is that why you're such a firecracker this morning?" Bluebonnet asked.

"Mmm." Petty nodded after taking a sip of the coffee.

"Oh, wait. Then perhaps you *shouldn't* be drinking the magic bean juice?" Jonquil dared to ask.

Petty growled at her and clutched the coffee close to her chest.

Jonquil held up her hands in surrender. "Calm yourself. I swear, you're acting like Grammy on a full moon."

"Sorry." Petty slouched. "It's just we have so much to accomplish." She glanced skyward, then over both shoulders. "Not that I'm complaining. It's a blessing to be so busy. Ever After is flourishing, as are our charges, and our wedding planning business. But it is a lot of balls to keep in the air."

Bluebonnet snorted her coffee and spewed it out of her nose like a geyser. "Balls!"

The three of them cackled, and with a wave of Bluebonnet's wand, she cleaned up the mess as if it had never happened.

"You're worse than me, I swear." Petunia took the opportunity to swipe the last brownie that her sisters had so lovingly left for her.

"Can this be right?" Bluebonnet nodded to the seven different columns on the far wall, each column allocated to a different wedding. Then she turned her head to the opposite wall, which had been plastered with their ideas for the spring carnival.

"We have a lot of work ahead of us," Jonquil said. "Don't get me wrong, I'm thrilled that after Ransom and Lucky's debacle we've still gotten so many bookings. The magic wells in town are full and we're able to begin exporting. I just don't know how we can keep up this pace."

Bluebonnet squealed so loudly that Petty's spectacles cracked.

Petty sniffed and wiggled her nose, trying to get the glasses to move without touching them with her fingers.

"Sorry," Bluebonnet apologized. "I'm so excited. Zuri will be here tomorrow."

Jonquil zapped Petty's spectacles, mending them instantly before she said, "I'm afraid she's going to be a project as well. More so than any help to us."

"She's a modern woman." Petty gave up and adjusted her glasses with her fingers. "She can do both."

"Hmm. But should she have to?" Bluebonnet asked.

"I have been noodling on this," Jonquil said. "First, we shall start her testing the wedding favors and services from the local vendors. That way she gets to meet everyone, she knows what we have to offer clients, and I think it especially important we get her set up with one of those wish favors."

Petty clapped gleefully. "Oh, you're brilliant. Just brilliant."

"But there's more," Jonquil teased in a sing-song voice.

"For an additional twenty-nine ninety-five?" Bluebonnet asked.

"For free." She tapped her wand on the long table. "Listen. We put her on the Petrovsky-Markhoff wedding. It's important."

Petunia narrowed her eyes. "Are we sure? I mean, the last wedding she worked on the bride took her dress off in front of everyone and lit it on fire. *FIRE*, Jonquil."

"Hmm. Quite." Jonquil nodded. "Don't tell me that you'd have done any less if you'd discovered your groom had been having an affair with the wedding planner. Actually, that's really rather mild in comparison."

"Oh yes!" Bluebonnet agreed. "The bride was quite reasonable. After all, it's not like she turned a prince into a frog. *Forever.*"

Petunia rolled her eyes and flopped back in her chair. "Oh my gods. Will you two give it a rest? I have apologized profusely to Charming. And really, he hasn't yet apologized to us, Bon-Bon. I mean, he's sorry. I made him sorry." Petty narrowed her eyes at the memory. "But the actual apology, being sorry for his actions because they were wrong, he hasn't owned that."

Jonquil shrugged. "His problem, I suppose. Maybe that's why none of the kisses have worked to free him from his green hell?"

"Hmm," Petty mused.

"Hmm," Bon-Bon agreed.

"When you have time, dears, you should really look at their threads. They're all tangled up like a cat in a basket of knitting," Jonquil advised.

"I should start brewing headache powder now, shouldn't I?" Petty asked.

Bluebonnet waved her off. "Oh hush. You know this is your favorite part."

Petty grinned. "It really is."

"Seven weddings. I can't believe it. I didn't think this crazy scheme of yours was going to work." Jonquil shook her head.

"Ha!" Petty pointed her wand at each of her sisters. "I knew you doubted me!"

Bluebonnet swatted her hand away. "Don't point that thing at me."

Petty pocketed her wand. "Sorry. But really."

Jonquil grinned at both of them. "We're awful. Absolutely wretched. If we didn't use our powers for good, we'd be wicked witches."

"Evil queens," Petty giggled.

"Damn," Jonquil swore. "I almost forgot. Our own evil queen Ravenna is going to be a problem."

"On purpose?" Bluebonnet wrinkled her nose. "I mean, she's always a problem, but is she going to try to thwart us because we already lived that story and I'm not about to tolerate any of her nonsense again. If she's not careful, why . . . I'll . . ."

"You'll what? Make her more miserable than she already is? She's not ready for love. It would be particularly unkind to give her what she's always wanted before she's ready for it," Petty said.

Bluebonnet crossed her arms over her chest. "I am feeling unkind. She thwarts us at every turn."

"Love is a gift, not a punishment, Bon-Bon."

Bluebonnet harrumphed. "I know. She just irks me."

"It seems she'll be at the center of the tangle." Jonquil gestured to the wall. "Of all of our threads."

"This calls for more fortification," Petty declared.

"Loose the dogs of war!" Bluebonnet cried, shaking her fist.

"Um, no. I was going to suggest we eat more treats," Petty said.

"I seem to recall someone telling me I simply needed more sugar," Jonquil offered soothingly. "And I did and it all worked out just lovely for Ransom and Lucky."

"I suppose. Perhaps an ice cream soda?" Bluebonnet replied softly.

"That's the spirit," Jonquil said.

"Wait, so what about the Petrovsky-Markhoff wedding is so important for our new assistant?" Petty brought them back to the subject at hand.

"Closure, as far as the threads of fate seem to be concerned."

Bluebonnet shook her head. "That doesn't bode well. Weddings are about beginnings, not endings."

"We'll all find out soon enough," Jonquil promised.

This definitely called for ice cream sodas all around. Perhaps the kind that could only be had at the pub.

"I say we take a break with a more adult kind of fortification at Pick 'N Axe," Petty suggested.

"Why Petty, it's not even noon." Bluebonnet pretended to be scandalized.

"It's brunch somewhere, dearies!" Jonquil said. "They have those delightful shakes. The ones with the mango ice cream and the rum."

"Sugar is always the answer." Petunia nodded. "If it can't be fixed with a brownie, try an ice cream soda. If that doesn't work, well, we go to the sugarcane spirits."

Bon-Bon giggled. "That's what I'm going to call it from now on. We're consulting the spirits."

Jonquil cackled. "Let's go consult the spirits."

Petty linked arms with her sisters. "I wonder if they'll have any answers for us."

As they started on the short walk to Pick 'N Axe, Petty saw a geyser of water shooting out from one of the mushroom-capped cottages beyond the square.

"Right on time," Bluebonnet said. "Roderick should be running to her rescue at five, four, three, two . . ."

Petty squinted through her spectacles and they enhanced her view just enough so that she could see the door to Roderick's cottage as it opened and he sprinted to Gwen's.

She grinned. "A decent round of meddling before brunch."

"Quite." Jonquil said, obviously pleased with their efforts.

Even if the shrieking from mushroom cottage number two said rather the opposite.

# Connect with Us

Visit us online at
**KensingtonBooks.com**
to read more from your favorite authors, see books
by series, view reading group guides, and more.

**Join us on social media**

for sneak peeks, chances to win books and prize packs,
and to share your thoughts with other readers.

**facebook.com/kensingtonpublishing**
**twitter.com/kensingtonbooks**

## *Tell us what you think!*

To share your thoughts, submit a review,
or sign up for our eNewsletters, please visit:
**KensingtonBooks.com/TellUs.**